DEADLY BUSINESS . . .

Reporters waited. Dr. Mosby glared at them. "Each and every victim ordered and ate a precooked chicken dinner from a nationwide franchise chain."

Dr. Mosby raised a hand to quell the uproar.

"By virtue of the authority vested in my agency, I hereby declare that every franchise operating under license from the Chicken Tonight Corporation in all states east of the Mississippi River be closed until further notice!"

"Miss Lathen is noteworthy for her quiet, dry humor and her skill in making big-business intricacy clear and plausible."
—*The New York Times Book Review*

"A masterful plotter, an elegant stylist, a comic genius and an old-fashioned purist who never sacrifices logic for surprise effect."
—*Newsweek*

Books by Emma Lathen

Accounting for Murder
Ashes to Ashes
Banking on Death
By Hook or by Crook
Death Shall Overcome
Double, Double, Oil and Trouble
Going for the Gold
The Longer the Thread
Murder Against the Grain
Murder Makes the Wheels Go 'Round
Murder to Go
Murder Without Icing
Pick Up Sticks
A Place for Murder
A Stitch in Time
Sweet and Low

Published by POCKET BOOKS

MURDER TO GO

EMMA LATHEN

PUBLISHED BY POCKET BOOKS NEW YORK

 POCKET BOOKS, a Simon & Schuster division of
GULF & WESTERN CORPORATION
1230 Avenue of the Americas, New York, N.Y. 10020

Published by arrangement with Simon and Schuster
Library of Congress Catalog Card Number: 69-84128

ISBN: 0-671-45529-X

First Pocket Books printing September, 1971

10 9 8 7 6

POCKET and colophon are registered trademarks
of Simon & Schuster.

Printed in the U.S.A.

CONTENTS

MURDER TO GO

CHAPTER 1

PREPARE FOR COOKING

WALL STREET is the financial nerve center of the world. Million-dollar transactions are almost commonplace in dozens of institutions dotted from the Battery to Foley Square. Rich men in opulent board rooms finance new products, new communications media, new worlds. At the same time, high-school graduates earn modest salaries in the back rooms of brokerage houses, shuffling stock certificates worth a king's ransom. One way or the other, Wall Streeters from senior partner to uniformed messenger deal with sums that stagger the imagination.

This has earned Wall Street censure, and worse, from some quarters. There are men and even nations for whom Wall Street is the enemy; in many tongues and idioms they accuse Wall Street's bankers, lawyers, brokers and traders of confusing money with value in the larger sense. Robber barons, they claim, stalk down Exchange Place and up Pine Street, intent on defrauding widows, robbing orphans and trampling upon the poor.

None of these activities is exceptionally profitable in a century of affluence. Moreover, Wall Street knows full well that there are things other than money important to man: beauty and truth, autonomy and commitment. After all, Wall Street can read, too.

John Putnam Thatcher had long felt that Wall Street's view of money did not differ markedly from that of mankind at large. On the contrary. The oddity was that Wall Street's dealings in billions of dollars, pounds and liras did not immunize it from irritation with petty sums.

John Putnam Thatcher was the senior vice-president of the Sloan Guaranty Trust. The Sloan Guaranty Trust is the

1

third-largest bank in the world. Thatcher's particular concerns, the Trust and Investment divisions, routinely handled seven-figure transactions. At the moment, they were tied in knots by a rancorous disagreement over twenty-five dollars.

"I'm not altogether sure I follow you, Miss Corsa," said Thatcher to his secretary.

Miss Corsa patiently explained financial details to Mr. Thatcher once again.

"Well," she said, "the Committee agreed that it wouldn't be fair to assess everybody the same amount. So Mr. Bowman suggested a different system. Everybody on the clerical roll would contribute what they wanted. Then everybody else"—this was one way to describe his stable of highly skilled professionals, thought Thatcher—"would be asked to contribute twenty-five dollars. But Miss Prettyman objects . . ."

Miss Corsa proceeded to outline a financial proposal that would not have disgraced many a small electronics firm. Thatcher repressed his smile, for this was no laughing matter. His comfort had been increasingly impaired by Miss Corsa's attendance at what was known throughout the Sloan as The Committee. (And the Senate Foreign Relations Committee was, comparatively speaking, small potatoes.)

At issue was Charles Trinkam's forthcoming anniversary, twenty years at the bank. Charlie was Thatcher's second-in-command, a resilient bachelor who yoked an exuberant private life with outstanding ability as a banker. In a casual, offhand manner Charlie Trinkam supervised the Utilities Section with notable success; in the same way, he commanded affection and respect from his colleagues.

All of Charlie's colleagues certainly wanted to do the right thing by him. A dinner, a briefcase, a contribution—fine! What had put the fat into the fire was Charlie's immense popularity with the rank and file. The Sloan's secretaries, file clerks, messengers and elevator operators did not feel, it developed, that Mr. Trinkam could be fobbed off with the standard: a dollar from each secretary, twenty per trust officer and whatever else necessary coughed up by the top brass. Not for a minute. Every single member of the Trust Division, from Miss Lelyveld (Statistical Typing) to Sheldon the messenger boy, was determined to do the thing brilliantly. (Thatcher's Miss Corsa, who carried calmness to unnatural lengths, was not involved in the roiling passions. But as the days progressed, she decided that Mr. Thatcher's presence must be made felt, and, acting as Mr. Thatcher's presence, Miss Corsa could outdo any zealot.) The net result was a committee, instead of one secretary passing the hat. Creation of a committee had flushed other personnel from all parts of the great Sloan family who wished to be associated with the festivities.

For some weeks the Committee had been mulling over various proposals concerning contributions and contributors. Once these weighty questions were settled, Thatcher feared, the problem of what to buy Charlie with the extravagant funds on hand could occupy Sheldon, Miss Lelyveld, Miss Corsa and many others for a long time indeed.

The only member of the staff not being inconvenienced was, predictably enough, Charlie Trinkam.

Fortunately, he strolled into Thatcher's office. This cut off Miss Corsa's meticulous account of Miss Prettyman's suggested pro-rata contributions system based on take-home pay.

"Say, John," said Charlie after Miss Corsa withdrew, "what's this about the twelve million dollars that Commercial Credit is playing games with?"

Thatcher did not require repetition here. "What twelve million dollars?" he asked crisply. Nor did he have to ask about Commercial Credit; it was the Sloan division concerned with advancing short-term loans to business. As such, it was not in Thatcher's immediate purview. But he was keeping a weather eye on it. In the last two years, Commercial Credit had shown a tendency to finance businesses that the Trust and Investment divisions would not touch with a ten-foot pole.

Charlie, who knew and appreciated the delicacy of the situation, grinned.

"The twelve million that Maitland anted up for one of those franchise operations. This one delivers chicken dinners to your door."

Thatcher almost groaned as he reflected on the reports of Walter Bowman's research staff. For the most part they dealt scathingly with the current rash of franchises for coin-operated car washes, big-name cleaning establishments, Wild West Bar-B-Cues and Teen-Age Night Clubs.

"I suppose," he said wearily, "that Maitland has just read one of those come-on brochures, and got swept off his feet."

Charlie nodded instant understanding.

"I know the sort of thing you mean. They explain how you—and the little woman—can own your own business by investing fifteen to twenty thousand bucks. Then you just sit back and rake in the money. Betty's Baked Beans will train you, they will big-brother you so you don't do anything wrong, they'll advertise twenty-four hours a day. You're practically guaranteed a fortune."

There is a sucker born every minute, and Thatcher had learned to live with the fact. Nevertheless, he did regret that one of them was in charge of an important Sloan division.

"Tell me, do you think anybody told Maitland about the rate of failure, about the mistakes in location—for that matter, did anybody tell him about the sharp dealers who are getting onto this merry-go-round?" he asked irately.

Charlie was reassuring. "It's not as bad as that. Trust Bowman. When Maitland discovered franchises three months ago, Walter kept an eye on him. So this loan wasn't to one of the dogs. Far from it. The twelve million went to Chicken Tonight. That's Frank Hedstrom's outfit."

"Ah!" Thatcher relaxed.

"Yes, the boy wonder himself."

Charlie's ironic tone made Thatcher reconsider the silver lining. No one on Wall Street was issuing anything but glowing reports on Frank Hedstrom these days. Like a comet, he had shot up through the ranks of other franchisers. Most of the innovations were his; most of the problems were his competitors'. Chicken Tonight had automated more than cooking. By the time Frank Hedstrom was done, a congenital idiot would be able to operate one of his franchises—profitably.

"All right, Charlie," Thatcher asked cautiously, "what's the catch?"

A gleam of sheer deviltry swept over Charlie Trinkam's face.

"Maitland went ahead and okayed a take-over by Hedstrom."

Thatcher sat bolt upright.

"A take-over? Who does he want to take over?" he demanded.

Charlie's smile broadened. "Southeastern Insurance. It's a small company in Philadelphia and—"

But Thatcher shook his head impatiently. "I know," he said and sank back into thought.

It is one thing to lend twelve million dollars to a profitable enterprise which is daily growing more profitable. It is another thing to finance diversification into an alien field.

"How far has this thing gone?" he finally asked.

"Too far," Charlie said bluntly. "The formal bid has been made, Southeastern has called an extraordinary stockholders' meeting and the proxies have been mailed. The reason I know anything about it is that one of the bright youngsters working for me owns a couple of shares of Southeastern. He showed me the proxy statement. Here, have a look."

Trinkam tossed one of the familiar statements on the desk. Expertly Thatcher flipped to the material he wanted. There it was, in black and white.

"Two for one," he murmured. "It sounds good. Have you checked the figures?"

"Sure. It's a real buy for Southeastern's stockholders. And they'll be getting glamour stock too. Everybody wants a piece of Hedstrom these days."

"We're going to have to find out more about this," Thatcher said decisively. "And a lot more about Hedstrom too."

Charlie came up with another ray of light. "That shouldn't be too hard. I hear that our old buddy Robichaux is handling Southeastern's end of the deal."

"Oh, he is, is he? Well, that at least gives us our first step." Thatcher buzzed the intercom. "Miss Corsa, will you get me Mr. Robichaux, please?"

With Tom Robichaux, any step at all required lunch. A friend of Thatcher's since their first encounter in Harvard Yard many years ago, he was a partner in Robichaux & Devane, investment brokers, and a man of far-flung interests.

"So I said to McBride that the next thing you know, they'll be proposing cost-of-living clauses in these damned alimony settlements. Talk about inflation!"

Thatcher was briefly worried. They were in Fraunces Tavern, and his plan to extract information was going to founder if it developed, as it so often did, that Robichaux was in the throes of marital upheaval. But as Robichaux rumbled on, it developed that his liaison with the current Mrs. Robichaux—a Loël, Thatcher seemed to recall—was

reasonably secure. He and McBride had simply been discussing common interests: McBride was the well-known
divorce lawyer, and God knew how much of Robichaux's
large income was earmarked by various courts for enterpris-
ing ladies. Still, this might be a straw in the wind. Thatcher
reminded himself to be watchful and firmly steered the
conversation back to productive lines.

"Chicken Tonight!" said Robichaux when the headwaiter
seated them. "John, Chicken Tonight has been the surprise
franchise success of the last two years. Hedstrom's already
got four hundred Chicken Tonights from New York to California—and they're all coining money. He's opening at least
twenty-five new shops every six months. He's got customers
beating down the doors—or the telephone—for these meals
he delivers. You know, it isn't just fried chicken. He's got
over thirty different kinds of— Eh? What's that? Oh, yes.
I'll start with oysters. Then, let's see—oh, I'll try the duck
today, yes, just olive oil and vinegar on the salad . . ."

Tom's ordering, protracted as it was by precise instructions
to the kitchen, came to an end, and he returned to the subject
at hand. "What was I saying?"

"You were saying," Thatcher said with mild sarcasm,
"that Chicken Tonight's twenty-five varieties of chicken were
all delicious."

"Oh, for God's sake!" Robichaux protested. "I was saying
that they sold!"

Thatcher managed to order roast beef and potatoes, then
indicated that he had already received a rundown on Chicken
Tonight's spectacular past from Maitland down in Commercial Credit. It was, he reminded Robichaux, the future he
was interested in.

"I've already gathered that you—and Maitland—think that
Chicken Tonight is a gold mine," he began

Robichaux blew out his cheeks, every inch a Colonel Blimp.

"Think?" he interrupted, heatedly taking up the defense.
"I know it. Let me tell you, Frank Hedstrom's got the golden
touch! Do you know what he's done? He's virtually automated the entire process of handling these chickens. It's really
amazing. . . ."

Thatcher listened carefully. Tom Robichaux was not a
man to go overboard about young men on the make. "John,"

he was saying earnestly, "Hedstrom is a born money-maker if ever I saw one."

Thatcher did not dispute the reading. "What do you think about him—as a man?"

Robichaux, who recognized his own weakness, expostulated. "Hell, how should I know?"

Thatcher persisted. He knew that Robichaux was not the man to supply a perceptive character study—as witness his marital career. Still, Robichaux & Devane were in this up to their necks. Robichaux could at least supply some salient characteristics.

Pressed, Tom did his best. Frank Hedstrom was very young—"Oh, around thirty, I'd say. Looks like a kid. From someplace out in Illinois—Oak Park or Park Oak or River Forest or River Grove or one of those damfool places." Hedstrom had started with one small diner, then moved into the take-out business. Then, using borrowed money—"and a lot of savvy"—he had launched into the franchise business. And in two short years . . .

"No, no," said Thatcher hastily. "I know he's got good inventory control. I know he's automated chicken cooking —whatever that means. I want to know what kind of man Frank Hedstrom is, Tom."

Over oysters, Robichaux was resentful. "What kind of— Oh, for God's sake! Doesn't say much, knows his business . . ."

"And knows how to make money," Thatcher summarized for him.

Robichaux suspected mockery. Downing a fork, he looked around Fraunces Tavern for financial spies, then reiterated the main point as he saw it.

"Look, John, don't think this take-over business came easy to the people down in Philadelphia. Their management had us check Hedstrom and Chicken Tonight backwards and forwards. They were dying to find a good, solid reason to put up a fight. But we couldn't find a thing. Hedstrom's a natural."

"Still, Southeastern's management was against the merger," Thatcher said. This was the kind of information he had hoped for. And more was coming.

"Use your head, John. Why do you think Southeastern has always stayed so small and conservative? Because of its management! Most of them are living back before World War One. Hell! Some of them are over seventy-five. They were surprised that there are chicken franchisers, let alone chicken franchisers big enough to take control of an insurance outfit!"

Thatcher could understand Robichaux's vehemence. In modern America, where cigarette firms were buying hotels and where frozen-food producers were diversifying into razor blades, such surprise argued a powerful insulation from the forces of the marketplace.

"I'm not sure that Southeastern Insurance is such a good catch," he observed calmly.

"Now, don't get me wrong," Robichaux urged, tacking sharply. "Southeastern isn't composed entirely of fossils. When we gave them the report on Hedstrom, most of the management was ready to bow to the inevitable. Hell! The offer was too good to pass up. Only a couple of the old trouts stood out."

Thatcher grinned. He often thought that Robichaux's own private calendar had become permanently stuck during Prohibition. "But still no real enthusiasm?" he persisted.

"What could you expect? The simplest thing for Hedstrom to do with that management is sweep it out!" Robichaux spoke with an enthusiasm which might have surprised his clients in Philadelphia. "But it was still too good not to recommend to the stockholders."

"Very altruistic of them," Thatcher said dryly. "I suppose Southeastern's management owns stock, too?"

Robichaux drew his head back like an affronted walrus. "Well, what do you think?" he demanded indignantly.

"I'd like to think that Hedstrom knows what he's doing," Thatcher said gloomily.

"That boy isn't taking shots in the dark. He probably figures that with the right management, Southeastern can take a real spurt. You can bet that he took a long cold look." Suddenly Robichaux was reminded of his own grievances. "He probably made up his mind in half the time it took me to persuade Southeastern. I'd still be at it if one of the directors didn't happen to be a big broiler king. He was hot for the deal, knows all about Hedstrom."

"A broiler king?" Things were worse than he had thought, Thatcher decided.

"He owns one of these huge chicken places. God knows what they call them. It can't be farms. They raise thirty thousand birds at a time. They sound more like factories. Anyway, he supplies Hedstrom, so he knew all about him."

Thatcher nodded. "All right, Tom. You've sold me—for the time being, at least. Hedstrom is a reasonable bet and so is Southeastern. I'm willing to go along."

Robichaux signaled to the waiter for coffee and relaxed. "Amazing when you stop to think of it," he said. "Hedstrom may well give Getty and Howard Hughes a run for the money."

"If what you say is right . . ."

"And the whole thing rests on a chain of chicken restaurants . . ."

A spoon hovered as Robichaux continued, contributing some personal philosophy.

"Just between the two of us, John—and I wouldn't like it to go any farther—I'm old-fashioned. I still think of railroads and oil—or even cars or soap. But chickens? Well, that's one helluva way to make big money!"

CHAPTER 2

TOP WITH CRUMBS

WALL STREET financiers might well view Chicken Tonight with incomprehension, but Wall Street financiers have time, money, cooks and *canard à l'orange* at their disposal. In less rarefied strata it is otherwise. For years young wives have pushed their carts along supermarket aisles, done a little comparative pricing and turned chicken into America's economy food, not its luxury. "What chicken again?" has become the lament of the rising young executive.

But while husbands asked rhetorical questions, American housewives got to the root of the matter: "Why cook?"

The answer was promptly provided by pioneers in the field of food delivery. Call us up, they said, and we'll deliver fully cooked chicken, with side orders of cole slaw, to your front door. But the frontier days of primitive fried chicken and cole slaw were numbered. Almost overnight, the food-delivery field was revolutionized. While purists and conservatives stuck to fried chicken, Chicken Tonight with its twenty-five, thirty-two, forty-one delicious varieties of chicken was born. And, with lightning rapidity, it grew and prospered.

One reason that this phenomenon (and the soaring price of Chicken Tonight stock) bemused Tom Robichaux and most of Wall Street was that, unlike the neon-lit hamburger stand, Chicken Tonight was largely invisible to its patrons. Frank Hedstrom did not waste money on showy downtown locations. Chicken Tonight in Willoughby, New Jersey, was typical. It occupied three converted storefronts in an old building two blocks off Main Street. It boasted only a modest sign. Many of its steadiest customers did not know where it was. The important thing, however, was that regularly every Wednesday night they phoned in their orders:

"For the seven o'clock truck, OK? One chicken Oregano, one chicken Mandarin. Two side orders of fried apples, one cranberry relish, two muffins . . ."

When it rained, snowed, grew very hot or very cold, regulars and others called Monday and Tuesday as well. On the weekends, everybody called.

What customers did recognize was the gaudy gold-and-orange Chicken Tonight truck, currently parked behind the store. Its dazzling stripes were always carefully polished; there was a model chicken over the driver's cab, and, inside, a heating system from which each order was plucked, already packed. The trucks, driven by high-school boys, sped around Willoughby after dark with youthful exuberance.

Indoors, the Willoughby Chicken Tonight was like every other Chicken Tonight in the country. There was a vast array of stainless-steel equipment, from ingredient bins to microwave ovens to giant refrigerators and pumps dispensing prepackaged mixes. A telephone order, taken by one of three girls, was relayed instantly to the tall young man standing near the phone desk; he pushed buttons and sent a complete order down an assembly line of dippers, turners, cookers, packagers and wrappers. In seven minutes your order was cooked, packed in heat-retaining containers and whisked to the waiting truck. The truck left every twenty minutes. Vernon Akers, who owned the Willoughby franchise, had reported these speeds to the home office and was still trying to match Chicken Tonight in Needham, Massachusetts, where orders took five minutes to fill and trucks left every fifteen minutes.

And the meal delivered to your door, while it could not rival a French chef's quail under glass, was guaranteed (money back) to be hot, tempting, ample and cheap.

This, in short, was what had mystified John Putnam Thatcher—automated chicken.

From four o'clock in the afternoon to midnight, Chicken Tonight in Willoughby was an orderly bedlam. Just now it was ten in the morning.

". . . and two boxes of chicken Paprika, two of chicken Tarragon and four of chicken Mexicali. Right?"

Vern Akers nodded.

"Say, that chicken Mexicali is really going over big, isn't it?" Clyde Sweeney drove the weekly supply truck from Chicken Tonight's Trenton warehouse. He sounded incredulous. "What the hell is it?"

"Don't ask me. I don't know what's in half the flavors." Akers was busy checking invoices against his order list. "Dodie! What's in the Mexicali?"

His wife looked up from a ledger. She was a bustling energetic woman with a short crop of wiry dark hair. At the moment, her face was marked with a long streak of ink where she had rubbed a finger against her cheek.

"Chili powder," she said absently. "Oh, hello, Clyde, you're early this week."

"I've been rushing to get to the Akerses'. They have the best coffee on my route."

Dodie grinned. "All right. I can take a hint." She pushed back her chair. "It'll be a relief to get away from these damned books."

"Now, Dodie," her husband said, "it's a lot less work than cleaning out all these tanks. And, if you're getting coffee, how about some of those breakfast rolls you made?"

While his wife was out of the room Vern Akers finished checking the invoices and handed back the flimsies. Clyde Sweeney slapped his order book closed as a signal that business was suspended. He became social.

"I've got a hot tip on the second race at Garden State tomorrow, Vern. Be a crime to pass it up."

Vern Akers shrugged. "No, Clyde. I don't know how it is. I used to get a real kick out of the ponies, but not any more."

Clyde Sweeney shook his head dubiously. He was a small, jaunty man with long carefully trimmed sideburns. He was wearing the gold-and-orange uniform of all Chicken Tonight drivers. Off duty, however, he was a dapper dresser, recognizable two blocks away as a sport, a bachelor, a man who always had money riding on the horses, the World Series, the Celtics or the Rangers. Now the missionary spirit moved him.

"Give yourself a break, Vern," he urged. "You work plenty hard. You deserve a little fun."

"That's just the trouble, Clyde," Akers explained. "It's no fun any more. I tell you, once you've gambled your life savings on starting your own business, marching up to the five-dollar window isn't much of a thrill. In fact, playing dominoes is a lot more exciting."

Sweeney was pained but tolerant. "Now, look, Vern," he protested, "you can't be in any real trouble. I deliver your orders. They're getting bigger every week."

Vern Akers struggled to express himself. His bewildered frown had become almost permanent in the last eighteen months.

"Oh, it's not how much we're selling," he said.

"Well, then?"

"I'll tell you what," said former Master Sergeant Vernon Akers in a burst of frankness. "Running your own business isn't like being in the Army."

"Christ! I should hope not! Wasn't twenty years enough for you?" Clyde Sweeney had never been in the Army, but he had heard about it.

Akers was unresentful. "There's a lot to be said for the service," he ruminated aloud. "You've got your own job to do, and you don't worry about anything else. But here you've got a hundred things to worry about. If it isn't the help not turning up, it's figuring out what supplies you're going to need. And as for getting anything fixed—well, that's hopeless. Honest to God, I sometimes think Dodie and me spent too long in Japan and Germany and Alaska. We're out of touch."

Clyde Sweeney broke into the recital. "But you're making a go of things here. So what are you complaining about?"

"I'm not complaining. I'm just trying to get things straight. If it weren't for the way Chicken Tonight has got things organized, we could never have gotten off the ground. We lease all this equipment from them, you know, and that training program they gave us was great. And of course the whole preparation of the orders is standardized."

"Coffee!" Dodie announced, returning with a tray. She helped them to cream and sugar and then extended a plate to Sweeney. "Try one of these, Clyde. They're homemade, believe it or not. The only thing around here that is." She looked around with mock disgust at the array of ovens and freezers lining two walls. "When Vern broke it to me that we were opening a Chicken Tonight, I thought my twenty years of cooking was going to come in handy. Instead, he's running a factory while I'm a bookkeeper."

Vern grinned. "That's what I was explaining to Clyde. They've got the whole thing down to a science. We get the different mixes in a dry powder. All we have to do is to dump them into the pumps. Just the right amount of water is automatically added. Then, when you slide a chicken under the spigot, the right amount is pumped out. Then the ovens do everything but make change for you. That's what I call management."

Dodie was unimpressed. As she poured more coffee, she said, "If they're so smart, why don't they automate the bookkeeping?"

"Maybe they will," her husband replied. "They're putting in a new system to cut down on the work in the warehouses and the trucks. You watch your step, or you'll be automated right out of a job."

"Like me," said Clyde Sweeney. "I was meaning to tell you. This is the last time I'll be around. I've already got my lay-off notice. They're cutting back the drivers by fifteen percent."

The Akerses looked at him in concern.

"Oh, Clyde," said Dodie with quick sympathy. "That's awful. What are you going to do?"

Sweeney gave a snappy little thumbs-up gesture. "Don't worry about me, Dodie. Mrs. Sweeney's little boy learned how to take care of himself a long time ago. I've already got something else lined up."

"That's good. But I still say it's too bad," Dodie persisted. "We'll miss you. Will you still be in these parts?"

"I expect to do some traveling. But don't tell Sue yet. I still want to see if she'll break down and come out with me Saturday night."

Dodie was not encouraging. Sweeney had been trying to date her daughter for the last six months. "It's no good, Clyde. I think she's just about ready to get married."

"Let me make one last try. I just saw her out in the parking lot. By the way, here are the new menus. I think I'll go out and start unloading the truck."

He left, and clucking gently, Dodie turned her attention to the familiar cardboard folders, zebra-striped in gold and orange.

Vern too had returned to business. "Well, what do you know?" he said, looking up from some literature from the home office. "You know how many delicious flavors of chicken we've got now, Dodie? We've got forty-three!"

Specialization has its drawbacks. Wall Street, including John Putnam Thatcher and the Sloan Guaranty Trust, concentrated on Chicken Tonight, Inc., its assets and liabilities, its rate of growth and earnings per share. Chicken Tonight proprietors, like the Akerses in Willoughby, charted the success of the new chicken Mexicali and reviewed the sales of chicken Magyar (sour cream) and chicken Arabian (pistachios). On balance, both Wall Street and Willoughby were cautiously optimistic.

The view from Philadelphia was rather more comprehensive. Possibly because of this, the prevailing mood was not particularly sunny. Twelve sober businessmen in an ancient board room not far from Rittenhouse Square were coming to the end of a long meeting.

For once, the board of directors of Southeastern Insurance had not gone through the motions of a meaningless ritual. For the first time in many decades, the board had had real business to get its teeth into. Chicken Tonight's bid to take over Southeastern Insurance had seemed like a vision of

Frank Hedstrom. But others, it developed, were only too willing to share the vision. The board had just learned that Southeastern stockholders were returning proxies at an astonishing rate, eloquent testimony that they wanted nothing more than to have their company absorbed by Chicken Tonight. At the present clip, the necessary two-thirds-approval would be in hand weeks before the stockholder meeting.

The prevailing mood was well-bred astonishment punctuated by elderly regret.

"I can't get over it," quavered the chairman of the board, an eminent septuagenarian. He flicked over a pile of garish brochures. "Chicken Mexicali! Chicken Neapolitan! I never thought I'd live to see the day when Southeastern became part of a hash-house operation."

"Oh, now sir . . ." said several voices.

"Chicken Hawaiian!" said the chairman, with deep disgust. "Oh well, I'm an old man. You younger fellows have to have your way. Chicken Polynesian!" He rose from his place at the head of the table and, like minor royalty, made his way toward a waiting Rolls-Royce, punctiliously escorted by several junior officers of the company.

"Poor old Cadwallader," said another director, relaxing now that business was over. "I don't think he'll get over it. Of course, at his age he can't be expected to see what a real opportunity this is."

"Careful," said somebody in his ear, but it was too late.

Buell Ogilvie, president of Southeastern Insurance, was even older than the chairman of the board. He too was clambering to his feet.

"Well, well, well!" he said testily. "I think I'll be going on, too, Morgan. Sad day—sad to see an old firm go. But, Roberts, you never get too old to see profits when they're under your nose! Not if you're an Ogilvie—or a Cadwallader! Well, I'm on my way. Give my regards to Margaret, won't you, Morgan?"

Only after a second ceremonial withdrawal did conversation become genuinely unbuttoned.

"Whew!" It was a long breath, expelled with triumphant relief. Pelham Browne was not only a member of Southeastern's board, he was a prime mover in the proposed merger. He had taken a modest (by Philadelphia standards) inheritance and parlayed it into a million-dollar poultry farm on the Eastern Shore of Maryland. A large, florid man, he was not particularly sensitive to atmosphere, but he knew better than anybody else in the room just how good an opportunity Chicken Tonight offered.

"It's going better than I thought," he said to no one in particular. "Of course, change always hurts—even when it's sweetened by a good healthy chunk of dough. But I tell you, Chicken Tonight's offer was too darned good for us to turn down. They're really going places. Do you know they've upped their purchases from me five times in the last year?"

He had finished by sounding rather defensive.

Morgan Ogilvie, the executive vice-president and the real head of Southeastern Insurance, nodded absent-mindedly. "There's no doubt you're right, Pel."

Pelham Browne was the kind of man whose feelings showed. At the moment, he was indignant. "For God's sake! We're all on our way to making big money, by merging with Chicken Tonight. And you'd think we were attending a wake!" he exploded.

Morgan Ogilvie smiled thinly. "Well," he said reflectively, "I confess I don't like this move any better than Uncle Buell does. But, like him, I see the financial advantages. I do wish we had had more time to get used to the whole idea. After all, Pel, Chicken Tonight and Southeastern Insurance—well, it's going to take time to get used to. You don't give up a company that's had an honored name for one hundred years without a twinge or two."

"I'll take the twinge," said Pel Browne rather coarsely, "when it comes sugar-coated this way."

His fellow-directors had heard Pelham Browne before. One of them turned to Ogilvie. "Morgan," he said, "I know you voted to go ahead, but tell me, do you have any real reservations now we're in the home stretch?"

Ogilvie pursed his lips. He was a tall, bald man with a handsome presence who prided himself on a strong sense of responsibility. In the reassuring voice that stood him in good stead as chairman of the United Fund, he replied, "I've done what I can to insure that this move is the best one we can make at the time. Robichaux and Devane have done a thorough job of stock valuation. I spent a week in Trenton, at Chicken Tonight's regional headquarters, and, as I said before, they showed me everything I asked to see. I have hired investigators to look into their over-all operations. I've tried to find out how stable their top management is, how their cost programs are working—everything!"

"And?" demanded his interlocutor.

Ogilvie shrugged well-tailored shoulders slightly. "As far as I can see, Chicken Tonight is going to be even more successful than it has been. I know that it's not our sort of business, but it's profitable. There's no doubt of that. And, in these days of conglomerates . . ."

When they finally went their separate ways, Southeastern's directors allowed themselves to be even more frank.

"Sure, Ida," said one well-known lawyer to his wife, "it's a sentimental loss—like tearing down Liberty Hall. But between you and me, if we get a little more money and a little less high-minded Old Philadelphia, well, I think we can handle that boat you've been talking about."

Morgan Ogilvie, whose family had founded Southeastern Insurance, was just as forthright.

"No, of course I'm not happy, Margaret. I had hoped young Morgan would succeed me. And Midge's Ted is doing very well in Sales. It's a real pleasure to see the next generation coming along. For that matter, I don't think I'm going to enjoy working as part of Hedstrom's outfit. But in this world it's money that counts. And there was absolutely no denying . . ."

Mrs. Morgan Ogilvie, a majestic woman, did not incline toward sympathy.

"Perhaps," she said ironically, "we should give Lena the night off and call Chicken Tonight."

CHAPTER 3

ADD TOMATOES

MRS. OGILVIE did not call Chicken Tonight, but millions of others did. All in all, chicken Mexicali looked like another triumph, one of an unbroken string.

Accordingly, headquarters, in a large office suite on the fifteenth floor of the Hotel Montrose, did not ring with self-congratulation, but with purposive bustle directed toward the future. At Chicken Tonight they were learning to take triumphs in stride.

". . . sales figures from New England are here," said a shirt-sleeved youth. "Up twelve per cent. And there's a breakdown on the motel business that that guy in Edgartown tried out. He's got seventeen motels tied up, and he did over eight thousand dollars each night in July and August. It's a real idea, Frank."

"Good," said Frank Hedstrom. "I liked that motel tie-up myself. Tell Wally I want to push it. Start advertising in the motel journals. OK, Bill, leave the stuff. I'll go over it later."

The door closed behind Bill. Hedstrom and his closest associate tried to continue their talk.

"That motel angle is a good one," said Hedstrom, glancing idly through the bulky report Bill had deposited. "Oh, and by the way. Mexicali is going to be our most successful promotion yet. I owe Iris something nice."

"Iris?" said Ted Young, looking up from a folder of cost studies.

"Mexicali was your wife's idea, boy," said Hedstrom. "Remember? After you went to Acapulco? You came back scared to death I had really gotten out of hand. Iris came back suggesting Mexicali."

"Oh, yes," said Ted Young.

18

Hedstrom watched him withdraw into private calculations. Good old Ted—great with facts and figures. People—even Iris, his wife—were something else. But without Ted could Frank Hedstrom have made the long haul from Oak Park, Illinois?

Hedstrom did not honestly know. The ideas were always his, the fierce, driving ambition. Ted had supplied the prudence, the doubts, the brake. The ideas and the daring were paying off, and a lot of people knew it. Just where did the prudence and doubt fit into Chicken Tonight's high riding?

"Frank," said Young, "Southeastern's proxies are pouring in. I hear they've got at least thirty percent of the stock already."

The telephone trilled. "Hedstrom," he said. "Yes, put him on. Yes. . . . Yes, Ted was just telling me. Better than we thought. . . . What? . . . Yes."

Young waited patiently, a permanently middle-aged man with rimless glasses and an anxious mien. He had been a high-school classmate of Frank Hedstrom's, but he had always been the wizened schoolteacher. Frank, it seemed, would go on being the basketball star forever.

"Robichaux," said Hedstrom, cradling the phone. "He wants us to lunch with him tomorrow."

"Old gasbag," said Young.

Frank Hedstrom raised almost colorless eyebrows. "He's done all right by us, Ted."

"We could have done it without him," said Ted Young stubbornly.

"I'm not so sure."

"What do you mean, Frank? Listen to me."

The door opened to cut off an argument, and admitted a secretary.

"Here's that cost breakdown you asked for, Mr. Hedstrom," she announced breathlessly. "All about those new pumps we've got to bid on—"

She was interrupted by an elderly man brandishing telegrams. "The test-kitchen studies on chicken Bavarian give it the OK."

"OK," said Hedstrom quickly. "Angie, put that stuff down here. And, Phil, tell them to go ahead. We'll get Jack to schedule a Bavarian Month."

"At Christmas," said Angie raptly.

Hedstrom was reading the telegrams. "Not a bad idea," he said.

Chicken Tonight was a business where every minute, every hour, every day produced news—about costs, about equipment, about men, about contracts. Ted Young and Frank Hedstrom thrived on interruptions. In the beginning, it had been from wholesale grocers, truck rentals, unions; now it was Wall Street bankers, real-estate developers, and chambers of commerce. But the tempo was the same, and so was the message; here was movement, here was drive, here was money being made.

Newcomers to the Chicken Tonight organization, whether at headquarters in New York, at the Chicken Tonight Test Kitchens, at any of the six regional warehouses or in any individual shop, got used to a ceaseless flow of spot checks, of detailed instructions, of questionnaires, of improved methods, of new products. They got used to them—or got out.

"There's your weak spot," Tom Robichaux had said during an earlier inspection visit. "It all rests on you."

"And on Ted here," Hedstrom had answered calmly. "He's been my right arm from the beginning."

Robichaux was bored by visits to industry. He had fallen back on a truth long obvious to him. "If Chicken Tonight grows the way I think it can grow, you need more than a right arm. You need an organization."

"He's right," said Ted Young colorlessly.

"Eh? Oh yes. Yes, indeed," Robichaux had said. He had forgotten that Ted Young was present.

Even so, there was now a director of marketing, a corporate-development manager, a product-studies specialist —all well-paid professionals, all ready to make the run for the roses with Chicken Tonight.

But when Frank Hedstrom thought aloud, he still did it with Ted Young.

"Ted, we're going to have to think about producing our own chickens," he announced. "I've said it before. This buying them from Pelham Browne and the rest is costing us too damned much money."

Young frowned.

Hedstrom was used to that frown. "I don't like being tied to these long-term contracts."

And Ted Young was used to Frank Hedstrom; he knew that this was only the beginning, in more ways than one.

Five flights up in the Hotel Montrose, the same topic was being discussed before a large mirrored dressing table in a suite fragrant with expensive perfume.

"You know, Frank has this bee in his bonnet about producing his own broilers. Ted doesn't like the idea at all."

"Well, they'll settle it one way or the other," Joan Hedstrom replied casually as she stooped to place her street shoes neatly on the rack.

"But which way? The right way or the wrong way?" Iris Young demanded.

"I don't suppose it makes all that much difference."

Iris Young laid down her hairbrush with a familiar sense of exasperation. "Honestly, Joan! Anybody would think you didn't care. Don't you know that Chicken Tonight can't afford to make mistakes at this stage of the game?"

Joan Hedstrom sank back on her heels. Her mild blue eyes widened. "What makes you think they're going to make a mistake?"

Under that clear, inquiring gaze, Iris became even more urgent. "Sometimes I think you don't realize what's at stake. Chicken Tonight is one of the miracle stocks on the market right now. But it's still new. It wouldn't take much to upset it. Why, if Frank and Ted go into raising their own broilers, that would mean canceling all their contracts. Then if they hit a snag or their costs went too high, they'd be sunk. Don't you see that?"

Joan Hedstrom remained as placid as ever. "I'm sure they'll figure out something."

"That's not good enough. Chicken Tonight could come down as fast as it went up. And particularly now, when they've got this merger on their hands."

"I don't know how you know all these things, Iris. You must spend hours reading those financial pages. Why bother? Everything will work out. It always does."

"And if it doesn't?" her friend asked almost menacingly.

"What in the world do you mean?"

"What if Chicken Tonight folded?"

"Then Frank would just have to start something else," his wife said with unimpaired serenity.

For want of a better outlet, Iris Young recaptured the hairbrush and attacked her hair with stinging vigor. She was not really surprised at Joan's response. For the better part of fifteen years, she had been trying to goad Joan Hedstrom into reactions that matched her own tempestuous surges of excitement and despair. And never successfully. At sixteen, Joan had been a calm, friendly, optimistic girl. She had not changed.

She was now inspecting her companion's appearance. "You look stunning, Iris. I'm so glad you settled on the sea green. The black wasn't half as good on you."

Iris had finished her cloud of black hair and was now fastening long gold earrings. Her tilted image smiled back from the mirror. The slight irony in that smile was lost on Joan. That too was a feature of the past fifteen years. As far as Joan was concerned, Iris often smiled that way.

"You're right, Joan," Iris Young said. "But I would have bought the black if you hadn't been with me."

Years ago, it had been accepted between them that Joan was the authority on fashion, just as Iris was the arbiter of social protocol. Joan Hedstrom herself was undramatically good-looking; her carefully lightened sandy hair and darkened brows required conventional clothing. But her unerring eye found ample scope in dashing creations that suited Iris' sinuous figure, raven hair and hazel eyes. Similarly, as Joan Hedstrom's income grew, it was Iris who prodded her into country clubs, riding lessons for the children, caterers for her parties.

But now they were at a crossroads. This much was clear to Iris Young, if not to Joan Hedstrom. Now they had moved into circles where women gowned in Paris and jeweled on Fifth Avenue were the visible symbols of their husbands' success. At the reception today, people would be more interested in the wife of Frank Hedstrom than in the wife of Ted Young, no matter how beautiful she was.

For one dizzy moment at Bergdorf's, Iris had almost forgotten this great truth. The black dress had beckoned because in it she would have been an important man's wife.

Which was absurd. Her husband was an employee of Frank Hedstrom.

"You were right," she repeated firmly, "absolutely right."

"Yes," said Joan, happily unconscious of Iris' thoughts.

"You know, Iris, I am really looking forward to next weekend. It will be our first weekend at the new house. And with the boys working this way, I'm really happy we've got it. I don't know why you had to work so hard to convince me we needed a place out in the country."

Iris was affectionately mocking. "You always fight change."

"But now I see that you were absolutely right. It will be just the way you said. A place on the Chesapeake, miles from the city or even the suburbs."

"Not exactly the way I said. I'll never know why you insisted on building a new house. What I had in mind was an old Southern Colonial, a plantation house. You know perfectly well you can afford it. A showplace, with a veranda and acres of lawns and gardens!" Iris' eyes sparkled at the picture she was painting. "You could have had waxed parquet floors with Oriental rugs. French windows opening out from the drawing room and living room. We could have found some Southern Georgian furniture and Chinese wallpaper. It would have been perfect!"

Joan laughed. "Perfect! Until you put Frank and Joan Hedstrom into it. Not to mention the kids! It would never have been right for us. Oh, Iris, we talked it all out. And you did agree with me in the end. We wanted a place where we could all relax, where Frank and Ted could get some fishing and duck hunting, didn't we?"

"Oh, yes!" Iris said quickly with the half-gasp that sudden recollection of her husband always evoked. In her enthusiasm for gracious living she had momentarily forgotten him.

"And the boys need a good rest," Joan continued persuasively, "with all their worries. They're in the office day and night."

"Ted burns himself out," Iris said with sudden intensity. "Frank is just a cockeyed optimist."

It was not the way Iris Young had planned things. In her senior year of high school she had fallen in love, with a passion that was almost shocking to a girl accustomed to playing the belle of the ball. She had known instantly that she would work and scheme and slave to make a good life for Ted Young. The future had been very clear to her. She would take a job so that Ted could go to accounting school. Then they would have children, carefully spaced so as not to be a drain on the financial resources of their early years. Then they would reap their reward. In the evenings she would leave a house lovingly designed to provide comfort and warmth for its owner; she would drive to the station in a convertible and wait for Ted. On weekends they would go out. They would still be young enough to enjoy themselves. They would travel, they would give their children all the advantages. They would be conscious of having built a good life together.

As the first stages of her program unfolded, she had watched the young Hedstroms with disapproval. Joan had her first baby as soon as propriety allowed. Frank worked days and went to school at night. Joan had a second baby. Then Frank, with utter irresponsibility, decided to go into business for himself. The Hedstrom standard of living, already marginal, plummeted sharply. Frank needed money to keep going. He borrowed from everybody and tried to talk Ted into a partnership. He was refused. Still, he kept going on a shoestring, in spite of babies, in spite of debts, in spite of everything.

And now here they all were. Iris had all the things she had dreamed of, even more. The convertible, the house, the parties. Her imaginary picture had been realized. Except for one thing. If Joan had had a place in that picture—and it was very hard for Iris to imagine a world without Joan—it had been as a loyal admiring chorus. Not for one moment had Iris visualized herself playing second fiddle to Joan. But she was, however little Joan realized the fact.

Iris Young smiled ruefully at her brilliant reflection. As she applied the final drops of perfume behind her ears and in the hollow of her throat, she could see Joan conscientiously emptying her street purse. Dear Joan! No one could really grudge her success. Then the wide, moist lips tightened. But Joan's husband was something else again. Little Frank Hedstrom! It was ridiculous.

Because, thought Iris with a sudden, bitter insight, it didn't much matter what she did. But Ted? Ted wasn't going to play second fiddle to anyone. Not as long as she could do anything about it!

"Ready?" asked Joan sunnily.

"Ready as rain," said Iris Young.

CHAPTER 4

BRING TO A BOIL

AMERICAN CUISINE and American television have many points of similarity, some of them the subject of ill-natured books by visiting British academics, French lady intellectuals and Italian journalists. Both industries have markets big enough to make the Common Market look like the corner delicatessen; both advertise with superlatives designed to whet jaded appetites: "sun-kissed, dewy-fresh," "an hour of impeccable taste," "from icy mountain streams," "from the entertainment capital of the world." The essence of American culture can be found where they coincide, in the food commercials on TV. Revolting as this may seem to visiting and domestic intellectuals, U. S. immigration data—like U. S. supermarket sales—prove that "rich creamy mayonnaise with that homemade flavor" and "luscious strips of delicious coconut" are just what a lot of people, Americans and otherwise, eat up, figuratively speaking.

So it was doubly ironic that TV delivered the initial blow to the food industry. First blood was drawn during prime time: ten-thirty, Eastern Standard Time.

A situation comedy pursued its relentless course. The young, lovely widow dithered between laughter and tears as her three photogenic (if genetically improbable) children machinated to get themselves a new daddy.

"Oh, Jeremy!"

"Gee, Ma! I just asked Mr. Perkins if he wanted to marry us."

(Maniacal audience laughter. Close-up of widow.)

"Oh, Jeremy."

Whatever towheaded Jeremy was going to say (after "Gee, Ma!") was lost. Suddenly an adult voice intruded into the world of Peter Pan: "Stand by for a network alert. We interrupt this program . . ."

Millions of Americans stiffened. Who had been assassinated this time?

". . . the Public Health Service has just announced that seventy-two persons in six states along the Eastern seaboard have been hospitalized with symptoms of acute food poisoning. According to spokesmen, victims had recently eaten chicken or other poultry. Until the source of the contamination is isolated, the Public Health Service is issuing a provisional warning to the public to avoid chicken and chicken products. Emergency investigations are under way and all possible personnel . . ."

Jeremy still wanted a new daddy, but from Maine to Maryland household attention was elsewhere.

"Thank God we had meat loaf tonight," said a housewife in Nashua, New Hampshire. "I was thinking of chicken."

In Olean, New York, no thanks were being offered:

"I knew it! I knew something was wrong! I've been feeling lousy since we got up from the table. No, Doris, an Alka-Seltzer isn't going to help! Didn't you hear what he said? I'm going right down to the hospital! God, I'm feeling worse by the minute."

It was a long hard evening in every emergency ward on the Atlantic.

The morning newspapers had the grisly details. The outbreak had felled people in Elmira, New York, in Lancaster, Pennsylvania, in Hackensack, New Jersey, and in Darien, Connecticut. The toll was stil mounting, and many of the stricken were in critical condition. As for symptoms—well, close reading of *The New York Times* alone caused severe nausea to several unusually sensitive commuters.

"There has not been an incidence of food poisoning on this scale in decades," said a U.S. Public Health official grimly. "Several hundred people are involved, at least. Nor can we pinpoint the source of the tainted chicken. We are pursuing every possible avenue and investigating warehouses, interstate shipments . . ."

In a word, the Public Health was leaving no chicken unturned. There was, however, a snag.

"At this time of the year," continued Dr. Mosby disapprovingly, "with colleges opening and summer vacations ending, many people are traveling. This has complicated the entire situation. Many of the patients admitted to the hospitals have been in transit. And, I regret to say, some of them still cannot tell us where they ate their last meal. At the moment, the extreme points of the affected area are Cleveland, Ohio, and Greenfield, Massachusetts. But it is quite possible . . ."

Clearly, Dr. Mosby himself would not touch chicken anywhere in the continental United States. He ended his statement by urging the public to see a doctor immediately should certain symptoms develop.

"It is nothing," said Dr. Mosby severely, "to fool around with."

In several large cities, local health authorities inserted bold-face advertisements in the major newspapers. The unappetizing text instructed the public, with trenchant candor, on how to void the digestive tract. In New York, experienced city officials did not rely on the written word. The live demonstration on television was presented six times in one day. This effectively squelched whatever appetite for chicken lingered in the metropolitan area.

By the next day, the immediate health emergency was over. Hospital admissions fell to the vanishing point.

So did the consumption of chicken. Supermarkets were the first to reel under the impact. Morning shoppers stocked up on meat, fish, eggs and anything else. By lunchtime, restaurants ranging in caste from the ninety-nine-cent blue-plate special to Cordon Bleu specialties were adjusting to the new facts of life. Charlie Trinkam reported on this facet of the situation when he returned to the Sloan and stopped in John Thatcher's office.

"This is a honeyfall for the printers," he announced, perching on a corner of the desk. "I understand every restaurant in town has put out a rush order for new menus. Crossing things out isn't good enough. They don't want the word *chicken* mentioned on the premises."

"You can't blame them," Thatcher replied. He was idly leafing through a report that Everett Gabler, a senior trust officer, had just delivered. "They poison enough customers without external assistance."

"Of course," Charlie continued, "the Chinese restaurants won't have any trouble at all. They'll just give their dishes new names and no one will ever know the difference."

Everett Gabler, a long-time devotee of health foods, took exception to this remark. Carefully he explained that Oriental diets, high on unbleached rice and vegetables, were nutritionally superior to their Western counterparts.

Wholesome asceticism had no appeal for Charlie. "Almost anything would be nutritionally superior to deadly poison, Everett," he said lightheartedly.

"Come, now, Charlie," Thatcher corrected him. "No one has actually died."

"Not yet," said Trinkam irrepressibly.

In Willoughby, New Jersey, the Akers family was not at all lighthearted. When Sue Akers returned from her nursing classes, she hung up her jacket and looked at her parents a moment before speaking. Instead of the usual predinner madhouse in the Chicken Tonight kitchen, there was only silence. The high-school assistants were missing. Her parents were sitting across the desk from each other, an overflowing ashtray the only evidence of their occupation.

"How are things?" she asked cautiously.

Dodie Akers did not beat about the bush.

"Terrible!"

"One call since we opened." Vern Akers laughed shortly. "For a tray of corn bread and a side order of sweet tomato relish. I told the kids to take off. I'm not going to have any trouble handling the business alone."

Dodie Akers looked at her husband with concern. Then she forced a smile and spoke to her daughter.

"Vern's right. We're not going to need any help. Why don't you and Bob go out tonight?"

She shook her head. "I don't feel like going out. I've already called Bob and told him to come over here. You always say we don't have enough free time to really straighten out the stockroom and polish the pumps. Well, now's our chance."

"What's the point?" said Vern Akers hopelessly. "We might be closing down this place in another couple of weeks."

But he was no match for his womenfolk, who were in silent agreement that he needed activity. Dodie rose decisively. "Then we'll close down with the best-polished pumps in town! Come on, Sue."

Sue paused at the back door to look at her father. "Don't worry so much, Dad. It's bound to blow over."

Sue Akers was not the only optimist. In the St. Paul offices of a major soup canner early next morning, worried executives scanned a list and suddenly realized that far too many of those red-and-white cans contained chicken or chicken stock.

"It could be worse," said one middle-aged and balding Pollyanna, "it could be tomatoes."

"God forbid! Well, what do we do?"

A lengthy conference with expensive market researchers and the firm's glossy advertising firm, as well as the beloved Millie Malone ("I'm Millie Malone, and I've got a wonderful suggestion for those cold-day blues! What about a mushroom soup pick-me-up, with cheese surprises . . ."), produced a high-level forecast: things were bound to blow over.

Day after day, interested parties in St. Paul and elsewhere studied the economic barometer. Finally, one full week after the chicken catastrophe, light appeared at the end of the tunnel.

"Hullo? This Chicken Tonight? Listen, I want chicken for eight. . . . What? Oh, four of the Creole and four of the chicken Kiev. And potato salad, and cole slaw . . ."

Harry Krebs, who ran Chicken Tonight in Pittsburgh, had tears in his eyes.

"Sure he was drunk, Betty. But it's a beginning, it's a beginning."

The ladies in charge of the Little League dinner in Utica were not drunk.

"But how can you feed seventy-five youngsters without creamed chicken on toast? We always have creamed chicken on toast! Besides, this was just another one of those accidents."

Then, on Saturday morning, the other shoe fell.

The U. S. Public Health Service, sounding perilously antagonistic to the entire public as well as its purveyors of chicken, released another terse announcement.

"Mr. Duane B. Bonfils, a victim of the food poisoning caused by eating tainted chicken from a source still not identified by this agency, died this morning in Elmira Community Hospital."

The Public Health then withdrew to its own work, which included investigation of every aspect of chicken production in the country. It left a scene of carnage in its wake.

There were a few doomed attempts to strike back amidst general demoralization.

From the Catskills to the Poconos, Jewish caterers and delicatessen owners stared incredulously at a world without chicken soup, chopped liver and chicken fat, and hoarsely reminded their clientele that kosher chickens were subject to purification rituals proven effective by whole millennia of human history. The response to this stirring ethnic cry was negligible.

The refrigeration industry, with hundreds of federal and local investigators in its warehouses and freight cars, bought time on radio and television to point with pride at the uncontaminated meat and fish it handled. But refrigeration could do only so much. It could not preserve a product that was already tainted.

The National Poultry Institute, already harassed, took instant umbrage and threatened a libel suit.

Two major supermarket chains announced that they would no longer handle any liver sausage containing the slightest trace of chicken livers.

The American Kennel Club urged all dog owners to boycott canned dog foods listing chicken by-products as an ingredient.

"In fact," said Walter Bowman, chief of the Sloan's research department, as he summarized these developments, "everybody's going ape."

After a lifetime at the hub of the American financial community, John Thatcher was not surprised. "They always do, Walter. Now, what about the stock market?"

Bowman reported that every listed stock remotely connected with poultry was sagging. "That's all the big food processors, of course. Everybody who puts out TV dinners and frozen chicken pies, or any of the canned chicken products. But the stocks that are really nose-diving are the franchises. Hell, there are at least fourteen franchise systems that rely on chicken."

"How badly are we hit?"

Walter Bowman let a disingenuous smile crease his face.

"Not badly at all," he said modestly. "I thought the hamburger franchises were a better buy."

Not for the first time, Thatcher marveled at Walter Bowman's ability to sidestep disaster, whether predicted or not. Now he smiled.

"And, of course, you've never been enthusiastic about franchises, anyway."

"They're all right for a quick killing. But in the long run the help problem will get them. The only one really getting anywhere was Hedstrom."

"I thought we'd come to him."

"Twelve million," said Bowman sadly. "That's a lot of credit for a business that's selling poison."

"I don't think we have to worry about that, Walter," Thatcher said dryly. "Chicken Tonight may be selling it, but I doubt if anybody's buying."

"No. Boy, you wouldn't believe everyone could stop buying anything so fast. Have I told you the latest? Now the egg boys are worried it may spread to them. They think the next step will be for people to stop eating eggs."

Thatcher was quick to reassure him. Most Americans, he said authoritatively, had left the farm so far behind that the chicken-egg relationship was lost on them.

"You may be right," Walter said, rising to leave. "All this excitement will die down once the Public Health people find the sleeper."

He was wrong.

The search for that sleeper had been quietly but painstakingly pursued. Patients groggily struggling to their feet after four days in a coma found that young men from the Food and Drug Administration were their first visitors. Relatives waiting in hospital corridors were cross-examined. Motel proprietors and roommates were asked to sign formal statements. All the questions were to the point. When did the patient last eat? What did he eat? Where did it come from?

When the answers came in, Dr. Mosby called his second press conference.

"There is no doubt about it," he declared militantly.

Reporters waited. Dr. Mosby glared at them. "Each and every victim ordered and ate a precooked chicken dinner from a nationwide franchise chain."

Dr. Mosby raised a hand to quell the uproar. He was going to make this announcement in his own way. Like a hanging judge he passed sentence.

"By virtue of the authority vested in my agency I hereby declare that every franchise operating under license from the Chicken Tonight Corporation in all states east of the Mississippi River is closed until further notice."

CHAPTER 5

STUFF AND TRUSS

DR. MOSBY's blitzkrieg tactics would have flattened most front offices. But not Chicken Tonight's. Characteristically, Frank Hedstrom and Ted Young fought back in different ways.

Young was in favor of counterattack.

"You can't do it!" he yelled. He was standing behind a chair, hands digging into its back, his weight thrust forward. Across from him in Frank Hedstrom's office was a representative of the Food and Drug Administration, stubbornly silent.

"You can't do it! We'll get a restraining order! We'll get an injunction!" Young shouted, looking furiously at Chicken Tonight's own lawyers. "What are you two sitting there for? Tell him they can't shut us down."

One of the lawyers closed his eyes wearily. "But they can," he repeated for the third time.

"I'm sorry," said the FDA man, looking both tired and embarrassed.

"Sorry!" Young mocked savagely. "You kill Chicken Tonight, and you say you're sorry! Sweet Jesus!"

The FDA man looked in silent appeal to the figure behind the desk. Frank Hedstrom finally spoke.

"Take it easy, Ted," he said dispassionately. "Don't let it throw you. There's no use fighting this one head on."

Young wanted to challenge him, but Hedstrom put up a hand and continued. "Start thinking, Ted. Even if they hadn't shut us down, do you think anybody would be buying from Chicken Tonight? Particularly when every paper in the country has headlines that say we're selling poison?"

The second lawyer roused himself. "Mr. Hedstrom, that's not accurate. There was a zinc adulterant in one mix and only one mix. The Mexicali, I believe you call it."

"All right, they've proved it was some zinc salt! How do they know it was our Mexicali that did it?" Young asked belligerently. "How do they know?"

Shaking his head, Hedstrom rose from behind the desk, grimacing as he did. They had spent too many hours listening to the FDA's painstaking report. One hundred and thirty-three people had eaten Chicken Tonight's Mexicali; one hundred thirty-three people had collapsed with zinc poisoning.

"It's our Mexicali all right," he said.

The FDA man rose to leave. "Obviously we had to close you down. At least until we zero in a little more. We have no real alternative."

Hedstrom smiled humorlessly. "Of course not."

The FDA man was pleased to be leaving Chicken Tonight. Hedstrom escorted him to the door. "You'll get all the cooperation we can give you."

"Good," said the official.

Hedstrom glanced back at his own lawyers. "I'll be in touch with you," he said pointedly. The lawyers took the hint and collected their belongings.

When Hedstrom returned to his desk, only two others remained in the room with him. Young was sunk into a black reverie of his own. The stout gray-haired woman in the corner was weeping.

"Chicken Mexicali!" Miss Collins moaned through her sobs. "Oh, Mr. Hedstrom, it's impossible! We tested and tested."

Tearfully she continued, telling him what he already knew. Mexicali, like every other Chicken Tonight flavor, had been exhaustively proven in the test kitchens. Chicken Mexicali was absolutely wholesome and fresh. Yet chicken Mexicali, packaged in model kitchens, dispatched to Chicken Tonights where standards of cleanliness were outstanding, had made hundreds of Americans ill and killed one old man in Elmira, New York.

"It's impossible, but it happened," Hedstrom said finally, cutting short Miss Collins' lament. "Now we don't have much time, if we're going to survive all this. We've got a major salvage job on our hands."

Young looked up. "How the hell can we salvage anything when they've shut down every one of our stores? God almighty, do you know what this will do to us when the stock market opens?"

Impatiently Hedstrom brushed this contribution aside. "Ted, forget about the problems. I know what they are. Our stores are shut, and if they were open we wouldn't have any customers. Our franchises are losing money every minute. We're committed to buying thousands of dollars' worth of broilers, whether we can sell them or not. On top of that, we've got a merger on our hands. We've got problems enough to last a lifetime. What we don't have is time."

Young was taken aback by this cavalier dismissal of their difficulties. But without pause Hedstrom went on to the strategy for orderly retreat. "Listen, they're going to let us open someday. We've got to be ready for it," he explained patiently. "Miss Collins, you're going to have an army of people going over your kitchens. I don't have to tell you to bend over backward. We'll get Basil to run down all our outstanding contracts and check our liability to our franchisees. Ted, you've got to get in touch with every one of our warehouses and alert them. Then we'll have to think of some sort of press release."

By sheer force of personality, Hedstrom singlehandedly kept Chicken Tonight headquarters functioning. Even though it was Saturday morning, almost all the staff was on the premises. The secretaries alternated weeping bouts in the ladies' room with savage typing. The marketing division was desperately reviewing cost projections for the forthcoming week. Executives answered phones, snapping curt replies. In its worst hour, Chicken Tonight was still bustling.

This surprised at least one visitor.

"Christ, I don't know how you can do it," said Pelham

Browne bluntly. "It's been one helluva week. Really got to me."

He tossed a flamboyant topcoat on the sofa and settled across from Hedstrom.

"Listen, Frank," he said, "my wife and I were just having a weekend in New York. Hell, I thought I deserved it after this damned chicken scare. Then I caught the news about Chicken Tonight. Do you know any more?"

Browne, owner of Browne Poultry, Inc., supplied nearly two thirds of Chicken Tonight's requirements for Pennsylvania, New Jersey and parts of New York State.

Ted Young looked up from the paper he was checking. "The trouble is in our Mexicali mix," he said abruptly. "That's all anybody knows so far. Your chickens have been used in our other dishes, and there hasn't been any trouble."

Browne heaved a noisy sigh of relief. "It would be a terrible responsibility to live with. Of course, our birds are all inspected—"

He broke off, belatedly aware of Young's open contempt. Hedstrom, he noted, remained expressionless. Browne was spared the need to dig himself out of his own blundering by the phone.

"Hedstrom here. . . . What? . . . Yes, Carl. It's terrible. We're hoping that by the end of the weekend it will be over. . . . What? . . . Why, then we're going to pitch in and triple the advertising budget, for openers. . . . Sure I know this puts the squeeze on you fellows, but remember, it's temporary. We're going to pull through. . . . Yes. . . . Thanks for calling."

Hedstrom put the phone down. "Carl Zabriskie," he explained. "He runs three Chicken Tonights in Buffalo. Worried as hell—and I don't blame him. This is catching our people hard, Browne."

Pel Browne's jowly face crinkled into heavy sympathy. "Boy, I sure hope you're right, Frank. About reopening soon, I mean. Otherwise those chickens you have to buy from me will be a dead loss for you, won't they?"

Young made no effort to hide his derision. "That's the problem, Browne. If we stay closed for three or four weeks, why, we have to keep paying you for chickens we can't use. Because you've got a contract. And you're going to stick to it, aren't you?"

Browne was genuinely startled. "Well, what else can I do? You contracted for an eight-week supply, didn't you? I've already laid out money for feed and supplies—"

Hedstrom cut him off. "Don't worry. We're honoring our contracts. We can still meet our obligations."

Browne's open satisfaction goaded Ted Young. "But just ask yourself what happens when this contract runs out," Ted said viciously.

"Now, Ted . . ."

"No, let him face it the way we have to. Either Chicken Tonight goes out of business, and Mr. Browne is left out in the cold, or else Chicken Tonight will be riding high again. Then we may be making other arrangements."

"Are you threatening me?" Browne blustered at him.

Frank Hedstrom remained detached. "Nobody's threatening anybody, Browne. Ted's just giving you the picture. At the moment, we're concentrating on getting back on our feet."

"Because I've been a damned good friend to Chicken Tonight," Browne continued. He had the trick of not listening very much to others. "You know I've always given Chicken Tonight top priority. And hell, who's been pushing the merger with Southeastern Insurance—Say!"

Browne was stopped in his tracks. He blinked his prominent blue eyes once or twice. "My God," he said slowly. "What about the merger now? I never thought . . ."

"We've thought about the merger," Hedstrom said quietly.

But Browne rolled on. "The agreement is to swap stock at two for one," he remembered aloud. "But when the stock market opens, and Chicken Tonight shares take a nose dive—Frank, what do you think Morgan Ogilvie will do?"

Hedstrom shot a warning look at Ted Young. Then he said, "Ogilvie's your friend. What do *you* think he'll do?"

For an instant Browne goggled at him. Then: "What do I think? I don't have the slightest idea! Why should I? And what makes you think I'm in Ogilvie's confidence?"

Even to his own ears this was unconvincing.

"The first vulture," said Young when Browne finally talked himself out of the office. "Or maybe I mean rat."

Hedstrom looked at him soberly. "Ted," he said, "we're in bad trouble. It isn't helping things when you lose control. You can't blame Browne for holding us to those damned contracts. You can't blame Ogilvie if he welshes on this merger. You can't blame our franchisees when they cry. What would you do in their place?"

Young muttered something inaudible, but Hedstrom went on. "Look, we've been in tight spots before, and we got through by keeping our cool. With luck, we'll make it this time. But right now, Ted, you're not helping a helluva lot."

Young bit his lip. Then, without a word, he turned and left the room.

Hedstrom looked after him until the telephone again summoned him.

"Hedstrom. . . . Oh, yes, Dr. Mosby. . . . What? Are you sure? Oh, yes, yes! Of course it's good to hear that Chicken Tonight was not negligent in any way. . . . What? . . . *What?*"

The voice at the other end of the line spoke at length, and, for once, Frank Hedstrom looked immature as well as young.

"But, Dr. Mosby!" Hedstrom liked to spell things out, no matter how bad they were. "What you're talking about is murder!"

CHAPTER 6

GREASE THE PAN

IN VERY short order, John Putnam Thatcher too was talking about murder.

"Look, Tom, will you please stop shouting and say what you want to say?" he demanded irately.

Telephone exchanges with Robichaux were trial enough during the normal working day. From Friday to Monday (or Tuesday), Robichaux was rarely in the financial district. Away from Wall Street, he compensated for additional distance and bellowed incomprehensibly.

Fortunately, since Robichaux's comments were becoming more thunderously inarticulate by the moment, Walter Bowman strode unceremoniously into Thatcher's office, brandishing a portion of the UP news wire.

Murder, said one word.

Without qualms, Thatcher hung up on the fulminations from an uptown steam room and obtained his information from the telegraphic word:

Federal officials announce Chicken Tonight deliberately sabotaged. . . . Contaminants in Mexicali mix responsible last week's mass food poisoning . . . now identified as zinc derivatives not used in food preparation. . . . Company officials silent possibility disgruntled employees or business competitors . . . DA states murder charge warranted. . . .

The phone rang again. With Miss Corsa absent, Thatcher indulged himself and let Tom Robichaux stew in his own juice. Of course, with Miss Corsa on guard, Bowman would never have enjoyed such breezy access. It was six of one and half a dozen of the other, in normal times. But these trying Trinkam Anniversary days were not normal times. Hence Saturday morning at the Sloan for Thatcher, and for many of his subordinates. Although not, of course, for Charlie Trinkam.

"You know, John," said Bowman comfortably, "this doesn't look so good."

"I suspect Robichaux is ready with a variation on just that theme," said Thatcher, but sarcasm could not deflect Bowman.

"I wasn't happy about our twelve million when the whole chicken industry was supposed to be poisoned. Then, when it was only Chicken Tonight, I got a lot less happy. But now things really look bad. Somebody's out to get Hedstrom."

"Oh, come, now," said Thatcher. "It could be some passing lunatic."

Bowman, who inclined to a Machiavellian interpretation of American business, would not settle for a passing lunatic.

"Maybe," he said with a wealth of doubt. "But from where I sit, the whole setup is as phony as a three-dollar bill. Hedstrom is just the kind of guy to attract trouble. He runs a high-pressure operation. He was beating his competitors hollow. He was going places—fast. I'll bet somebody was out to stop him. Well, I'd better get back to work."

He left Thatcher with food for thought. Finally, unable to put Bowman's views from his mind, he took an unusual step. He tried to reach Maitland down in Commercial Credit, to discuss the Sloan's current position vis-à-vis Chicken Tonight.

Maitland was not in his office. Maitland was not at his home. (Maitland was driving to Syracuse to install his daughter in a freshman dormitory.)

Balked by the phone, a state of affairs Miss Corsa did not tolerate, Thatcher thoughtlessly fell prey to it.

"John!" Robichaux exploded when Thatcher answered. "What's going on there? Now, listen, have you heard the latest? We're going to have to do something. . . ."

"But why does doing something involve driving to Trenton?" asked Thatcher early Monday morning as the Sloan limousine sped down the New Jersey Turnpike.

Robichaux was letting his attention wander. "We can lunch at the Nassau Inn . . ."

"I hope there's a better reason than that," Thatcher commented. He was sure there must be, but it was Frank Hedstrom who produced it.

Hedstrom was waiting for them at Chicken Tonight's giant Trenton distribution warehouse. This was a long modern building that was as carefully landscaped as its neo-Bauhaus neighbors in the Trenton Industrial Park. To all outward appearances, it was not only spankingly clean, it was antiseptic.

As the limousine pulled up, Hedstrom hurried forward to greet them.

"I thought," he said after Robichaux had performed the introductions, "the Sloan might be interested in what's come up."

"What now?" Robichaux rumbled as Hedstrom led them indoors to a severely elegant foyer. There was a decorative receptionist; there was a large sculpture on the wall over the foliage. And there was a small gray-haired man ensconced on the black leather sofa.

"Mr. Denton," said Hedstrom as the small man spryly rose to his feet.

Mr. Denton, it developed, represented the Public Health people. He was one of their senior field men. He acknowledged introductions rather absently and plunged ahead.

"Captain Johnson thought you'd be interested in hearing how we broke this," he said. "Crackerjack work, if I say so myself."

Robichaux, Thatcher could see, was beginning to fret at all these promises of interesting material to come.

"Who is Captain Johnson?" Robichaux asked peevishly, but Mr. Denton, who had an immense air of benign authority, was well and happily launched.

"Yes, indeed," he said, rubbing his hands together. "There's absolutely no question about it now. There was poison in the Mexicali mix, Mr. Hedstrom. Undeniably."

Hedstrom did not reply. But Robichaux protested.

"Good God, the newspapers have been full of it! You don't mean we came all the way down here—"

Mr. Denton eyed him censoriously. "We have more than that."

During this exchange, Hedstrom had been leading them down a corridor. Now they entered a small office complete with desk.

Mr. Denton was still talking. "As I say, we have more than that, although it took us time to get it. Most victims couldn't talk to us until several days after their collapse, you understand. In the meantime we talked to their relatives and studied your distribution system. We started with this map."

Mr. Denton shook out a large map of northeastern United States and laid it on the desk. A portion of the area had been outlined with thick black ink, and small red crosses were dotted irregularly throughout.

"The black line includes the area serviced by your Trenton warehouse," he said, using his pencil as a pointer. "The green circles show the location of individual Chicken Tonight franchises. The red crosses represent victims. You can see why those Cleveland cases bothered us."

Thatcher leaned over the map to follow the argument. All red crosses were within the black line except two in Cleveland, Ohio, which were almost a hundred and fifty miles from the nearest other victim.

Hedstrom was nodding gloomily. "You thought other regional warehouses might be affected."

"Exactly." Denton beamed at this ready comprehension. "I can't tell you how relieved we were that the Cleveland cases pulled through and could talk to us. They turned out to be two college boys."

Robichaux, who was less familiar with the driving habits of the American public than his companions, was still mystified. But Hedstrom seemed to understand.

"All-night drivers," he said.

"Yes. They were driving straight through from Boston to Wisconsin with no stops. At eleven o'clock at night they picked up some chicken Mexicali in New York State to have something to munch. They continued on, alternately sleeping and driving, and occasionally having a bite of chicken. It took much longer for the toxicity to build up than if they had had a regular meal. In fact, they made it to Cleveland before collapsing."

"Well, that pinpoints it at least." Hedstrom accepted the inevitable. "All the poison came from this warehouse." He looked at his bland neutral surroundings appraisingly.

Denton now sprang his surprise. "Not necessarily from the warehouse. If you look at the map again, you will see that, although all the victims bought their chicken within the regional area, only certain franchises were affected. Many Chicken Tonight shops in this region served perfectly wholesome chicken Mexicali."

"God knows what they have on their shelves!"

"Now, now." Mr. Denton was reproachful. "Naturally, we checked that. As soon as we knew it was a zinc additive, we worked out a field test. We went through your stocks here in the warehouse."

"And?"

"Absolutely clean. Then we went through the stocks and pumps of your franchises—with some rather interesting results."

Thatcher could see that they had fallen into the hands of an enthusiast. "And what did those results tell you, Mr. Denton?"

"They gave us a distribution pattern. What's more, the pattern told us that all the poison had been delivered by the same truck, on the same round. It even gave us something else." Mr. Denton's voice ended on a note of triumph.

Frank Hedstrom wasn't playing any games. "What was that?" he asked sharply.

"The truck did not start to deliver poisoned Mexicali until after it had made its first few stops. So I played a hunch. I asked for the driver's time sheet for that particular round. And, sure enough, there had been a truck breakdown early in the morning which forced the driver to leave his truck unattended for an hour. Consequently, he was late for all subsequent deliveries."

Mr. Denton flourished his glasses at this climax.

"That was good work, Mr. Denton," said Hedstrom unenthusiastically. "But it still leaves a lot up in the air. Unless you claim somebody with a pocketful of poison just happened to stumble across that abandoned truck?"

"And then," said Thatcher, equally skeptical, "casually broke in and did a massive adulteration job, when the truck driver was likely to reappear any minute."

Mr. Denton deprecated their attitude. "Certainly not! The breakdown of the truck must have been engineered. And, in any event, the boxes of mix are sealed. I should think you'll find that substitution was involved. But there is only so much that we at the Public Health can do. At this point I turned my findings over to the State Police. I understand they've made further strides. Captain Johnson wanted you to have this background."

"Oh, that's who this Johnson is," Robichaux began.

"You've been most helpful," Thatcher said hastily. Frank Hedstrom was lost in thought.

"Captain Johnson is waiting for you in Willoughby. But there is just one further item. You know how your trucks are loaded with mix?" Mr. Denton looked dubiously at Frank Hedstrom. He had learned that the most obvious details of operation were often a secret to the front office.

But Hedstrom had every detail of Chicken Tonight at his fingertips. "Four boxes deep, four boxes high and as wide as necessary to fill the orders," he replied.

"See what I mean about Hedstrom?" Robichaux whispered at this display of expertise.

Denton, meanwhile, had become a seer, eyes closed, fingertips together. His body rocked slowly back and forth.

"I do not say it is certain, mind you, but it is probable, extremely probable, that you will find that every sixteenth box has been adulterated."

"I figure it out," Captain Johnson said, after laborious calculations on the back of a dirty envelope, "as one out of every sixteen boxes."

They were standing in the parking lot behind Chicken Tonight in Willoughby, New Jersey. A light wind playfully sent leaves scuttling across the asphalt while clear autumn sunlight bathed the scene in brilliant visibility. Thatcher had rarely seen Tom Robichaux looking more out of place.

"You can see how this joker pulled off the job," the captain continued. "He was here, ready and waiting, when the warehouse truck arrived. The driver made his delivery to the Akerses, and then he had a cup of coffee. Apparently that's standard routine." The big policeman looked a question at Hedstrom.

"That's right. Every driver has coffee somewhere along his route. And this driver isn't new, Captain. He's been employed by us for over two years. He's just new to this route."

"We'll come to that later. I just want you to get the picture. The driver has his coffee. When he comes out, he starts up and discovers his fan belt is broken. So he goes inside, tells the Akerses, borrows a car and sets off to get a new one. I suppose that's in order?"

Hedstrom was scrupulously fair to his employees. "Those are our standard instructions to drivers. If they need replacements of standard small units, like fan belts and spark plugs, they buy them locally, get a receipt and continue with the job. Of course, in the event of a major breakdown they're required to call in."

"OK, so you can see what happened. Our joker frayed through the fan belt while the driver was having coffee. Then there's a good hour free for the doped boxes to be substituted."

"You're sure it was a substitution?" Hedstrom asked. He was frowning as if he saw some unpleasantness ahead. "You do realize that there wouldn't have to be any stirring of the poison. These mixes are emptied into a pump which reconstitutes them and does a thorough stirring in the process."

"My God!" ejaculated Robichaux, awed.

It was clear that, by now, Captain Johnson's knowledge of Chicken Tonight was almost as exhaustive as Frank Hedstrom's. "There's no question about that, I'm afraid. We've got some of the doctored boxes, and they were very carefully resealed. That was done at home with plenty of time in hand—not in the back of the truck. I know what's bothering you. You want to know how our joker got hold of mixes to use in the substitution. Well, we'll clear that up in due time."

"I must say it sounds reasonable to me," Thatcher remarked as the frown remained fixed on Hedstrom's face. "I'm already bothered at how much was done right here in the middle of the parking lot. It seems a very public and dangerous place for such an operation, Captain."

"Not as dangerous as you think. In the first place, the truck itself blocked the view from the back window of the Akerses' store."

"Yes, but what about all the other windows? Or what about other people driving up and parking? This lot seems to service all those stores."

Thatcher waved around the little compound. In addition to the Akerses', there were a bakery, a hardware store and a shoestore in immediate view. Not only personnel but customers also used the lot. As they watched, a woman came out of the bakery with two boxes tied together, entered her car and drove off.

"It didn't matter. Anybody but the Akerses could see what was going on. In fact, several people did. We've questioned the whole block till they're sick of us. They saw a man in the orange-and-yellow uniform loading and unloading boxes. Naturally they paid no attention. They see that sort of thing all the time. Our boy simply brought the doped boxes in his own car. When the coast was clear, he substituted them. Then he drove away with the good boxes."

"Christ!" Robichaux exploded. "That's a damn simple way to ruin a million-dollar company."

The captain interrupted him. "It's more than that. It's a damn simple way to commit murder!"

Robichaux was taken aback. Thatcher, however, had seen this coming. "Of course, with what you've uncovered, Captain, that death in Elmira has become murder. There's no question of a mishap any more."

Captain Johnson grunted. In his own way, he turned out

to have some of Mr. Denton's spark. "I don't know if you know how your stuff is unloaded and loaded, Mr. Hedstrom?"

"Four deep, four high, and as much as they need across," Frank Hedstrom repeated his litany.

"Yes, but that's not exactly what I meant. The drivers are told to unload from right to left in each bin. It's got something to do with your first-in, first-out system on inventory."

Hedstrom nodded, waiting for Johnson to continue.

"As nearly as we can tell, the damage was done by substituting the top front row. That way every sixteenth box to be unloaded would be poisoned."

Frank Hedstrom began to curse bitterly.

Captain Johnson was almost sympathetic. "Now, that could be coincidence. But I don't believe it for a minute. A lot of your franchises take multiple orders on the popular flavors. And your Mexicali was going over big. There were two to five boxes going out at each drop. With this system, our boy managed to spread the damage as far as possible. He wasn't taking any chances that all his poison would end up in one or two places, where it would be caught after a couple of people went to the hospital. He wanted a mass epidemic."

As Hedstrom seemed beyond speech, Thatcher marked time. "I suppose that's why he chose the Mexicali."

"Sure thing. That chili powder would cover the taste of almost anything. Not to mention that a lot of people wouldn't be sure of what it was supposed to taste like."

Hedstrom had recovered himself. His voice was now very hard and adult. "All right, Captain. A couple of times you've said we'd get to something later. I suppose I can see what's coming. You haven't even mentioned the fact that the truck was probably locked while it was unattended." He paused aggressively.

The captain contented himself with a silent nod.

With a twisted smile, Hedstrom continued. "So let me list the points for you. Whoever pulled this stunt had access to boxes of mix available only in Chicken Tonight warehouses. He knew the schedule of our drivers. He knew about coffee breaks and instructions in case of breakdowns. He knew which was our most popular, strongly flavored mix. He could get hold of a uniform and a truck key. He knew the physical layout in this parking lot. And, if your first theory is right, he knows how the trucks are unloaded. I don't have to be a mind reader to guess your conclusion. This was done by one of my employees." Hedstrom paused for a deep breath. "You see where this leaves me, don't you? Ordinarily, once the source of contamination was spotted, I'd expect the Public Health people to let me open up. But, hell! Even if they let Chicken Tonight open—and don't think for a minute they will—how can I prevent this from happening again in a week, in two weeks? I'm helpless until I know who did this. And that's as big a mystery as ever!"

This was the moment for which Captain Johnson had been waiting. "I wouldn't say that, Mr. Hedstrom. I think I can name the man right now."

Hedstrom's face went blank. "You can?"

"Not that it's going to do you much good. You've been laying people off at your warehouses, you know. One of the men you let go was a driver called Clyde Sweeney. In fact, he was the driver on this route until almost two weeks ago."

"Are you telling us someone poisoned over one hundred people because he was fired? But he'd have to be insane!" Robichaux, the gourmet, was genuinely indignant. "After all, he'd have no trouble getting another job these days."

"It's not that simple," Johnson replied. "If it was, we could find Sweeney, and then your problems would be over. This is what we know so far. Clyde Sweeney got his pink slip about four weeks ago. A week later he suddenly deposited a thousand dollars in cash at his bank. The next day the pilferage in your warehouse started. It went on for about a week. It stopped when Sweeney left. By that time, ten boxes of Mexicali mix were gone. Incidentally, he never turned in his uniform. The day after he left, the substitution took place in this parking lot. He'd already arranged to sell his car. That afternoon, Sweeney delivered his car, cleaned out his bank account, packed his bags and left town. Incidentally, his landlady tells me that he got a fat envelope, registered, in the mail that morning. The way I see it, somebody else planned the whole thing and paid Sweeney to do the dirty work."

For a moment they all stood silent. It was not a pretty story.

"You're looking for Sweeney now, of course?" Thatcher finally asked.

"Looking!" Captain Johnson barked. "We're about to send an alert across the country. His picture will be blasted across every television screen from here to Frisco. But in the meantime we're working on leads here. Somebody had to make contact with Sweeney, hire him for the job, give him his thousand. And, of course, there may be something in Sweeney's background that will tell us where he's likely to bolt."

"A thousand dollars! It's not much, is it?" Robichaux commented.

"It is in some circles, Tom. And don't forget the registered envelope," Thatcher advised.

Hedstrom was grim. "It looks as if someone's out to destroy me—or Chicken Tonight. I'd like to think that Sweeney rated the job as worth more than a thousand dollars."

"That's jumping to conclusions," the captain intervened. "From what I hear of him, this Sweeney may not have known what it was that he was pulling."

Hedstrom looked at him sharply, but said nothing.

Thatcher was interested. "Oh, you have some idea of the kind of man he was? Have you been talking to people who knew him?"

"Sure. Some of them are right here. The Akerses took it pretty hard."

"Clyde Sweeney! It's unbelievable," Dodie Akers repeated to them when they entered the kitchen by the back door.

"They've just about proved it, as far as I'm concerned." Vernon Akers no longer looked bewildered or defeated. He looked alarmingly angry. "And I remember all that gab of his about being on to something new."

"But he must have been planning it even when he was sitting here the last time! And he always seemed so friendly."

The visitors were tactfully silent. Not so her husband.

"Sue never liked him," he replied with clenched jaw. "Did you, Sue?"

"No, I didn't. And I'll tell you something, Mother. That last time he was trying to date me. He didn't really think I'd say yes. He was getting a good look around the parking lot."

Dodie Akers stared at Sue in something like horror. For

Mrs. Akers, Thatcher realized, the greatest shock was that a mass poisoner had been near her daughter.

Robichaux was not the man to let a pretty girl speak in vain.

"Why didn't you like him?" he asked.

Sue Akers was thoughtful. "He was always so pleased with himself. And not for any good reason that I could make out. He was full of big talk. I don't say there's anything wrong with that. But it was all very dull."

Neither Dodie nor Vern was inclined to quarrel with this assessment.

"From what you say, he sounds gullible," said Thatcher, happy with their witness's youthful frankness. "Do you think he could have been persuaded to do this—the substitution of mixes—without realizing how serious it was?"

Suddenly Sue Akers sighed with a depression beyond her years. "Clyde thought he was so smart. That would make him very easy to fool, wouldn't it? I suppose you could say it would make him very dangerous."

CHAPTER 7

STRAIN THE INGREDIENTS

THE AKERSES were not the only source of information about the kind of man Clyde Sweeney was. After seeing the New Yorkers on their way, Captain Johnson drove swiftly to a rooming house on the other side of town. Here his men were already busy searching the room that had been rented to Sweeney, but before Captain Johnson could join them his path was barred by an angry landlady.

"This is a respectable house," she screeched at him. "But today it's nothing but one squad car after another. What do you think the neighbors are saying when they see all these cops?"

But Johnson had done his homework. "Well, Mrs. Menotti," he said calmly, "I suppose they'll say the same thing they said in April 1966, in November 1968, and last August."

"These men!" Mrs. Menotti moaned, extending her arms passionately. "Is it my fault? I do everything but X-ray them!"

"Let's see," Johnson continued. "The first time it was a convict jumping parole, the second time it was a guy pushing reefers, and last time one of your boys got beered up and tried to pull a bar apart."

Unexpectedly Mrs. Menotti softened. "Ah, that!" She dismissed the incident with an airy wave. "That was Joey Dorfman. He's a good man. A little excitable when he drinks, yes. But a heart"—again she extended her arms generously—"a heart like this."

"Mmm," said the captain noncommitally. The report had listed an astonishing amount of personal injury and property damage for one man with a heart like that. "Well, never mind about Dorfman. I want to know about Sweeney."

"Him!" Mrs. Menotti snorted. "Such a fuss about a little nothing. That's what he was—a nothing. What do you want him for? I can tell you right now—if it was anything big, then Clyde Sweeney didn't do it. He was small, through and through."

"And if it wasn't big?"

"Then he probably did it all wrong!" the landlady snapped vindictively.

Johnson nodded thoughtfully. At least he couldn't complain that his witness was biased in favor of the suspect. "How much did you see of Sweeney? I suppose you did his room, that sort of thing?"

"I cleaned his room and changed the sheets and towels. That's all, absolutely. I've got enough to do. Just the bathrooms and stairs can keep you going all day." Mrs. Menotti's brows drew together in a fierce scowl. "No meals!" she said sharply, as one who has seen a trap and evaded it. "No meals served and no hot plates in the rooms either!"

"Then I suppose he had a tavern somewhere he used?" Captain Johnson knew these rooming houses with no home comforts. Inevitably the men drifted to some nearby com-

mercial establishment and adopted it as a clubhouse. It was
where they ate, where they drank and where they fraternized.

Mrs. Menotti's answer was prompt. "The bar and grill two
blocks down on the corner of Lake Street. Not that they
have to go there to drink. I've got a nice little refrigerator in
the hall upstairs for them to keep their beer in."

She must have noticed the look of surprise on the captain's
face, because she hurried into justification. "It makes it
nice for them. Most of them have these little TV sets. Weekends, they like to watch the ball game and drink a can of
beer. There's no harm in that. A little beer keeps a man
sweet."

It occurred to Johnson that all of Mrs. Menotti's rare
moments of indulgence seemed to center around beer. Sternly
he kept to the issue at hand.

"He went to this bar most nights?"

"Yes, he ate there regular, except on Wednesdays."

"What happened on Wednesdays?"

Mrs. Menotti brought out another surprise. "Wednesdays
he ate with his mother. She lives over in Bellsboro."

After extracting an address for Mrs. Sweeney, Johnson
moved on to his critical question.

"Now, Mrs. Menotti, I want you to think back. Did any-
thing unusual happen with Sweeney about four weeks ago?"
The captain paused hopefully. Four weeks ago Clyde
Sweeney had deposited a thousand dollars in the bank.
Johnson knew that the Sweeneys of this world want cash
down when they agree to do a job.

"You mean that phone call," she sniffed. "I knew no good
would come of it. Sweeney had just come in from work when
this call came for him. I'd seen him come in. So I stood at
the bottom of the stairs and shouted. But nothing happened,
so I finally climbed all the way to the third floor. And never
so much as a thank-you. But I heard what he said. He was
going to meet someone. It must have been someone he didn't
know, because he described what he'd be wearing and asked
about the other guy. Sweeney went out about ten minutes
later. And he didn't come back until late. He was all excited,
and he'd been drinking. Said he was celebrating." Mrs.
Menotti became sarcastic. "I can see he had a lot to celebrate
—getting in trouble with the police!"

"Did you hear the other man's description?"

"Sure. At least what he was wearing. An orange-and-brown sport shirt, tan slacks. Oh, yes, and he'd be carrying a windbreaker." Mrs. Menotti paused, curiosity getting the upper hand. "Say, what is this? Do you mean Clyde Sweeney is really mixed up in something big?"

"Big enough for a coast-to-coast search."

"Oh, my God! Who would have believed it?"

When Johnson finished at Mrs. Menotti's it was still too early, he judged, for the regulars to have arrived at the local bar and grill. Accordingly he headed for the neighboring town of Bellsboro. Pulling up before Number 53, he noticed that the name on the mailbox was Gallagher, not Sweeney.

This was soon explained. Mrs. Sweeney was living with her daughter and son-in-law. "That's why Clyde comes on Wednesdays. Ray goes to his lodge and Ellen goes to the Guild. I baby-sit and Clyde keeps me company," she said.

"He comes then to avoid me," said her son-in-law truculently. Ray Gallagher was a salesman in Trenton.

"There, dear," soothed Ellen. "You and Clyde never hit it off."

Her husband's jaw tightened. "We don't get on because Clyde is a good-for-nothing."

Ellen leaned forward and squeezed her mother's hand. "Don't mind Ray, Mother. He doesn't mean that the way it sounds."

Mrs. Sweeney took a firm grip on her handkerchief and sat up straighter. "I'm sure there's some mistake. I don't understand why the police should be looking for Clyde."

At the rooming house, Captain Johnson had been prepared to be mysterious. The evening papers would have the story and Mrs. Menotti would enjoy them thoroughly. But here it was only common decency to break the bad news. In a neutral voice, he announced the suspicions of the police. Three startled faces stared at him.

"Poison!" gasped Ellen.

"Oh, I know there's some mistake," Mrs. Sweeney wailed.

"Christ!" muttered Ray. "That doesn't sound like Clyde."

Johnson pounced. "What do you mean by that? I thought you said he was a good-for-nothing."

"That's what I mean. Clyde never does anything." Ray Gallagher struggled to express his frustration with his broth-

er-in-law. "Year after year goes by and he isn't getting anywhere. He just drifts from job to job, from rooming house
to rooming house. He can't even manage to get married.
Hell, he isn't that much of a drifter. I don't think he's ever
lived more than twenty-five miles from home."

Mrs. Sweeney ignored irrelevancies. "He's waiting to meet
some nice girl."

"Well, he isn't going to meet one in those joints where he
hangs out."

"But he met one where he worked," said Ellen, a born
peacemaker. "He told us so himself."

"But I know Clyde wasn't planning to go away for good,"
Mrs. Sweeney protested. "He said six months. That shows
he didn't poison all those people."

"He told you he was going away?" Johnson asked alertly.
"When was that?"

Mrs. Sweeney was indignant. "Of course he told me!
Whatever can you be thinking of? After he lost his job, he
said he had a chance for something out of town. Then, the
day he left, he stopped by and asked me to keep some of his
things. He said if his chance worked out, he'd be away for
about six months, that he'd write me his address as soon as
he was settled."

Johnson's request to view the belongings left by Clyde
Sweeney roused a demon of perversity in Ray Gallagher.
Not without a search warrant, he declared, startled into
family solidarity by the charge against his brother-in-law.
Mrs. Sweeney tearfully proclaimed that Clyde had nothing
to hide. Ellen, as usual, was left trying to reconcile the ir-
reconcilable.

Half an hour later Johnson was examining the contents of
a large cardboard box. He found them rather pathetic. There
was the famous television set. There was a trophy from
a bowling tournament. There was an intricately worked
model ship. All treasures that a man would want to keep,
even if he were taking the first plane out of town and
planning to lie low for six months. Captain Johnson was
very thoughtful as he left the Gallagher home.

"Clyde was strictly small-time," said the bartender with
finality. He jerked his head toward a corner table. "All of
that bunch is, but Clyde most of all."

In less derogatory terms, this was the judgment of the table too.

"Sure, I remember the night he was so excited. He came roaring in here like a house afire. Said he was on to something really good, the chance of a lifetime. But with Clyde, the chance of a lifetime was usually a tip on a horse. Though this time it wasn't a horse." The small bald man drew circles with his wet beer glass.

"How do you know it wasn't a horse?"

"Because he stayed up in the air about it. A horse, it would have been over, one way or the other."

A large, soft-looking man agreed. "He was excited right up to the end. Even when he didn't get the price he wanted on his car. Said a couple of hundred bucks didn't make any difference any more."

"He claimed losing his job was the best thing that ever happened to him," the third man at the table contributed. "I figured that meant he'd found another one. All Clyde's jobs were going to be great—at first. You know, the first step on the road to the top."

The bald man dissented. "The way he talked, it didn't sound like a job. You weren't here that first night. After that he didn't talk about it much."

"Well," Johnson asked patiently, "what did he say when he did talk?"

"Said he was the right man in the right place at the right time." Baldie frowned as he tried to remember. "He said all it took was a little luck, and you ended being worth real money to someone. Oh, yes, he said some people got their kicks in the damnedest ways, but what the hell, so long as it didn't really hurt anybody."

"Clyde," said the large, soft man proudly, "was very broad-minded."

"Sure, Captain, sure I bought his car. But this won't be in the papers, will it?" the thin man asked anxiously.

"I don't see why it should. But why the sweat?"

"You don't understand women."

Captain Johnson, who had several sisters, one wife, three daughters and a two-month-old granddaughter, waited.

"Look, I got that car for four hundred dollars under the blue-book price. And it's a real cream puff! But if my wife

ever finds out it belonged to a mass poisoner, that'll be the
end. I'll have to sell it!"

"I wouldn't worry about that, Mr. Baumer. Where did you
two meet when the car was delivered?"

"At my bank. Sweeney wanted to be paid in cash."

"And that was the last you saw of him?"

"No. I offered to drive him to the station in Trenton."
Baumer had the grace to blush. "It's only forty miles, and I
wanted to let her out on the expressway."

Further inquiries disclosed only that Sweeney had been
carrying two suitcases and was bound for New York. It did
not take much imagination to realize that in New York
Clyde Sweeney had probably changed his name. After that
he could have gone anywhere.

When Mr. Baumer left, Captain Johnson tilted back his
chair and stared unseeingly into space. A picture of Sweeney
was slowly developing. A man who spent his money on
clothes and cars. A careful reader of the racing sheets and
the tabloids. A timid, unadventurous kind of man. And, most
important of all, a man about whom such disparate people
as Sue Akers, Mrs. Menotti, Ray Gallagher and the bartender were in accord. With one voice, they said that Clyde
Sweeney would never do anything big, anything startling.
He would never really hurt anybody. He was a simple,
stupid optimist.

If they were right, thought Captain Johnson, the conclusion was clear. Clyde Sweeney had fulfilled his manifest
destiny—by becoming somebody's patsy.

CHAPTER 8

DISSOLVE THE SUGAR

IN THE Sloan limousine speeding back to New York, John Thatcher was speculating, less professionally, along the same lines.

"Has it occurred to you," he asked Frank Hedstrom, "that this wretched Sweeney may not have realized what he was doing?"

Robichaux snorted. "Then what did he think he was doing?" he demanded, turning from an uninspiring view of the Jersey flats. "Did he think he was getting a thousand bucks for fun?"

"No," said Thatcher, with a sidelong glance at the immobile Frank Hedstrom, "that's not what I mean, Tom. Sweeney knew he was adding something to the Mexicali mix. But he might not have known it was poison. Perhaps he thought it was something that simply altered the taste. After all, a good dose of quinine would be enough to put people off Chicken Tonight for quite a while."

"I should think so!" said Robichaux, who had been known to blacklist restaurants for a misplaced lettuce leaf.

Thatcher continued to muse aloud. "If Sweeney was only a dupe, then he must be terrified right now. First a wholesale poisoning, then that death in Elmira, and now a nationwide manhunt!"

Hedstrom roused himself. "Maybe you're right. But what difference does it make? Whoever hired Sweeney knew all this was going to happen. Hell, that's why he didn't do the job himself."

"Still can't get over what a thousand dollars will buy these days!" Robichaux marveled to no one in particular.

Thatcher ignored him and replied to Hedstrom. "But whoever did plan this must have taken precautions to keep Sweeney under wraps during the police hunt. Unless——" He broke off to examine a new thought, then went on. "Do you think it's possible that Sweeney does not know who hired him?"

"Oh, for God's sake!" Robichaux expostulated. "You don't do business that way."

"You do, Tom, if your business is mass poisoning. Put yourself in Clyde Sweeney's place," Thatcher said sternly.

Robichaux looked affronted.

"You wake up to find yourself a murderer. You don't know who hired you, and you're too scared to go to the police."

If there was one thing Tom Robichaux knew about, it was money. "It doesn't make any difference how scared he is. They'll get him. If he's only got one thousand dollars, he can't go far."

Hedstrom objected. "Chances are, Sweeney does know who hired him. He's probably sitting pretty."

"You don't sound very interested," Thatcher said dryly.

For the first time, Hedstrom stopped staring out the window and gave his companions his full attention. "I'm not," he said. "I'm interested in Chicken Tonight. Let the police take care of Sweeney. I've got my own problems."

"That's the line to take," said Robichaux with approval.

As the conversation proceeded to business matters, Thatcher found himself only half listening. He was wondering if Frank Hedstrom really believed that Clyde Sweeney was not one of his most serious problems.

"Levelheaded boy," Robichaux observed after the limousine had dropped Frank Hedstrom at the Hotel Montrose.

"Possibly," said John Thatcher, "possibly a little too levelheaded."

Frank Hedstrom, meanwhile, was taking off his raincoat and delivering an unemotional account of the morning's discoveries in Trenton and Willoughby. But Ted Young was given no opportunity to react. Hedstrom immediately swept on to future plans.

"I want to reopen Chicken Tonight right away," he said briskly, settling himself at his desk.

"Right away?" Young repeated. "Listen, Frank. I think we

should take a few days until this uproar about Sweeney dies down. People are asking too many questions. Opening too soon could be a mistake."

There was an interval. "No," Hedstrom said. "No, Ted, we're opening all the Chicken Tonights as soon as we can. We can get permission from all the health authorities now, and, by God, that's what we're going to do! Tell the lawyers to get on the stick. We've got to come on strong. I want you to get Phil and tell him to go all out on the newspaper and radio promotion and—"

Ted Young slumped farther down in his chair. He sounded morose. "It's suicide, Frank," he said. "You're going to regret it. Give it a week, at least!"

Hedstrom twirled a pencil. "It's the only thing to do. Every day we're shut is costing money. We've got to get back into business."

"If we can!"

"If we can," Hedstrom agreed. "But now—well, we've got the Sloan loan, which should help us over the rough spots. If we can just get things going we've got a chance. Otherwise, those contracts with Pelham Browne will eat us up alive. You know that!"

Young looked at him somberly. "What do you think of the chances for the Southeastern merger, Frank?"

Hedstrom shrugged. "I wouldn't give ten cents for them. But Robichaux will try to find out," he said.

"Robichaux," said Young wearily. "He won't put up a fight for us."

Frank Hedstrom had never heard Ted Young sound so defeated. Instinctively, his own voice became more cheerful.

"Well, that's it. We open up Chicken Tonight and we pray. And then we get the hell away from business next weekend. Part of the trouble is that we're all clutched up."

Ted Young grinned tiredly at him. "I'm all clutched up, you mean. No one's ever going to make that complaint about you, Frank."

Hedstrom nodded. "No, the complaints about me are different, aren't they?"

Young gave his rare, short bark of laughter.

"That's better," Hedstrom said. Just then the door opened and his secretary showed in his wife and Iris Young.

Iris Young was visibly surprised by the laughter.

"Well, you two seem to be shucking your problems," she said. "Did you find out anything new, Frank?"

Hedstrom bent over to give his wife a careful kiss. "Now, Iris. I'm not going to bore the two prettiest girls in town with a lot of business."

Joan Hedstrom responded simply and directly. "Then why don't you two take us out for drinks? It would do both of you good to relax a little."

"Tempting," said Ted Young, "very tempting!" He stepped forward to scoop up a woman on either arm.

"Watch him," said Hedstrom indulgently. "He's turning dangerous, Ted is!"

Joan Hedstrom sparkled flirtatiously. She looked up at Ted Young provocatively.

"So Ted's dangerous, is he? And you've been hiding it from me, Iris. Not that I blame you. But fair's fair. Everybody has to take her chance."

Iris tried hard to get into the spirit of things.

"Not me. I saw this coming and I immunized Ted against you a long time ago, Joan."

"Ha! Wait until I get him alone this weekend." Joan was conscious of no restraint. She was smiling happily as she turned to her husband. "Iris still isn't happy about the house. We're not elegant enough for her."

Hedstrom's shrug was barely perceptible. "Oh, Iris," he said almost indifferently.

It was then that Iris Young's good intentions collapsed. The unfairness of everything swept over her. There was Ted, strained, tired and taut. And there was Frank, despite days of crisis, looking calm and unruffled. She yearned to puncture that self-possession.

"Come on out with us," she said. "We'll be as gay and unconcerned as we can manage. After all, Frank, you're front-page news. Everyone is going to be watching us. Looking for the first crack in the Hedstrom façade."

She knew she was being malicious, and ineffectively so. Ted Young lost his ebullience and became truculent.

"Goddam ghouls," he growled.

Frank, the target of her shaft, was unshadowed.

"Don't let it get you down again, Ted," he advised.

It was at moments like this, Iris realized, that she came perilously close to hating Frank Hedstrom.

CHAPTER 9

OMIT HORSERADISH

TWO DAYS later Tom Robichaux made an announcement.

"Chicken Tonight has reopened."

"I would have to be deaf, dumb and blind to have missed it," John Thatcher replied with some asperity.

Six hours after a green light from the Public Health, Chicken Tonight flung open its doors—with as much hoopla as possible. From Maine to California, Chicken Tonight could once again dispatch a gold-and-orange truck to any doorstep, delivering succulent chicken Kabob with tempting side orders of cranberry wriggle and brandied onion rings. Full-page ads were urging Americans to have Chicken Tonight from St. Paul to St. Petersburg. High-priced singers interlarded the top ten hits on dozens of radio stations with a catchy jingle:

> To-oo Make Life Bright
> Have Chi-i-cken To-oo-nite!

But during the same twenty-four hours, the front pages from Atlantic to Pacific hammered another refrain: "POLICE HUNT CLYDE SWEENEY. NO MOTIVE, SAYS HEDSTROM. FBI ENTERS CASE."

Irrational or not, Americans were boycotting Chicken Tonight. And not only Chicken Tonight. The best efforts of the American Poultry Institute were unavailing; broiler sales still ran seventy to eighty percent below normal.

As for home deliveries . . .

It was Thatcher's private opinion that the appearance of

the famous gold-and-orange truck on many a quiet suburban street could incite to riot.

"It's like a newspaper strike," Robichaux said.

"What is, Tom?" asked Thatcher, happy to have a respite from the clamors of the Trinkam Anniversary Committee.

"This chicken crisis. You know, every time there's a newspaper strike, people get out of the habit of reading papers. Then, when the strike is settled, they're surprised that a lot of readers have gone away forever. I tell you, some of my wives had more brains than these unions and publishers."

"Oh, I scarcely think Americans have given up chicken for good," Thatcher remarked.

But the real reason for Robichaux's pessimism turned out not to be chicken consumption. "I might have to go down to Philadelphia myself," he announced, making it sound like Hanoi.

"To see if you can salvage the merger?" Thatcher asked. "Isn't that visionary, Tom? After all, the board of Southeastern Insurance reads the papers, too. They know what's been happening to Chicken Tonight—and it scarcely makes it a desirable partner for a corporate marriage, does it?"

This earned him a stately lecture on the subject of looking on the bright side of things.

"All right, Tom," said Thatcher, repressing the temptation to ask where it was. "You may be right."

"You think so?" Robichaux was touchingly eager for reassurance. But, in good conscience, Thatcher could not offer more.

His own research department had surveyed the Chicken Tonight debacle with its customary bleak eye. The upshot was a warning to any trust officers who had been out of the country during the preceding weeks to eschew Chicken Tonight in any way, shape or form. This excellent advice, of course, was too late for Commercial Credit. Maitland had scarcely returned from Bates Residence for Freshmen Women before he was hospitalized with what was officially described as extreme fatigue.

Despite this overwhelmingly negative picture, Thatcher suspected that Frank Hedstrom might pull through. This was guesswork on his part. Thatcher's trip to Trenton had raised the possibility that the motives of Frank Hedstrom were as mystifying as those of Clyde Sweeney. But one thing was certain: Hedstrom was not a born loser. He might still make this a horse race, for Thatcher's money.

Since this approach was not really respectable for an eminent Wall Street banker, Thatcher wished Robichaux well and tried to put Chicken Tonight from his mind.

Both events and Robichaux conspired against him. Before the day was out, Miss Corsa announced yet another call from Robichaux & Devane.

"Yes, Tom," said Thatcher, a shade wearily.

Resolute cheeriness was gone. Indignation had replaced it.

"Philadelphia!" said Robichaux in tones of pure loathing. "John, you wouldn't believe it!"

This did not prevent him from providing considerable detail.

The call from Robichaux requesting an appointment had arrived at the staid offices of Southeastern Insurance Company at a most inconvenient moment. Morgan Ogilvie had been planning an early departure. Very early.

Hat in hand, he had been caught leaving by his venerable uncle.

"Want to talk to you about this Chicken Tonight fiasco, Morgan."

"Yes, of course, Uncle Buell," said Ogilvie with a quick glance at his watch. "I've promised Margo . . ."

But Buell Ogilvie, president of Southeastern, had not reached his figurehead eminence by undue concern for the promises of others.

"Where do we stand on the merger?" he demanded abruptly.

"Of course, the board—"

"Oh, damn the board. What I want to know, Morgan, is what the situation is! And what you propose doing about it!"

His nephew resigned himself to delay. He tossed his hat on a chair.

"Well, as you know, we have a commitment—"

"Commitment be damned!" Uncle Buell sputtered. "Yes, we sent out proxies to our stockholders! But we can go to the SEC and send out other proxies. What kind of commitment is this, anyway, Morgan? We voted to merge with a going concern, not one headed for bankruptcy!"

"We don't want to act hastily."

"What do you mean, hastily? Do you want to merge with Chicken Tonight now? Just give me a plain yes or no!"

Morgan Ogilvie tried to hold on to an ebbing temper. Although he was the man who actually ran Southeastern Insurance, he was always meticulously correct with his uncle. Still, he did not enjoy having to account to this aged and querulous man for his business decisions.

Particularly now, when he was very worried about one of them.

In his grave, measured way, he said, "Perhaps we can discuss this later, Uncle Buell—"

At that moment his secretary emerged. "Oh, are you still here, Mr. Ogilvie? There's a Mr. Robichaux on the line from New York. I told him I thought you might have left."

"Put him through, put him through!" Uncle Buell trumpeted.

Cursing his luck, Morgan Ogilvie, who wanted to be elsewhere, was forced to converse with Robichaux under his uncle's unwavering eye.

"Yes indeed, Robichaux. No, I'm afraid you caught me just as I was leaving. . . . Yes, I agree we should have a serious talk about the merger. Naturally you see our difficulties. We've always been a conservative firm. . . . What? Well, obviously, there's something seriously wrong at Chicken Tonight when somebody will sabotage their operations for a paltry few thousand dollars. We want to know what's behind it. . . . Yes. . . . Yes, we're giving the whole situation our undivided attention." Here Ogilvie carefully fixed his eyes on the portrait of a forebear safely dead instead of the simmering relative at hand. "Absolutely. I agree, we don't want to be hasty. Possibly we can talk about this later in the week, after our thinking has jelled. Yes. . . . yes. . . ."

He was irritated to find that he was perspiring slightly when he finished.

Uncle Buell eyed him coldly.

"Sometimes I wonder, Morgan. Sometimes I wonder. Let me recommend that you do some thinking—and soon. It looks to me as if you've nearly made a very serious mistake."

When Morgan Ogilvie finally made good his escape he was in a thoroughly troubled frame of mind. This despite the fact that he was not hurrying to a business appointment, but to the opulent quarters of the Jockey Club at the Garden State Race Track, in Cherry Hill, New Jersey, where the first horse ever to wear the Ogilvie colors was running today in the Garden State Futurity. If Ogilvie, unlike his wife, was only moderately interested in horse flesh, he thoroughly enjoyed the camaraderie of the Jockey Club, where the owners mingled with members in an atmosphere of unobtrusive luxury and cushioned comfort, far from the run-of-the-mill two-dollar bettors. His place in this kind of world was as dear to Ogilvie as Southeastern Insurance; in many ways, they were one to him.

Shortly after three o'clock, when he reached the entrance to the Jockey Club, a slight mist had given way to brilliant sunshine. Upstairs, the Jockey Club was thronged. There were tanned, handsome men, mostly lean and fit from lives of sport, outdoor exercise and expensive living. Their women, all tastefully turned out, were also lean and fit, although on the whole looking rather less pleased with their lot than did their consorts. Men and women alike, however, had what Ogilvie felt was the unmistakable hallmark of good breeding. He had been more affected by his wife's interest in stables than he knew.

He sighted many acquaintances from Philadelphia, from Baltimore, even from Princeton. Ogilvie looked around for his wife. Instead, he came upon Pelham Browne, resplendent in a vibrating plaid. In an instant Ogilvie's contentment dissipated as his worries crowded back.

Browne, hallooing greetings to friends, edged his way over.

"Hi, there! Good to see you, Morgan," he said heartily, very much the country squire rather than the poultry entrepreneur.

For some reason, this piqued Ogilvie.

"For God's sake," he muttered.

Browne shed his role. "Come over here, Morgan, and let's sit down," he said quickly, leading the way to a small table near the window overlooking the track. "Now tell me, how are things going?" This question was made with an urgency that had nothing of the country squire about it.

Ogilvie recovered his self-control.

"Everything's in a state of flux," he said coldly. "What did you expect? At the moment, we're still committed to that

merger with Chicken Tonight. But I'm afraid we may have
to take action. There's a good deal of opposition—"

But this was not what interested Pelham Browne. "What's
Hedstrom's position?" he interrupted to ask bluntly. "Do you
think he's going to go under? Do you have any idea how long
he can hold out?"

Ogilvie was looking unseeingly down at the graceful oval
where entries in the third race were just beginning their
long approach to the starting gate. He gave no sign of having heard Browne.

"Frankly, Pel, I'm very worried."

This was a tone of voice that no one on Broad Street, and
very few people at Southeastern Insurance Company, heard
from Ogilvie. Gone was the businessman, the Philadelphia
civic leader. But Ogilvie's summer place was fifteen miles
from Pelham Browne's lordly establishment on Chesapeake
Bay. Ogilvie's wife, like Browne's, hunted with the Chesapeake Hunt. It would be too much to say that Morgan
Ogilvie regarded Pelham Browne as an intimate. He accepted him as one of his own kind.

Browne was beckoning for a second drink.

"You know, I'm in a helluva position," he said. "I've got
to make a decision one way or the other. Either I go on
producing for Chicken Tonight or I don't. It's a risky prop-
osition. That contract is the real backbone of Browne
Poultry . . ."

In short, he had not listened to Ogilvie, either.

This mutual inattentiveness seemed perfectly normal to
both men; their universe had a healthy respect for self-
interest. They sat in silence amidst the sounds of merriment
behind them. Browne was still weighing sales to Chicken
Tonight. Ogilvie was thinking about Southeastern Insurance
and its problematical merger. Finally the common denomina-
tor emerged.

"The key is Hedstrom," said Ogilvie heavily.

"Always has been," said Browne.

"No, I mean the key to the future. Look here, Pel, what
do you suppose is behind this? After all, somebody deliberately set out to poison Chicken Tonight. Have you thought
of why?"

Pel Browne was not much of a theorist. "God knows," he

said shrugging bulky shoulders. "Probably some nut with a grudge—"

He broke off as the bell signaled that the starters had opened the gate. A group of spectators moved closer to the windows as the horses pounded out of the chute and onto the straightaway.

Ogilvie ignored the spectacle. "If it's just that, Hedstrom is lucky," he said. "But I've been thinking. What do we know about Hedstrom?"

Browne was being towed beyond his depth. "What do we know about—? Hell, Morgan, what are you talking about?"

The horses were rounding the far turn, and from beyond the insulating windowpanes came an uproar like distant thunder.

Ogilvie pulled at his lower lip. "What I mean is this. Here's Frank Hedstrom, a nobody who suddenly appears from someplace in Illinois. The next thing we know, he's built up a million-dollar business—almost overnight. And he has the Sloan Guaranty Trust financing him. He's big enough to buy all your broilers, to take over my insurance company. And God knows what other plans he has! I understand he was getting ready to go into broiler production on his own, before he was struck by lightning."

The horses pounded across the finish line, the favorite winning by a nose. Glancing idly down, Ogilvie missed the unguarded emotion on Pelham Browne's face. He returned his attention and said, "Now, look at it this way. Hedstrom is something of a mystery man. We don't really know where he came from, or how he became so important. He could have a connection with the underworld."

This time he saw the emotion on Browne's face. Browne was gaping.

"Look here, Morgan, are you saying that Hedstrom is just a front?"

Whatever Ogilvie was going to say was forestalled.

"Well, there you two are! Margo told me to be sure to get you down to watch them saddling up."

Antonia Browne's public manner consisted of a sustained brilliant smile. It did not falter when her husband and Ogilvie, although dutifully rising, did not respond with their usual heavy playfulness. "Come on down," she coaxed.

But as they rode the escalator down to the paddock area,

where horses were being saddled under the watchful eye of track officials, where jockeys were receiving instructions from trainers, where grooms were checking equipment and rich owners were beaming impartially, she hissed in her husband's ear, "What on earth is the matter, Pel? You look sick!"

"I'll tell you later, Tony," he said, conscious of hundreds of eyes upon them. Horses, jockeys, owners, guests, all were part of the strange spectacle that fascinated the average man, and the fence held back hundreds of average men and women looking at the show with wonder.

Mrs. Browne was concerned, but maintained her smile as she joined Mr. and Mrs. Morgan Ogilvie outside stall six.

Mrs. Ogilvie, a large-boned woman with a deep tan and smart white hair, was more interested in her horse, Nagrom, than in her husband's frame of mind. Her penetrating eyes were fixed on the aged trainer who was whispering something to the jockey.

"Jockeys up!" commanded the loudspeaker.

In eight stalls, undersized riders were swung aboard thoroughbreds to become part of a powerful muscular machine. The red-coated starter began the long slow amble under the grandstand, onto the track. The horses, their grooms riding beside them, fell into line. Stepping carefully, the owners, their friends and relatives departed to watch the race.

"Well, Morgan," said Mrs. Ogilvie in a deep voice. "Did you have a good day?"

"Yes, dear," said Ogilvie.

"Ben says Nagrom is ready," she told him, leading the way to the escalator that would deliver the party back to the Jockey Club.

From the track, the bugler signaled the horses coming out. In the grandstand, bettors began studying forms, watching odds, heading to the tellers' windows.

"Make your bets early," the loudspeaker advised. "The horses are coming onto the track for the fifth race, the Garden State Futurity. Ticket windows are now open. Make your bets early!"

Tony Browne and Margo Ogilvie, scanning their programs, were ahead of their husbands.

"Were you joking?" Pelham Browne asked in a husky undertone.

"I was never more serious in my life," Ogilvie replied. "Somehow or other I've gotten a very strange impression about Hedstrom, and I haven't been able to get it out of my mind."

"I'll be damned," said Browne. "My God, Morgan, do you realize what this could mean for us?"

"The horses will reach the starting gate in five minutes. . . . The horses will reach the starting gate in five minutes. . . ."

It is one of the customs of privileged persons to show pleasure at the small triumphs of their peers. This is why the weddings, debutante parties and other celebrations of the rich are frequently merrier than the occasion warrants.

"Here, Morgan!" yodeled a tall red-faced man. "Let's drink to Nagrom as if she had a real chance. C'mon over, Perry."

"But do you realize what that could mean for us?" Browne pressed.

It was unlikely that Ogilvie heard him. A crowd of well-wishers had surrounded both Ogilvies with dutiful hilarity. Other hopeful horse owners, with their respective claques, occupied other outposts of the Jockey Club.

"The horses will reach the post in two minutes . . . The horses will reach the post in two minutes. . . ."

"Pel! What is it?" Emotion was rare with the Brownes; it was all the more unnerving when it appeared.

Pel looked down at his wife, at a loss. The substance of his anxiety had suddenly become too disconcerting to put into words—to her, at least. Fortunately, he was released by the surge toward the windows.

"They're off!"

Nagrom started in fifth position, moved up to three at the far turn, made her bid on the back stretch, matched strides with Greengirl at the clubhouse turn and, five lengths from the finish line, loosed a tremendous last-minute spurt that winged her home ahead of the pack.

And Pelham Browne lost his opportunity to buttonhole Morgan Ogilvie for the day.

The Ogilvies were swept down to the winner's circle, almost on the shoulders of exhilarated friends, certainly in a happy cloud of bourbon and congratulations. They were helpless against the tide, yet somehow they ended up in the winner's circle, to be photographed with the garlanded

Nagrom and the mud-spattered jockey. Mrs. Ogilvie was lost to sight behind an enormous bouquet of roses; beside her, Morgan Ogilvie looked very dignified indeed.

Pelham Browne, meanwhile, watched the other races with lackluster eyes, while Tony Browne watched him.

"But what's the matter?" she asked during the long drive back to Maryland.

"Nothing," said Pelham Browne, intent on the road. "I had a touch of indigestion, that's all. I'm fine now. Just fine."

Uncertainly she inspected him. His words were faintly slurred—but that meant little. Pel prided himself on being able to hold his liquor, and Tony agreed that he could.

"You're sure . . . ?"

"Oh for God's sake, Tony!" he snarled. "Just leave it alone, will you?"

Astonished, she relapsed into hurt silence.

She remained ostentatiously silent at the breakfast table next morning.

"Here's a picture of Morgan and their horse," he said, signaling a cease-fire. "Seems that Nagrom broke the track record yesterday. That's pretty nice going."

"I'll ring them up and congratulate them," she responded.

But she could not keep her glance from his face. Pelham Browne was studying the photograph of Morgan Ogilvie with attention.

And there was something in his attention that almost frightened his wife.

CHAPTER 10

TIE IN A BUNCH

THE JOCKEY CLUB at the Garden State Race
Track embodied one form of togetherness. There are others.

Americans are passionate believers in organization, so
much so that it is virtually impossible for more than six of
them to share any interest without hankering after weekly
sociability and instruction. They lecture each other remorselessly. They give prizes to each other. They eat and dance
with each other.

The great family of Chicken Tonight was no exception. In
happier days it had regional banquets and annual clambakes;
it had suggestion competitions and guest lecturers. News of
all flock activities was broadcast by the house organ, *Chicken
Feed,* which arrived at each franchise on the first of the
month. There its smudged mimeographed pages were de-
voured eagerly. One spouse would read aloud to the other
items such as:

Congratulations to Jack and Anne Owen, who served
their one-millionth order in Cedar Rapids last week!
To commemorate the occasion Jack added a bottle of
champagne for the lucky customers!

In Pennsylvania Bob and Ginny Meyers are facing a
second-generation threat. Their son, Tommy, whose wed-
ding we announced last spring, has just opened a CT
franchise in McKeesport. "Dad and I are planning to
have a friendly competition," Tommy said as he cut
the ribbon. Father Bob will have to look to his laurels!

Al and Marge Pecek are shown receiving a check for
one hundred dollars from Regional Manager Glen

Davidson in Tucson, Arizona. Marge's suggestion for cleaning the Chicken Kabob pump won the Southwest area competition.

"Fire fighting was never like this," said Jerry Flynn as he announced plans to open his second CT franchise in the New Hampshire ski area. Jerry was a retired fireman from Saugus, Massachusetts, when he started his first operation in North Conway in 1962. He has made a specialty of delivering orders to ski tow lines. Readers in Vermont and Colorado take note!

Dodie Akers was always the first to grab *Chicken Feed* from the mailbox. After dealing with the front-page features and letters to the editor, which currently seethed with indignation about the poisoning ("As an old CT hand in Seattle I would like to extend my sympathy and encouragement to our friends back East . . ."), she turned her attention to the classified ads. Running a finger down the column, she said, "I don't see anything that would do for us. There are some uniforms for sale. If we stay in business, we'll need some. They have six of them, all size thirty-eight. They must have hired all skinny boys last year and hefty ones this year. I don't suppose so. It's hard enough getting help without tying ourselves to stringbeans. . . Oh, look, Vern. There's going to be a meeting."

Vern was philosophical. "Meetings, always meetings," he muttered.

"But this is different. Headquarters isn't calling it. It says here it's addressed to franchise operators in the Northeast adversely affected by the poisoning."

"And do they suppose it did anybody a lot of good?"

"Vern, maybe we should go. They say it's to take action."

"Let's see." Vern stretched out a hand for the paper and became absorbed.

"What do you think?" Dodie asked when he lifted his head.

"It doesn't say who's calling the meeting," Vern replied thoughtfully. "Two bits it's that troublemaker Gatto."

Mentally, Dodie reviewed her image of Joe Gatto, a CT operator forty-five miles north. For a moment her enthusiasm dwindled. Then she shook her head decisively.

"Well, what difference does that make?" she demanded.

"Just because he's called the meeting doesn't mean he'll run the show."

"A loudmouth, a guy who likes the sound of his own voice," Vern summarized dispassionately. "Aside from that, he's got a chip on his shoulder a mile wide. He's probably real glad he's finally got someone else to blame for his lousy operation."

Dodie had made up her mind.

"All the more reason for us to go," she announced. "After all, you're not sure that Gatto is behind this meeting. And even if he is, there'll be plenty of people who honestly want to know what to do."

"I suppose so," Vern said unenthusiastically. "Let's see. It's on Tuesday."

"Then that's settled. We're going."

Vern let the paper fall with a gesture of defeat. "All right. I hate to say it, but even if it is a waste of time, we don't have anything better to do with ourselves."

The meeting *had* been called by Joe Gatto, and he was in full cry when the Akerses entered the American Legion Hall in Newark that Tuesday.

"He's in great form today," a fellow franchisee whispered as he moved over to make room for Dodie. "He thinks we should start a counterattack."

The Akerses listened fatalistically.

". . . Hedstrom is out to ruin us little guys and take all the profits for himself. It's been the same all along. They send out inspectors, they spy on us, they give orders. Who does the work, I ask you that? We do, that's who! And now who's getting kicked in the belly? Us! Well, I'm here to tell you I won't stand for it and I hope you won't either. There's no point kidding ourselves. We're none of us big enough to take on Hedstrom by ourselves. We've got to plan things together. . . ."

As the speaker neared the inevitable conclusion that they were all going to hang separately if they didn't hang together, Vern raised eloquent eyebrows at Dodie. I hope you're satisfied, they said. This is what we drove fifty-five miles to listen to.

Things did not improve when Joe Gatto yielded the floor. The small, rumpled man who took over was hoarse with earnestness.

"I don't like to hear you say things like that about Chicken Tonight, I really don't, Joe. Look at it this way. I didn't have enough cash to go into any real business by myself. Most of us didn't. If it hadn't been for the kind of help we got from Mr. Hedstrom, I'd still be back on the line. Instead I've got a fine business." He scowled at the chorus of derisive cries. "Well, it *was* fine until a couple of weeks ago. I figure that the people who helped us, the people who got us started, are entitled to their share of the profits. I didn't have anything to complain about. Bessie and me were doing real good in Scranton." Here he paused to look defiantly at Gatto. "And I say that anybody who paid attention to the front office's advice about location, anybody who operated the way they told him to, anybody who really put his back into it, was making out all right."

This was the equivalent of challenging Gatto to a duel. Everybody knew that Joe had chosen his location in the teeth of management opposition, that he didn't go by the CT manual and that he was—in Vern Akers' words—the laziest s.o.b. to come down the pike in a long time. Happily, before Gatto could lash back, a calmer influence appeared. Chet Brewster, the largest operator in three states, did not descend to personalities.

"Now let's put aside any little discontents we may have felt with the management in the past. I don't say they don't exist, I guess you all know my own little gripes." Brewster gave the indulgent chuckle he always used with the smaller operators. He had opened one of the first Chicken Tonights in the Northeast. This gave him all the advantages of getting in on the ground floor. He had always been the man of substance at the area meetings, the man who could understand and appreciate what influenced headquarters. "But I do say that management is just as hard hit by this disaster as we are. This is no time to talk about forcing them to do anything for us. They've got enough trouble keeping their heads above water. We've got to work *with* them, not against them. What you may not understand is that a company like this lives by its reputation. Once that goes, you can kiss goodbye to the whole business of Chicken Tonight. If you want the advice of someone who's been in this business longer than anyone else here, I say this is the time to give our unqualified support to the front office."

Chet Brewster had settled everybody's problems, at least to his own satisfaction. He acknowledged nonexistent applause with a wave of the hand and returned to his seat wrapped in self-satisfaction. There was a long pause, as if forty-two couples were holding their breath. Characteristically, it was a woman who rushed in where angels feared to tread. She did not bother going to the platform. She simply rose and spoke as the spirit moved her.

"I don't pretend to understand high finance the way Mr. Brewster and a lot of you do. But I do know one thing. Mr. Brewster's rich. He can afford to sit this thing out. I suppose Mr. Hedstrom and all the people in the New York offices can, too. But we can't! Stan and I put our life savings into our franchise. It's not easy saving up fifteen thousand dollars on a mailman's pay, not when you've got kids to raise, it isn't. But we did and we never regretted sinking it all into Chicken Tonight. I don't want you to get the idea that we go along with Joe Gatto here. We were grateful to the front office. They were fair about everything. We knew it would take time to get off the ground, and with Stan's pension we could manage it. We didn't do anything wild, we didn't do anything that wouldn't work out with a lot of good, hard elbow grease and some patience. All those people who keep checking up on us will tell you that. But we can't take this!" She reached down to clutch the hand of the man beside her. Then, with renewed determination, she continued more calmly, "I don't know anything about how we split up here. I know a lot more of you are in our shoes than in Mr. Brewster's. You know the situation as well as I do. We haven't done a nickel's worth of business for two weeks. But we've still got payments to meet. They go on and on. Where can we get the money? We're all going to be wiped out, after we've worked so hard. And it isn't as if we were in this alone. We've all had our kids working in our places. A lot of us were hoping to set them up in the same business. It's so unfair!"

She sat down, now weeping openly. Several women near her made overtures of comfort. But the rumbling that spread down the rows suggested that most of her audience had been stirred into a more combative mood. Joe Gatto rose to say that Mrs. Horvath had said exactly what he said, that a united front was essential. Chet Brewster, still exuding confidence, denied that riches had cut him off from the problems of the less fortunately circumstanced. Gatto's foe claimed that Helen Horvath spoke for all of them in expressing gratitude to Chicken Tonight. There was a confused medley of seconding.

"This isn't getting us anywhere," Vernon Akers grumbled in an undertone. "I didn't come here to be cried at by Helen Horvath."

"Oh, Vern! You know that every word she said was true. You're just uncomfortable because she got so emotional about it." Dodie had put her finger on his trouble. "And why shouldn't she be emotional? I wouldn't mind lying down and having a good cry myself."

At this ultimate threat, Vern opted for appeasement. "I didn't say it wasn't true. I said it wasn't getting us anywhere. We know all about the payments we've got to meet. We should talk about doing something about them."

"Then stand up and talk!"

"Oh, now, Dodie." Vernon Akers disliked anything in the nature of a public exhibition.

"No, I mean it, Vern. We drove fifty-five miles in the hope of seeing something accomplished. And we're not going to if you just let this bunch of blowhards preen themselves. You know that all Gatto and Brewster care about is sounding off. On your feet, Vern."

If there was one thing to be said for the Army, Vern Akers thought nostalgically, it was lack of opportunity for public speaking. At least if you were a sergeant. Generals, of course, were born gasbags.

"You know I can't talk to meetings, Dodie," he hedged, convinced that it was exactly what he would soon be doing.

"I just wanted to suggest that we try a different tack," he heard his own voice growling as he climbed reluctantly to his feet three minutes later.

There were sounds of encouragement from the solid cadre of men who shared Vern Akers' dislike of wasting time.

"That's the boy, Vern!" a voice from the back called.

Akers looked more depressed than ever. But grimly he forged ahead. "I think we should take up where Helen Horvath left off. We've got a lot of financial problems. If Chicken Tonight goes under, I guess there isn't any solution. But if it doesn't, then most of us could probably survive if we got some help. That's the line we ought to take with the management. Now, they need us as much as we need them. That stands to reason. If we could work out some kind of deal, if they'll forgive payments until things get better, we might be able to sneak by. Anyway, I think it's worth a try. There's no point going to them and hollering a blue streak. We ought to make them see that if they don't give us a lift we may all end up in bankruptcy. Then they'll never see their money!"

This suggestion, introducing concrete detail, immediately prompted embellishment.

"That's talking sense, that is," said a heavyset elderly man. "And there's another thing. It's not just the payments on the equipment. We're going to need credit for supplies. Any cash we've got we're going to need to keep the trucks and the utilities going."

"Not to mention the help," grumbled someone. "It's hard enough to hire a high-school kid who'll do the work. He sure as hell isn't going to do it on an IOU."

"And publicity!" squeaked a suburban operator who had retired from the corporate rat race. Notoriously he was a true believer in the powers of advertising. "They'll have to give it the works! Papers, magazines, radios, even television!" He sat down, lost in the beauty of it all. For two years he had pleaded for a TV commercial.

"Sure," said Vern, trying to control the whirlwind he had sown. "But remember, we can't just ask for pie in the sky. We've got to try for as good a deal as we can get."

"They're in no position to fight us," cried someone who had bounced from despair to euphoria in less than a minute. "We're their bread and butter."

By this time Vern Akers had been carried away by his own arguments. "The carrot and the stick," he said with misleading clarity. "First we sweet-talk them. If that doesn't budge them, then we get rougher. Hell, they sent poison into our shops. We could probably sue them!"

Enthusiasm reigned. There were calls for a lawyer, calls for a committee, calls for a representative to negotiate with Frank Hedstrom himself.

And, to his unparalleled dismay, Vernon Akers left the building the unanimously elected spokesman of all Chicken Tonight franchises from Boston to Buffalo.

CHAPTER 11

RESERVE THE CARCASS

TWO DAYS later a letter arrived at the headquarters of Chicken Tonight.

"Nobody loves us any more, Ted," Frank Hedstrom remarked after rapidly scanning Vernon Akers' request for an early appointment. "Not even our franchisees. They've organized. Here, take a look."

He tossed the letter across the desk. Ted Young received it, after a quick look, with a blunt biological statement.

"Oh, come on, Ted," Frank reasoned. "They were bound to start sending out SOS's. At least this way we won't have the whole bunch trooping in here one by one."

Ted Young refused to be jollied up. "It's not the franchisees that bother me. But they don't help, coming on top of everything else. This is what I'm worried about." He brandished a communication on a printed legal form. " *'You are hereby summoned to attend and give witness at a hearing by the Public Health Service in Trenton, New Jersey, . . .' "* He mimicked the official language savagely.

Hedstrom shrugged.

"It could be worse. I've talked with our lawyers. We get a chance to trot out evidence and show them what safeguards we use."

"They can massacre us, Frank! Think of the questions they can ask! Why was a discharged driver allowed to hang on to a key? Why didn't anybody notice that the boxes had been resealed? Why didn't we withdraw chicken Mexicali as soon as the pilferage was reported?"

"Sure they can massacre us if they want to," Hedstrom agreed. "But what makes you think they do want to? They know as well as we do that anybody who's got a key can get duplicates. They know that pilferage doesn't normally lead to poisoning. Hell, this could have happened to any food outfit in the country. We're supposed to take precautions against spoilage and contamination, not against some criminal lunatic!"

Ted Young shook his head. "What's so lunatic about it? We've got plenty of competitors who'd be glad to put us out of business."

"Everybody's got competitors. For that matter, I'm not so sure that's the explanation."

Young lifted his head sharply. "Not sure? What else could it be?"

"Well, there was a time when we would have liked to put some of the big boys out of our way. Not so long ago, either. But did something like this ever occur to you? It didn't to me. You know who stands to gain the most by crippling Chicken Tonight. Can you see any of them pulling this Sweeney stunt?"

Hedstrom almost smiled as he saw Young struggling with this thought. Ted didn't take a relaxed view of the competition.

"I'd have a hard time putting a name to anyone," Ted admitted at last. "Do you think that's why the Public Health boys are planning this hearing? Because they have doubts, too?"

"I don't think they need any special reason beyond having a couple of hundred people poisoned." Hedstrom frowned. "I'm not crazy about it myself."

Young was exasperated. "So you think we don't have to worry about this hearing. You think we can work out a deal with the franchise operators. In fact, you think Chicken Tonight has touched bottom and is on the way up. Have you seen the stock-market quotes? I only wish you weren't a minority of one."

"Well," Hedstrom replied with a half-grin, "there's always Morgan Ogilvie."

"What's he up to?" Young asked sourly.

"He called before you got back from lunch. He wants us to drop everything, go down to his country place for the weekend and figure out some way to save the Southeastern merger."

"No wonder Southeastern has been losing money for

years," Young snorted. "He must have rocks in his head. Does he think anybody in his right mind would vote to merge with Chicken Tonight now?"

"He admits that's the problem. So he wants to work out some scheme to put the whole deal on the back burner for a three- or four-month period." Now Hedstrom was grinning outright. "He's sure we'll be back to normal by then. So I've got at least one backer."

"Some backer! That's not the way you handle mergers. If you can't go through with them when they're ripe, you drop them. If we're back to normal in three months—and I think you're both nuts—then we'll be looking at something else."

"Sure." Hedstrom nodded peaceably. "But try telling Ogilvie that. For a guy who wasn't so hot on this merger at the beginning, he sure has warmed up. He was pushing like hell. But I told him we don't have time to waste right now."

Although he did not know it, these sentiments were being echoed at that very moment by Tom Robichaux.

"You mean come down to Maryland for *this* weekend?" he was inquiring incredulously into the phone. "Ogilvie, do you realize it's Friday afternoon?"

The enormity of the situation rendered Robichaux incapable of further speech, leaving him prey to renewed persuasion. It was five minutes before he could object.

"I know that you put in a lot of work on this merger. I know Chicken Tonight was offering you a first-rate deal. Good God, man, I was the one who told you so! But the deal is dead now. This is no time to be going into a huddle with Hedstrom."

The phone buzzed persistently.

"But what makes you think Chicken Tonight is ever going to go up? No, Ogilvie, take my advice and thank God you missed this one by the skin of your teeth."

The next torrent contained a fact which caught Robichaux's wandering attention.

"I didn't know you had a place on the Eastern Shore," he said chattily. "I'm sorry I won't be seeing it. But I have other plans for the weekend."

The maxim about dripping water and stone is not entirely without foundation. Twenty minutes later Robichaux was saying wearily, "All right. I'll see if I can persuade them.

Mind you, I can't promise anything. But one thing I can tell you. Hedstrom won't make a move on this without the Sloan Guaranty Trust."

It was late Saturday afternoon before John Thatcher had an adequate opportunity to relieve his overcharged feelings. The morning had been spent traveling from New York with a disgruntled band consisting of the Hedstroms, the Youngs and Tom Robichaux. They had arrived at the spanking new Hedstrom house barely in time to swallow a pickup luncheon before Morgan Ogilvie had arrived—on a scene of total domestic confusion complete with opened suitcases, a bewildered maid, and Iris Young and Joan Hedstrom seething mutinously in the background. He had hurried the men away to his own home for their first futile session. Now they were back at the Hedstroms'. Still in store lay dinner at the local hunt club to round out the day's agenda.

"You know, Tom," Thatcher began with sinister mildness, "you have a good deal to answer for."

From the bathroom there came an anguished protest. "For God's sake, you don't think I like this any better than you do? And it's going to cost me plenty, too. Loël is very upset."

Thatcher ignored this tempting bypath. What would Tom consider suitable recompense for disrupting his latest bride's plans? A diamond necklace? A cruise in Greek waters? Sables?

"Never mind that," he admonished sternly. "You can make a start by explaining what we're doing here in the Hedstrom house."

A good deal of petulant splashing preceded the reply. "Hedstrom just built this place. It turned out that the Youngs and the Hedstroms were planning to spend the weekend here. As a sort of housewarming. That's why they wouldn't listen to Ogilvie's invitation. Then Ogilvie found out there was a bare fifteen miles between the two houses. So he said they could combine the two ideas—his and theirs. Then we got tacked on."

"But why are we here instead of at Ogilvie's?"

"Because Hedstrom wanted you with him." Robichaux appeared in the doorway clad in an exotic bathrobe. "And if you ask me, I got shifted over because Ogilvie saw his chance to get out from under. Not that these people are set up for this sort of thing."

Robichaux ran an appraising eye over their quarters. They had been allotted a suite of two bedrooms and a bathroom. In spite of the total lack of personalia and in spite of normal-sized beds, it was clear that they had commandeered the nursery. Without a word, Thatcher seized the adjustable closet rod, now at waist level, and started jacking it up to a reasonable height.

"Wait until you see the bathroom," Robichaux advised lugubriously. "There are little steps—and other things."

"Oh, go away and let me get ready, Tom. I suppose the children were intended to be along this weekend."

"That's why the women are so burned up."

"If they're burned up now, wait until they hear that Ogilvie has dragooned us all into a dinner party tonight."

Money was admittedly Robichaux's chief claim to human intelligence. But the social predisposition of woman ran it a close second.

"Probably be just the thing to cheer 'em up," he predicted.

An hour later Iris Young, in shimmering emerald green, and Joan Hedstrom, in fawn chiffon, bore his words out. Gone were the sulks which had marred the beginning of the day.

"It's really a good idea for us to be eating out," Joan commented. "Veronica is upset enough, having to open the house. This way she can take the evening off."

Iris leaned forward to the front seat. "Are you sure you're going the right way, Frank? We don't want to be late."

"I'm doing what Thatcher tells me to do," Hedstrom answered.

John Thatcher, who was navigating, conned the complex directions scrawled by Morgan Ogilvie. "Turn right at the second lane after the house with the yellow barn. Then it's straight ahead."

"They ought to hand out radar," Robichaux grunted as everybody peered into the inky darkness in an attempt to distinguish the color of barns flashing by.

But after the turn had been successfully negotiated, another problem reared its head.

"Do you think *this* can be it?" Hedstrom asked dubiously. Before them spread pandemonium. Horses were being walked before a large porticoed building. Grooms strolled about with buckets and brushes. Horse trailers backed perilously out of an immense parking lot, while gangs of men carted white wooden frames to remote destinations.

"This is it, all right." Robichaux pointed to a sign proclaiming the club's identity. It was almost obliterated by the more temporary announcement superimposed on it.

"It says they had a horse show today," said Young. "There's Ogilvie!"

Their host and hostess were just emerging from a Mercedes-Benz in the parking lot. They pulled alongside, and the party coalesced.

A short question elicited almost too much information about the horse show held at the Calvert Hunt Club.

"Margo was here most of the day," Ogilvie offered, "and did very well, didn't you, my dear?"

Margo Ogilvie was a woman who liked to share her triumphs with others. "I knew that bay could be schooled as a jumper. But never did I expect him to develop so quickly. First prize, and the Crowleys were entered with their Tenspot."

A discussion of Tenspot's downfall took them past the cloakrooms and into the lounge.

"Mr. Ogilvie and a party of eight," the headwaiter was confirming when he was interrupted.

"Wait just a moment, Wilson. I may change that." Morgan Ogilvie turned to his guests. "Look over there. The Pelham Brownes are here tonight. This is lucky."

He waved vigorously. Pelham Browne and Tony detached themselves from the bar and strolled over. Introductions followed.

"This couldn't be better," Ogilvie said enthusiastically. "You'll join us, won't you, Pel?"

Pelham Browne did not share Ogilvie's open pleasure at this encounter.

"Mighty nice of you, Morgan, but we won't butt in on your party. I expect you people have a lot to talk over. Tony and I don't want to cramp your style."

His intentions, whatever they were, were doomed by Ogilvie's laughing insistence and by the determination shared by Mrs. Browne and Mrs. Ogilvie to rehash the horsy events of the day. Instructions to the headwaiter to enlarge the table were being given while Browne was still protesting.

"Poor bugger!" Robichaux murmured as they trailed behind the others. "Can't blame him for not wanting to get mixed up with this wake."

"If he's a director of Southeastern, he probably doesn't want to lend public support to this insanity of Ogilvie's," Thatcher added.

"You know, Ogilvie did such a thorough job of checking out Chicken Tonight when he didn't want the merger that he ended up brainwashing himself. I have to hand it to him. He really gave it the works. Looked for any weak spot at all. Hired us, hired accountants, hired all sorts of legmen, even went up there himself. Now he's a convert. He probably thinks it'll take him just fifteen minutes to sell Browne on this damfool idea."

Thatcher shook his head as he stood aside to let a convivial foursome stumble past. "If so, Tom, Ogilvie's tactics are very strange."

Almost immediately Morgan Ogilvie's tactics moved from the strange to the bizarre. As the group settled at the table, with all the difficulties inherent in a party of four women and six men, he gave instructions to the waiter. "We're in no hurry and you can space out the courses. That will give us plenty of time for dancing."

Undeniably there was an orchestra. Ogilvie smiled benignly around the table at his paralyzed captives. Thatcher noted appreciatively that Tom's jaw had actually dropped. Robichaux was staring at his client with outright incredulity. Probably Southeastern Insurance was going to find itself drummed off the Robichaux & Devane roster in very short order. They would be lucky not to have their epaulettes stripped off.

"As soon as we've had our first drink," Morgan Ogilvie was continuing in bland disregard of audience reaction, "I hope Mrs. Young will let me show her what an old man can do on the dance floor."

Thereafter horror succeeded horror. Ogilvie's march to the dance floor made it mandatory that the other men choose partners. Thatcher, blind to all other perils in his determination to avoid Margo Ogilvie, was actually on the floor with Joan Hedstrom before he discovered that the orchestra of the Calvert Hunt Club was pandering to the swingers in their midst. He preferred to draw a curtain of amnesia over his subsequent attempts to acquit himself with credit. He returned to the table resolving that nothing would entice him out again until he had first identified the music. If necessary, he could emulate the wallflower at her college prom and spend the evening lurking in the cloakroom.

The table itself offered its own trials. Conversation was dominated by the Mesdames Ogilvie and Browne. First the company learned of the great triumph of Nagrom at the Garden State Race Track.

"It makes me wish Pel and I could take on a racing stable," Tony said enviously. "What a way to start!"

"All our friends have been so kind about it," gushed Margo Ogilvie, who specialized in simpering to an extent surprising in so large a woman. "All day Thursday the phone never stopped ringing."

Then there was an exhaustive recapitulation of today's horse show at the Calvert Hunt Club. "But, Tony, even if you only took one first yourself, three of the other firsts were bred by you. You're becoming one of the best breeding stables on the Chesapeake."

"That's Roanoke's Belle," said Tony happily. "She just goes on dropping winner after winner!"

By clever timing, Thatcher squeezed in two duty dances during the short interval in which the band played something he dimly recognized as dance music. He also suffered the humiliation of seeing Tom Robichaux, a man exactly his own age, lead Tony Browne fearlessly onto the floor in the midst of an incredible caterwauling, and there perform a highly competent version of some tribal erotica. Of course, Thatcher justified himself, that came of Tom's marital propensities. A man cannot make a habit of marrying women at first ten years, then twenty years, and now, alas, thirty years younger than himself without remaining *au courant* with courtship ritual. No one could expect the same expertise from a staid widower. Nonetheless, it was all salt in the wound.

With the arrival of after-dinner brandy, formal constraints relaxed. Several people from adjoining tables stopped by to offer congratulations on various equine achievements. Margo Ogilvie was chaffed, with inebriated freedom, on her submergence under a bushel of roses in the picture featuring Nagrom and her husband. Tony Browne was swept into a dauntingly technical discussion of stud services for the coming season and the resulting virtues of the hypothetical progeny. Frank Hedstrom was identified by several local squires as the man who had bought the "old Tyson place" and was welcomed as a new resident. Partners for the unengaged ladies emerged from nowhere, and Thatcher seized his chance to melt into the background.

But the Calvert Hunt Club, commodious as it was, offered no suitable resting place. The men's room, it soon developed, was definitely out. Pelham Browne, who was evading either the dancing, his host or his wife, appeared to have established some sort of squatter's claim. He was inclined to view the approach of another member of the ill-starred Ogilvie party with distinct hostility. The terrace, to which Thatcher subsequently fled, was also under enemy occupation. It offered a first-rate view of the parking lot and the driveway from the stables, where activity was at last subsiding. The view was being ignored by Mr. and Mrs. Young. They were in the midst of one of those fierce whispered marital exchanges.

"What was it, Ted?" Iris pleaded. "Please don't hide things from me."

"I'm not hiding things from you, Iris." Her husband sounded harassed. "I don't know where you get these ideas."

"I could feel your arm. You went stiff as a post. You know you did!"

Young's voice rose. "For God's sake, Iris. If you must know, I thought I recognized somebody in the parking lot."

"You're lying to me! Ted, if something else has gone wrong, I've got a right to know."

Thatcher felt that, under present circumstances, the terrace was unlikely to offer aid and comfort. Sadly he made his way back to the bar. There Morgan Ogilvie was roaming abroad, collaring stray celebrants. By this time Thatcher was ready to ring up Miss Corsa and demand a surreptitious rescue by the Sloan helicopter. Suddenly his thoughts were given a happier turn by a change in the evening's musical score. A staccato flourish of the mariachi signaled an insinuating change of tempo. Unconsciously Thatcher reacted.

Many years ago—in the thirties, to be precise—a much

younger Thatcher and his wife had made an extended stay in South America, bringing together the Sloan and the coffee bean. They had returned home with a new talent. By rights, Thatcher should now have sought out another lady in the party. But it was Joan Hedstrom who had witnessed his earlier mortification. It was only right she should see it expunged.

Joan was alone at the table when he asked her to dance. This deprived her of any excuse to malinger. But five minutes later she was all smiles.

"Mr. Thatcher! Wherever did you learn to rumba this way?"

A few dazzled onlookers applauded.

Emboldened, Thatcher had a few words with the bandleader. He and Joan did a spirited olla podrida of rumbas, tangos and sambas, before duty returned them to a table at which everyone else was waiting to leave.

The usual flurry over coats and hats covered the chill that had settled between the Youngs, the tardy reappearance of Frank Hedstrom, and the total evaporation of the Pelham Brownes. Mrs. Ogilvie led the way to the parking lot as commandingly as she could in view of the fact that she was, undeniably, drunk as a lord.

"Morgan," she trilled, pausing by the door of the Mercedes, "you'd better be sure that Mr. Hedstrom understands how to get back to his own place."

While Ogilvie was obeying, Ted Young politely opened the door. Unsteadily sweeping forward, Mrs. Ogilvie began to clamber inside. Seconds later an ear-splitting scream shattered the discussion of shortcuts home.

Everybody swung around.

Clumsily Margo Ogilvie was reemerging from the car. And, terrifyingly, she was still screaming.

"Oh, my God!" said Ted Young in a sick voice, peering over her shoulder.

Thatcher and Hedstrom sprang forward. In the front seat of the Mercedes a man was sprawled, thrown into harsh relief by the strip lighting overhead. Hedstrom reached inside to rouse him.

"What's wrong with him?" Robichaux asked from the rear.

Hedstrom did not reply. Instead he recoiled. At his touch

the body had shifted. Now they could see it more clearly. A colorful silk scarf and a simple wooden peg had been combined to form a lethal tourniquet around the man's neck. Colorless eyes, bulging in their sockets, stared sightlessly and reproachfully upward.

"Christ!" Hedstrom muttered. "He's been strangled!"

CHAPTER 12

TEST FOR TENDERNESS

WITH THAT, the nightmare began.

First, Margo Ogilvie slumped heavily backward against Ted Young. He sagged under her dead weight. Hedstrom, thrusting Joan and Iris away, turned to assist Young. In a stupor, Morgan Ogilvie was staring into his car.

Keeping the women shielded, Thatcher moved aside to let Young and Hedstrom support Mrs. Ogilvie to a nearby car. He could hear her spasmodic gasps.

"I'm all right," Joan Hedstrom murmured, shaking Thatcher's hand from her elbow. She moved toward her husband.

"Who is it?" Iris Young whispered. "Who . . . ?"

Hedstrom and Young left Mrs. Ogilvie for Joan to comfort. They rejoined Ogilvie, still paralyzed.

"Now what do we do?" Tom Robichaux asked almost angrily.

"Among other things," said Thatcher, "we call the police."

Behind him, Mrs. Ogilvie's painful whimpers eased into natural weeping.

From that point forward, the world became a confused kaleidoscope of fear and excitement, of light and dark, of morbid curiosity.

"The police?" somebody repeated almost dreamily.

"You're right," said Morgan Ogilvie, breaking his own

trance. He turned and went striding back toward the clubhouse.

"What's the matter?" asked a couple approaching them.

"Better stand back," Frank Hedstrom advised. His voice was steady, Thatcher observed. "There's been some kind of accident."

"Accident? Can I . . . Oh, my God!"

There was a choke of horror.

"Listen," Robichaux urged in Thatcher's ear. The sobbing from the next car had abated. An automobile sped down the highway. Insects were chirping in the green darkness around them.

"What is it?" Thatcher asked.

Robichaux was a man who took his symbols as they came. "The orchestra," he explained. "Stopped playing."

He was quite right. The festivities had come to an abrupt halt. At one moment the Calvert Hunt Club was middle-aged exuberance, overloud laughter, one more drink. The next moment Morgan Ogilvie stumbled to the phone—and the forest fire started. Already tuxedoed men were hurrying out into the night.

"Hedstrom!" Thatcher called out. "We'd better get the women inside."

Thereafter he lost all track of time. In its place there was a montage of rapidly shifting scenes: Hedstrom ruthlessly steering Mrs. Ogilvie indoors; Ted Young, arms around both Joan Hedstrom and Iris, marching behind him up the cinder path; the hallway, suddenly filled with spectators, with unanswerable questions, with strange rumors.

And, inevitably, the parking lot again.

Thatcher found himself leaning against the fender of a car, arms crossed, listening to a babble around him. Death, he noted, has a sobering effect. The voices he heard raised were tense, even hysterical; they were not blurred with liquor as they had been earlier in the evening.

"Must have been some junkies who had a fight . . ."

"Always lock the goddam car, that's what I say."

"Say, does anybody know who it is?"

"Jesus!" This was from someone who had peered into the car.

"Listen, do you think whoever did it could be hiding around here?" somebody asked nervously.

Beside Thatcher, Robichaux's cigarette lighter flared.

"Well, Tom?" Thatcher inquired agreeably.

"Knew this was a mistake," Robichaux remarked in an undertone. "These emergency meetings in crazy places—I've always been against them."

Since Thatcher could not honestly disagree, he turned his attention elsewhere. Not all the members of the Calvert Hunt Club were out here in the parking lot, speculating aloud, commiserating with Ogilvie or simply waiting for developments. From here and there in the parking lot, headlights blazed, ignition keys turned, and cars crept down the cinder driveway past the clubhouse toward the highway. Not everybody was staying to watch the fun.

"Where are the police?" Robichaux muttered irritably. "At this rate, we're going to have to hang around here all night."

"Here they are," said Thatcher as a thin sliver of sound crescendoed into the scream of a siren. A cavalcade of flashing lights sped toward them. "And, Tom, I'd count on a pretty long night if I were you."

He was right. Soon spotlights were beating down on Morgan Ogilvie's Mercedes. Instead of portly notables, the parking lot swarmed with uniformed men and a small army of technical specialists. Inside the clubhouse, Captain Stotz took control. His officers were questioning the kitchen staff, the waiters, the orchestra, the boys who normally fetched cars. Two detectives in the dining room were taking statements, which included confused recollections of earlier merrymaking, as well as names and addresses. They kept at it for nearly two hours.

Stotz himself, a large man with a soft voice, was heavily reassuring. As well he might be, Thatcher thought, watching him take Iris Young through an account of her movements. He had swiftly cut out the Ogilvie party and carried it off to the library, now bedraggled with overfull ashtrays and half-empty glasses. Its occupants were not happy at this special treatment, nor at Stotz's patient insistence on re-creating every moment in a long, movement-filled evening.

"How can anyone remember everybody he talked to?" Morgan Ogilvie asked blearily. "Look here, Captain Stotz, can't we defer this until tomorrow? Surely these questions can wait until then. It is very late now, and the ladies have already had a terrible shock."

Stotz seemed sympathetic to this appeal. He turned appraisingly to the sofa, where Iris Young sat clutching Ted's hand. Next to her, Joan Hedstrom was white-faced with fatigue. Frank Hedstrom kept a large hand comfortingly on her shoulder. Mrs. Ogilvie, bolt upright in an armless chair, was herself again.

"Exhaustion won't help anyone." Ogilvie declared. He had not been so confident earlier, Thatcher thought, when Stotz wondered aloud why Ogilvie's Mercedes had been singled out by a murderer. He had been shaken into vehemence. No, he had never seen the man before in his life. No, he did not know what the body was doing in his car. No . . . no . . . no . . .

This was what everyody else had maintained.

"Look," said Ted Young, surprisingly even-tempered, "how about letting us go, Captain? Nobody knows anything about the man."

Iris ground out her cigarette, and Hedstrom murmured something that Thatcher did not catch. Robichaux could not hide a huge yawn.

"Well, now," said Stotz in that soft drawl, "I suppose there's not much more we can do here. Sure, you can all go home. I'll be around tomorrow, after we've got a little more to go on."

There was a general stir of relief, and Morgan Ogilvie expanded visibly. At his most gracious, he rose. "I appreciate this, Captain Stotz."

Stotz nodded as he too rose.

"We'll have to send you home in one of our cars," he said. "The Mercedes is on its way to the lab."

Ogilvie was stiffly cooperative. "Of course. And, let me add, I understand fully." He glanced dubiously at his tight-lipped wife and said nothing further.

"A couple of other things," Stotz went on, almost thinking aloud. "This Mr. Browne and his wife. They spent a good part of the evening with you, according to what you say. Now, I guess they went home before you did? Before you found the body?"

The Pelham Brownes were not in the library, Thatcher realized. In the confusion, he had missed their departure. He knit his brows, trying to recall whether one of those hearty voices in the parking lot had been Browne's.

Mrs. Ogilvie broke the silence. "They must have," she said with majestic certainty. Again her husband glanced quickly at her. Like Thatcher, he knew that the Brownes might very well have left after the body was found. And Stotz did, too.

"Mmm," Stotz said ambiguously. He looked around benevolently and added, "Oh, second thoughts. Any of you have second thoughts?"

"Second thoughts?" Tom Robichaux roused himself to ask. "Second thoughts about what?"

Captain Stotz was not ruffled. "About not recognizing the man in the car."

The chill was immediate. So too was a negative murmur.

"I see," Stotz said, with unimpaired pleasantness. "Well, thank you for your cooperation. I'll have Brady drive you folks home. We'll probably have a lot more to get our teeth into tomorrow."

And John Putnam Thatcher, for one, did not like the sound of that at all.

Nor did his companions, Thatcher reflected over breakfast the next morning. Nobody had slept well. Even where this was not explicitly stated, it was painfully obvious. As in the case of Tom Robichaux, aggrieved since he prided himself on regular habits—in some realms at least. Iris Young held her second cup of coffee with a hand that trembled slightly. There were shadows ringing her eyes. Her vivacity was gone, she sat silent and remote. Joan Hedstrom too was withdrawn. She had faded overnight. Occasionally she frowned, deep in some inner calculation.

"Hell," said Hedstrom abruptly as the telephone trilled again.

"I'll get it, Frank," said Ted Young, pushing back his chair.

The phone had begun at dawn. Frank Hedstrom was back in the news—with a vengeance this time. Thatcher wondered briefly how these new headlines would affect Chicken Tonight.

And he wondered even more what Frank Hedstrom was thinking.

"Captain Stotz," Young announced laconically a minute later. "He wants us to stick around this morning. He wants to talk to us."

"Why?" It was a cry of protest from Iris. Joan Hedstrom closed her eyes against tears. "Why?" Iris repeated.

"Iris . . ." Ted began with a helpless look toward Hedstrom.

The answer was obvious, Thatcher thought, feeling as gloomy as Robichaux looked. And thirty minutes later Captain Stotz was spelling it out.

Looking even larger in Hedstrom's living room than he had looked at the Calvert Hunt Club, Stotz surveyed the company with an amiability that made Thatcher narrow his eyes. Stotz, it developed, had not had much sleep, either. But he had not tossed on a comfortless bed. He, and many other law-enforcement officials along the Atlantic coast, had been very busy indeed.

"The body has been identified," he announced without preliminaries.

There was a long silence, during which Captain Stotz sat placidly. Finally Robichaux could stand it no longer.

"Well?" he exploded.

Stotz was responsive. "The dead man," he said conversationally, "was Clyde Sweeney."

"Oh, dear God!" Joan Hedstrom cried.

Stotz glanced at her, then went on. "I guess you understand what that means. That means —" and his voice hardened suddenly—"that means that we take it all again from the beginning."

Later Thatcher realized that the moment had been photographed in his memory. Joan Hedstrom flinched, as if from a blow. Iris Young turned away, denying what Stotz had said. And Hedstrom and Young froze into immobility.

Was one of them acting?

Captain Stotz seemed to think so.

"That means we stop pretending this doesn't have anything to do with you," he explained. "It wasn't just one of those things. Clyde Sweeney. Got a lot of publicity, Clyde Sweeney did."

"All right," said Frank Hedstrom dully. "You've made your point."

Stotz exuded geniality. "I'm glad you see it that way, Mr. Hedstrom. Because it's pretty clear, isn't it? Sweeney wasn't down here by accident. He was here because you people are here. That's why he was at the club last night. And that's why he ended up dead."

Ted Young shot a warning look at Hedstrom and said, "Believe it or not, this is as big a surprise to us as it is to you."

"Sure," said Stotz briefly. "Sweeney poisons a couple hundred people, he ruins a big business, his picture is in all the papers—but you don't recognize him."

There was an edge of desperation in Frank Hedstrom's voice. "Look, Captain. We don't—didn't give a damn about Sweeney. We wanted to know who hired him. And the police haven't been much help there."

Did that ring true? Thatcher asked himself. Certainly it did not impress Captain Stotz.

"Oh, the police have been more active than you think, Mr. Hedstrom. We've just got a long report from New Jersey." Stotz paused deliberately. Then, swiveling dramatically, he turned to Ted Young. "They've been checking on Sweeney's contacts. Still claim you don't recognize him, Mr. Young?"

"For Christ's sake," Young stammered, flushing, "what the hell are you talking about?"

"I'm talking about those lectures you gave to Chicken Tonight warehouse people over in New Jersey. Remember? You spent four days in Trenton giving that course. And Clyde Sweeney was there, Mr. Young. Every single day."

Young stared back at him, speechless. Before Stotz could continue, Frank Hedstrom intervened.

"So what?" he asked angrily. "I know those courses we give. Hundreds of people sit in on them. How the hell could Ted remember one man . . . ?"

Stotz had the answer ready. "Mr. Young has somebody help him with his demonstrations and things like that. Guess who was Mr. Young's assistant for four days? Clyde Sweeney, that's who!"

Young had recovered. Due to the respite provided by Hedstrom's interruption, Thatcher suddenly saw.

"I'll take your word that it was Sweeney at my course," Young snapped. "But stop trying to trap me with it. I saw a body last night in the dark, with a rope around its neck. It didn't remind me of a casual contact four months ago. Why should it?"

He was openly defiant. That's my story, he might have been saying. Try to prove anything else.

Stotz was pained. "I'm not trying to trap anybody, Mr. Young. I'm trying to get you to open up. But we're not making progress, are we? I guess we'd better get down to work. Is there a room I can use, Mrs. Hedstrom?"

Numbly, Joan Hedstrom rose to show Stotz into a small study. At the door a uniformed trooper stood, almost on guard. Stotz took a manila envelope from him and turned to look back into the living room.

"Oh, by the way," he said. "Do any of you recognize this?"

It was a creased silken scarf, gay with brilliant yellow stripes.

It was also completely sinister. Words were not needed to correct Ted Young on one point at least. It had not been a rope around Clyde Sweeney's neck.

"Be careful!" Iris Young spat the words. As they turned to stare at her, Joan Hedstrom uttered a strangled noise of helplessness.

"Joan!" Hedstrom said in alarm, taking a quick step to her side.

But as he reached her she found a voice that was almost normal.

"It's my scarf," she said. "Is that . . . is that what . . . ?"

Stotz looked down at her almost pityingly. He did not answer her question. Instead he said, "I guess maybe I'll start my talks with you, Mrs. Hedstrom."

CHAPTER 13

PLACE ON RACK

FOR A MOMENT, Thatcher was afraid that Frank Hedstrom might attack Captain Stotz. But the trooper stepped into the room between them, and before anybody could react Captain Stotz and Joan Hedstrom were gone.

"What the hell is he trying to do!" Hedstrom yelled furiously.

The trooper stared stolidly.

"He can't . . ."

"Hedstrom," said Thatcher sharply. "He can question all of us. As he no doubt will. Don't make a bad situation worse."

He waited until he saw Hedstrom unclench his fists before adding, "Use your head. That scarf was used to murder Sweeney. Stotz has to ask your wife when she last saw it. And she's going to say that it was on the chair or on the desk or somewhere yesterday afternoon. There's nothing more to it."

"He's right, Frank," Ted Young said.

"Furthermore," Thatcher went on, "that isn't the most dangerous question Stotz will ask. Not by a long shot. We'd all better prepare for a good many questions."

He succeeded in lowering the emotional temperature. Joan Hedstrom's reappearance, some twenty minutes later, was even more helpful. She managed a wan smile.

"It's all right, Frank," she said. "It's just . . . oh, anybody could have taken my scarf. I know I packed it, but I couldn't find it when I was dressing last night."

Someone else, Thatcher thought, had noticed those open suitcases in the front hall yesterday.

"Captain would like to talk to you, Mr. Robichaux," said the trooper.

"Eh? What's that?" Robichaux, jerked out of a short doze, sputtered.

It was the one light moment in a dreary day.

And, as he waited for his own turn to come, Thatcher was formulating questions of his own. One of them concerned that revealing exclamation from Iris Young.

It was four-thirty in the afternoon before Captain Stotz left. If he had learned anything from his grueling catechism, he gave no sign of it.

"Thank you for your cooperation," he said.

"You mean that's all?" Hedstrom asked with a bitter smile. He had been closeted fully an hour with Captain Stotz.

"We're not ready to make any arrests—yet," Captain Stotz

replied placidly. "I'll have to ask you not to leave until tomorrow."

Accordingly, the departure of the police did not dissipate the tension.

"I guess I'll see about dinner," Joan Hedstrom said uncertainly. Thatcher did not think she wanted to see about dinner, or even to eat. She wanted to leave this room.

"I'll help," Iris Young said.

Silently, Frank Hedstrom moved to the bar and started to pour drinks.

"Well, one thing to say for the situation," Robichaux remarked to Thatcher.

"What's that, Tom?"

"We can leave tomorrow. I'm all for an early start."

There were further discomforts before that early start.

"Now, who the hell . . . ?" Hedstrom muttered as musical chimes announced someone at the front door. "If that's a reporter, I'll break his neck."

It was not a reporter. It was Morgan Ogilvie and Pelham Browne.

"Good God!" ejaculated Robichaux in subterranean explosion. "Does that idiot want to talk business now?"

"No, Tom," said Thatcher wearily. "He wants to talk about murder."

And, with the thinnest possible camouflage, this was what Morgan Ogilvie did talk about.

"I don't know what I can say," Ogilvie began after he accepted the drink that Hedstrom handed him.

"Well, I do!" Pelham Browne interrupted robustly. "I say things are getting out of hand. My God, just because some miserable little crook gets himself killed . . ."

From across the room, Ted Young spoke without looking directly at either of the newcomers. "That line won't get us anywhere," he said distantly. "That little crook was Clyde Sweeney. Or didn't the police mention that to you?"

Browne rounded on him. "Yes, the police mentioned it! But he's still a two-bit crook, isn't he? Why the hell should the police ask me if I strangled him? God almighty! Just because Tony and I drove peacefully home at a reasonable hour, we get a lot of damfool questions. . . ."

With detached interest, Thatcher listened to Pelham Browne's extended, if shapeless, tirade. Sentence followed

half-sentence, but the only thing communicated was Browne's
passionate resentment. Its cause was not altogether clear to
Thatcher. As a reaction to routine police inquiry, it seemed
disproportionately strong. Browne was now embellishing his
grievances with a string of obscenities. There had been nothing routine in the interrogation of Hedstrom and Young, but
they both had themselves well in hand. Browne was getting
angrier by the minute. His normal high color had deepened
into a dangerous flush; the veins on his brow throbbed visibly.

"Did Captain Stotz himself talk to you?" Thatcher inquired
idly as Browne paused to gulp his drink. And not his first,
either, Thatcher realized.

"Stotz?" Browne repeated. "No, it was a Detective Some-
thing-or-other. Who cares who it was? What burns me is
their goddam nerve . . ."

As Browne mumbled on, Thatcher decided that this outburst had been compounded of one part drink and three
parts outrage that the police dared approach the Pelham
Brownes with any questions at all. And this reaction followed
only cursory official attention. The Maryland State Police
had been training their big guns on Hedstrom and Young.

But Pelham Browne, he reminded himself, was almost as
intimately concerned with Chicken Tonight as the men who
ran it.

Thatcher looked around the room. Hedstrom was staring
into the middle distance over Browne's head. He was not
listening to this strange diatribe. Young was scowling mood-
ily into his glass. Ogilvie, who was making heavy weather
of dissecting his pipe, seemed torn between embarrassment
and distaste.

". . . told them I went home when I damn well pleased.
And why the hell shouldn't I? Why didn't they look for whoever killed that little rat instead of wasting their time and
mine? That's what I told them!"

To Thatcher's amusement, relief from these maunderings
was supplied by Tom Robichaux, possibly the one person in
the room giving Browne undivided attention. He was probably alone, too, in thinking that reasoned discourse with him
was possible.

"Now, look here," he remarked. "Somebody did kill
Sweeney, after all."

This innocuous observation stopped Browne dead in his

tracks. Abruptly, his disjointed remarks collapsed into outright gibberish. Robichaux might not understand this response, but Thatcher did; Browne, in his inflamed condition, thought that Robichaux was leveling an accusation. It might be prudent, Thatcher judged, to intervene.

Morgan Ogilvie did so. "That's undeniable," he said, abandoning his pipe. "And that leaves this Sweeney a mystery man to the end, doesn't it?"

Hedstrom returned his attention to the room. "You mean, he's a mystery because he came down here to Maryland?" he said.

They were heading toward thin ice again, Thatcher feared, but Ogilvie was more adroit than he had expected.

"Everything about the man seems to be extraordinarily puzzling to me," he said firmly. "Take his poisoning your Mexicali and, by doing so, endangering hundreds of lives and actually killing somebody. Now, that's not the act of a sane man, not as I see it."

"Money," said Hedstrom tersely. "You'd be surprised what people will do for money."

Ogilvie shook his head. "No, I would not. Remember, I've been in the insurance business all my life. But Sweeney's list of priorities isn't—or wasn't—normal. The crime he was willing to commit was too serious for four thousand dollars."

Ted Young took the conversation to the inevitable next stage.

"Maybe that's what brought Sweeney down here," he suggested. "Maybe he was out to collect more money—from somebody."

Browne, who was boring Tom Robichaux with some confused anecdotes about his various speeding tickets and other confrontations with police incompetence, looked up.

"What's that supposed to mean?" he demanded truculently.

Hedstrom exchanged an amused glance with Thatcher. "If you don't know," he said to Browne, "you're the only one in the room who doesn't."

Browne had now attained the drinker's hieratic wisdom.

"Well, lemme tell you," he said portentously, "it's nothing for you to grin about, Hedstrom. Not funny at all."

Out of the mouths of babes. Or drunks, Thatcher amended ruefully. Because Browne's whisky-powered insight hit the nail on the head. They could discuss Clyde Sweeney disinterestedly. What was he but a greedy fool, hired for dirty work and possibly murdered for his stupidity? His life, and now his death, had inconvenienced, if not endangered, everyone in the room, but in the larger sense the Clyde Sweeneys of the world did not matter.

No, the ghost in the woodwork of Hedstrom's expensive new home was not Clyde Sweeney. It was the man behind him. The man who gave him money to introduce poison into Chicken Tonight's deliveries. The man who wanted to destroy Chicken Tonight. The man who had taken a scarf . . .

Thatcher braked his overactive imagination.

"It is my opinion," Ogilvie was saying with gravity, "that Sweeney must have come down here to Maryland in order to speak to you, Hedstrom."

Hedstrom looked startled. Ted Young certainly was. "What?" Ted exclaimed blankly. "What did you say?"

Ogilvie was no Tom Robichaux. He hastened to eliminate the flavor of accusation from his words. "No, I mean that he probably came down here to give himself up. He probably thought that you were the right man to approach."

Tom Robichaux did not help him much.

"Why not go to the nearest police station?" he asked, reasonably enough. "That's what I would do. Unless, of course, the fellow just wanted to do a little traveling before he was put away."

Thatcher beat down the temptation to enlarge upon his sudden vision of Robichaux as errant fugitive-tourist.

"You'd be surprised at how stupid some of these people can be," Ogilvie retorted.

"The problem," Thatcher thought aloud, "is to determine the exact form their stupidity takes."

Ogilvie, together with Hedstrom and Young, looked at him curiously, but Thatcher was not inclined to pursue the issue. He did not intend to develop a line of thought that would inevitably culminate in another accusation, veiled or not. There were many reasons for Clyde Sweeney to descend upon the Eastern Shore, Ogilvie's implausible theory apart.

There was blackmail, for example. There was information to sell. There was help to solicit. There was even pure chance.

"Well, well," Ogilvie said heavily. "The whole situation is extremely unfortunate."

A snort from Pelham Browne did not deflect him.

"I just wanted to tell you personally how distressed I am, Hedstrom. And Mrs. Ogilvie is, as well. . . ."

As Ogilvie got going on a lofty statement with overtones of condolence, Thatcher pondered the many varieties of tactlessness. No doubt, Ogilvie's intentions were good. He explicitly expressed his profound hope that this latest development would not exacerbate the Chicken Tonight crisis. He promised to use his best offices to insure decorous police behavior, citing local politicians and civic pull. He urged everybody to remain optimistic and promised unspecified improvements.

Under the circumstances, Thatcher decided, good intentions were not enough. Ogilvie's benevolence was a mistake. It suggested Frank Hedstrom needed help—and badly.

Of course, anybody who chose to make courtesy calls accompanied by Pelham Browne could not be thin-skinned. Unless, Thatcher thought, observing Browne's glassy eyes, Browne had simply foisted himself on Ogilvie. On the whole, that seemed more probable. It presented, however, another small puzzle: why had Browne come?

Ogilvie at last had risen to leave. ". . . after the uproar dies down. And I still think that Chicken Tonight has a great future. I don't see any reason why this should hurt you a bit."

It took time and effort to transport Pelham Browne out to the car and to convince him that Morgan Ogilvie should do the driving.

Tom Robichaux, partner of Robichaux & Devane, considered his departing client and favored the world with a professional opinion.

"Trouble with Ogilvie is that he won't face facts," he rumbled over his third drink. "Don't want to offend you, Hedstrom, but—"

Frank Hedstrom did believe in facing facts. Without resentment, he finished Robichaux's sentence for him.

"But the survival of Chicken Tonight looks pretty shaky right now. Any idiot can see that."

"We'll pull through," said Ted Young from the bar.

Just then the ladies rejoined them. Under cover of the desultory conversation that ensued, Robichaux transmitted a personal opinion to Thatcher.

"And we've only got to put in, let's see"—he peered at his Accutron—"twelve more hours in this hellhole. What do you say to that?"

"What is there to say?" Thatcher replied. "Except amen!"

CHAPTER 14

STEAM IN DOUBLE BOILER

BUT FATE had yet another blow in store for Tom Robichaux, to whom the dinner hour was sacred.

"We're going to have to put dinner back a couple of hours," Mrs. Hedstrom announced uncompromisingly.

"I'm getting a little hungry, believe it or not," said Hedstrom, voicing the sentiments of every man in the room.

Joan Hedstrom was unsurprised. Like every wife, she knew that no catastrophe in the world could diminish a husband's need for three large meals each day.

"Veronica," she continued "is upset."

"That's torn it," muttered Robichaux, who knew what this meant.

She ignored him. "The police have been in the kitchen all afternoon."

"Probably stuffing themselves," Robichaux said resentfully.

Mrs. Hedstrom shouldered her domestic obligations. "Would anybody," she asked, "like some crackers?"

"I think," said Robichaux with considerable dignity, "that I'll go upstairs and rest before dinner, if you don't mind."

Thatcher was not unsympathetic to Tom's plight. He was hungry himself. But he was, in many ways, a more prudent man than Robichaux. He delayed his own departure until the appearance of a dish of saltines.

"I've brought you something to eat," he called out as he

entered their suite. "Dinner's coming in an hour and a half, according to Mrs. Hedstrom."

Robichaux, mouth full, tried to make the best of things. "Well, that means it won't be a TV dinner, at least."

"Oh, I don't think so. Veronica, I gather, is an excellent cook," said Thatcher.

He had gone too far.

"No woman," said Robichaux, disappearing into the bathroom, "really knows how to cook." There had been Alphonses, Pierres and Étiennes in the Robichaux kitchens to match the Amandas, Glorias and Brendas in the drawing room.

"Well, I'm going to while away this interval with alcohol," said Thatcher, turning to leave. "Sure you won't join us?"

Robichaux spoke from the nursery bathroom. Thatcher could distinguish only four words: ". . . own flask . . . tomorrow morning . . ."

Thatcher grinned to himself. There is, after all, something admirable about a relentlessly hopeful approach to life. Tom was simply rising above momentary discomforts and concentrating upon the coming moment of release, tomorrow morning. With Thatcher it was otherwise. Despite a reasonably optimistic nature, once he found himself inextricably mired in disaster, he developed a certain technical interest in its dimensions. It was this characteristic that steered him downstairs while Robichaux cravenly loitered amidst the spirit of stuffed animals and music-box lamps yet to come.

Fortunately, Thatcher could not foresee what he was letting himself in for.

Not that he was foolishly sanguine. Too much was conspiring against that. Modern architecture, for instance.

The new Hedstrom house, while large, really consisted of one spacious common room and assorted bedrooms, serviced by tiny utility areas. This meant that Thatcher's alternatives were a function of the construction plans: siege conditions with Robichaux and flask, or fraternization with everybody else. Well, he had opted for the latter and could not complain when he found the entire cast still assembled.

Frank Hedstrom sprawled in a large chair, legs stretched out. His head was tilted back and he was studying the ceiling. Ted Young was, once again, busy at the bar. Joan Hedstrom had curled up on the sofa and was knitting with demonic rapidity. Iris Young was just switching off the television.

"Any news?" Thatcher inquired dutifully.

There was no news, in the hard sense. Police inquiries were continuing, public cooperation was being solicited, but progress was scanty. This had not kept local and national pundits from an orgy of speculation about Clyde Sweeney, about Chicken Tonight and about every personality remotely concerned with either.

The conversation Thatcher had interrupted was resumed. Not unexpectedly, it centered on Clyde Sweeney. This was the price that Robichaux refused to pay. But, sybarite or no, if Robichaux & Devane instead of the Sloan had twelve million dollars riding on Chicken Tonight, Tom would have led the charge into the living room. Reminding himself to have a brutally frank talk with Maitland in Commercial Credit, Thatcher settled down to listen.

"No, I don't like it, Ted," said Hedstrom.

"Who does?" Young replied, adjusting his drink. "Naturally the networks are going to harp on the fact that we found the body. Everybody knows about Sweeney and Chicken Tonight."

"That's not what I mean. What I don't like is that our ideas about Sweeney were all wrong."

"Why were they wrong?" Young objected. "We know somebody hired Sweeney to sabotage us. Now somebody has killed Sweeney because the pressure went on. Hell, it's simple enough! Sweeney got to be too dangerous for the guy who hired him."

Hedstrom was shaking his head. "No, that's not good enough. Think of everything the police over in New Jersey dug up about Sweeney. Sweeney was planning to blow town for just six months. Then he was coming back. He talked about a little easy money. You know what the police told us, Ted. Everybody says Sweeney didn't know what he was doing—the Akerses, that landlady, and all Sweeney's cronies."

Thatcher, unlike Young, saw what Hedstrom was driving at. Logically, Sweeney's own ignorance should have protected him from murder.

"So he was a patsy," Ted Young retorted. "The brains behind this probably planned to kill him all along."

"That doesn't make sense, Ted," Hedstrom replied. "Remember, it was a stranger who hired Sweeney. He had to describe himself over the phone. Do you think he was handing out his real name and address? When he was planning to poison two hundred people? Why do you think Sweeney got his final payoff through the mail?"

Thatcher recalled the registered letter Sweeney had received the day of the poisoning. "Did the police find that it came from John Doe in Chicago?" he asked.

Hedstrom grinned briefly. "No, John Smith in New York."

There was an interval during which the click of knitting needles was the only sound in the room. Then, Hedstrom returned to his argument:

"And another thing, Ted. You say the brains planned to kill Sweeney all along, so it didn't make any difference if Sweeney knew who hired him. But that doesn't hold water. That way, Sweeney would have been killed right off the bat."

As Young still looked unconvinced, Thatcher weighed in. "Obviously, the critical point for Sweeney must have come when the headlines told him that he had been tricked into committing a serious crime. That was over a week ago. Whatever Sweeney did to get himself murdered, he should have done then."

"OK," said Young, "maybe you're right. But what difference does it make *when* Sweeney got murdered?"

Frank Hedstrom was suddenly impatient. "For God's sake," he snapped. "It makes a lot of difference. Sweeney came down here to contact somebody. He must have had a good reason. As for coming to me to give himself up—" He broke off contemptuously.

Ted Young could be mulish. "Don't be too fast, Frank," he advised. "Ogilvie was nuts, sure. But that doesn't mean a damned thing. Say Sweeney *did* come down here to contact you. No, not to turn himself in—that's crap. But what if Sweeney was ready to spill the beans? About who hired him, and why. Then it was pretty reasonable of him to head down here. He figured he'd tell you everything—at a damned good price. And whoever hired him figured out what he was doing, followed him down, and murdered him."

Outdoors, a storm was brewing. Somewhere in the distance there were dim flashes of lightning. Soon there would be thunder.

"But why should Sweeney try to contact Hedstrom here?"

Thatcher objected. "Why not call your New York office? Sweeney was less likely to be spotted in a big city than down here. After all, he was the object of a highly publicized manhunt."

Hedstrom supported this view emphatically.

"Ted's theory is as bad as Ogilvie's. How did Sweeney know I was here? The office wasn't giving out our whereabouts. For that matter, nobody but Angie knew—"

"Plenty of people knew," Young insisted.

"Come on, Ted," Hedstrom said bluntly. "Sweeney came down here to meet the guy who hired him—and you know it!"

"What do you mean by that?" Iris Young, who had been listening hungrily, trembled with emotion. Thatcher, like Hedstrom and Young, had forgotten the women. The brittle voice startled him.

Hedstrom was the first to recover. "I mean something funny's going on, Iris. That's what the police think. That's what we all think. Hell, that's what we're trying to cover."

"Nobody's covering anything," Iris shot back. "We all told the police everything we know!"

Here Frank Hedstrom made the first obvious mistake that Thatcher had witnessed. He tried to cajole her.

"Well, we didn't overburden them with details," he said with a smile, ready to dismiss the subject. Joan Hedstrom, her eyes on her knitting, seconded his efforts.

"I know I told Captain Stotz everything I knew about that scarf."

With a sharp gesture, Iris Young waved away these attempts to deflect her.

"Oh, no you don't!" she rasped. "I see what you're doing." She leaned forward, staring at Hedstrom. "Do you think you can get away with this? Or do you think you can justify letting Stotz go after Ted? Why didn't you do something?"

"Iris!" Both Joan Hedstrom and Ted were protesting, but Frank Hedstrom, stung, ignored them.

"How the hell could I do anything?" he asked roughly. "I never knew he met Sweeney in Trenton. Once that came out, there wasn't anything I could do. God, I went along when he pretended not to recognize Sweeney—"

"Hey!" Young shouted. "What do you mean, *pretended?*"

"Oh, for God's sake, Ted," said Hedstrom almost desperately. "Have it your own way. I didn't know whether you recognized him or not. I didn't care."

This may have mollified Ted. Iris, however, was derisive.

"Oh, you're clever," she almost crooned at Hedstrom. "First you let Stotz single Ted out. Now you come up with a theory that Sweeney came down here to get in touch with someone. *Someone*. When are you going to come right out with it? When are you going to tell us you think Ted hired him?"

Whatever Hedstrom had been expecting, it was not this. For that matter, Thatcher himself was jolted.

"Iris!" Again the cry of warning from Joan Hedstrom went unheeded.

"Iris," said Frank Hedstrom, "have you gone crazy? Why the hell should Ted hire Sweeney?"

"Oh, sure! I'm crazy. Because I can see what you're up to. I can see what that rotten little mind of yours is scheming. Well, Frank, you're the one who's crazy—crazy like a fox!"

Iris had gripped the arms of her chair. Her head was thrust forward. The fine-boned face was suddenly pointed, vulpine.

Ted Young half rose, but Hedstrom waved him back to his chair. "No, let's hear this out. What am I supposed to be scheming at, Iris?"

She smiled unpleasantly at him. "You want an excuse to get rid of Ted. You always have. Oh, sure, you make a big thing of being old buddies. But you're scared. Scared rotten! You know Ted's ready to step into your shoes. And that's really gotten to you, hasn't it, Frank? He's worth ten of you. You know people can see through you these days. You've lost the old magic."

"Can't we stop this?" Joan Hedstrom's placid suggestion was hurled back in her face.

"No, we can't!" Iris Young spat.

Hedstrom muttered something indistinguishable about getting it out of her system, and Iris pounced.

"Medical advice! From you? Don't you dare!" She looked briefly at her husband, slumped into white-faced misery. When she went on, her voice was broken. "Ted's done everything. He's slaved night and day for you—and for Chicken Tonight. And where do you think you'd be without him? Where? I'll tell you where. You'd be nowhere—"

"Iris," her husband began, but she swept on.

"And now you're scheming against him, because you're scared. Well I'm not standing for it—just you remember that, Frank Hedstrom! You can fool the rest of the world, but you can't fool me. I've known you too long. You're not using Ted as a scapegoat. Not as long as I'm alive. For all we know, you killed Sweeney yourself! You probably arranged everything! You're the one—"

"Iris!" Ted Young finally surged to his feet. "Iris, cut this out!"

"No!" she screamed. "Don't you try to stop me, Ted. You've got to listen, too. You've been brainwashed. You don't want to see what he's doing to you."

She too leaped to her feet and stood there, swaying almost drunkenly. Dramatically, she pointed at Hedstrom. "He's be-behind all of the trouble! Can't you see it? It's so obvious that it makes me laugh!"

Then, with terrible emphasis, she did begin to laugh. First it was an actress's mockery, then it became shrill, uncontrolled. As Young moved swiftly to her side, she broke into painful spasms of coughing. He grasped her shoulders and shook hard. For a moment this had no effect. Then, suddenly, Iris opened her eyes wide and gulped. Intelligence returned. She looked into Ted's face searchingly. Then she collapsed against his shoulder in tears.

Without a word, Young half carried her, half led her from the room.

He left behind frozen silence.

"Great!" said Frank Hedstrom at last. "That's exactly what we need. Our little Iris in hysterics!"

Thatcher, who had hastily snatched up a stray copy of *Vogue,* emerged from shelter. He was torn between a desire to forget the entire episode and curiosity. "Do you think she'll be all right?" he inquired of Joan Hedstrom.

"Oh, Iris will be all right," she replied with a calm worthy of Miss Corsa. "Ted will look after her."

Thatcher eyed her. "Does that mean that . . . er . . . do you mean that Mrs. Young has . . . ?"

She was almost roguish. "Oh yes, Iris has a tendency to get—carried away."

"Good God!" said Thatcher with real feeling. He was truly impressed with the understatement.

"That's just fine," Frank Hedstrom said irritably. "I've seen Iris go off before—but why make a dead set against me?"

That too was an aspect of the affair that interested Thatcher.

Serenely Joan counted stitches. "Well, every now and then Iris hates you, Frank."

Hedstrom was beginning to look punch drunk, and Thatcher could scarcely blame him.

"What!" he yelped. "Hates me? What have I done to Iris? Hell, I thought we were supposed to be friends."

Hedstrom sounded bewildered. Joan, on the other hand, might have ben dispensing immutable feminine lore.

"It's not anything you've ever done, Frank. It's what you are."

If she expected this to solve the problem, she was doomed to disappointment. Both men required further enlightenment.

"Er—do you think you could expand that, Mrs. Hedstrom?" Thatcher suggested, fully alive to the danger of plunging into murky areas.

"What do you mean, what I am?" her husband demanded, goaded.

Joan Hedstrom selected her words carefully, as if dealing with perversely slow children. "Iris hates you—sometimes— because she resents the fact that Ted plays second fiddle to you."

"Second fid—? You mean she thinks that Ted doesn't get a fair cut?" Hedstrom was trying to reduce this to manageable proportions. Thatcher decided that the effort was futile, and he was right. "Ted's getting rich from Chicken Tonight, and Iris knows it."

With gentle authority, Joan corrected her husband. "Money doesn't matter," she said, confirming Thatcher's worst fears. "Iris doesn't care about money. She cares about Ted. You know, it's a shame that we didn't reverse our husbands. I wouldn't mind being married to a second fiddle."

Hedstrom took a long gulp from the glass he had forgotten. "Look, Joan, baby," he said. "Whose side are you on? Maybe you and Iris wouldn't mind the switch, but what about me?"

His wife smiled at him warmly. "You know what I mean," she said. "The trouble is that Iris is too intense. And she's especially intense about Ted."

Hedstrom pondered this. "Yeah," he said doubtfully. "I follow you there."

Intensity, thought Thatcher, is one thing; accusation of murder is another.

Joan Hedstrom was continuing. "Of course, Ted is pretty intense himself. What I meant is that Iris got hysterical because she's so worried about Ted. She's not a good judge about him. When Captain Stotz turned on him today—well, that set her off. You know how protective she feels. Any threat to Ted, and Iris nearly goes insane."

Hedstrom was decisive, and Thatcher honored him for it. "Let her go insane in her own home, then. We've got enough troubles around here. For God's sake, Joan, she's as bad as Browne. We're in the middle of a murder investigation. You've got to expect the police to ask questions. What's she afraid of? That Ted will be suspected?"

She put down her knitting and spoke very slowly and distinctly. "She's afraid of more than that, Frank."

He stared at her blankly. Then: "What does that mean?"

Joan Hedstrom did not want to put it into words, so Thatcher did so for her.

"I take it Mrs. Young is afraid that her husband might actually be guilty. Right, Mrs. Hedstrom?"

Joan nodded, Hedstrom erupted, and Tom Robichaux, at his jauntiest, entered the room.

"Well, now," he said cozily. Then, with instinctive gallantry, he remarked upon the sparkle in Mrs. Hedstrom's eye, the roses in her cheeks.

Inconsequently, Thatcher suddenly wondered what a notable ladies' man would have made of Iris Young's performance.

Or of Joan Hedstrom's explanation for it.

CHAPTER 15

REMOVE FROM HEAT

MOST MEN returning to their offices after a weekend at the vortex of a sensational murder could safely rely
on being the center of spellbound, not to say ghoulish,
interest on Monday. If John Putnam Thatcher ever harbored
such unworthy illusions, they were speedily punctured.

At first glance, his secretary's greeting was encouraging.
"Oh, Mr. Thatcher, I'm so glad you were able to get in.
We do need you this afternoon," Miss Corsa said, her voice
barely able to contain surprise at this unlikely turn of events.

Thatcher was too experienced to suppose that her remark
had any reference to the financial activities of the Sloan
Guaranty Trust. Miss Corsa held a healthy, and perfectly
justifiable, opinion of her own abilities along these lines. Any
trifling question about investing in heavy industry in newly
emergent nations she could handle herself. Indeed, Thatcher
had long suspected that only her respect for protocol per-
mitted him a view of the documents daily crossing her desk.
As for those he did not see—well, he was too wily to raise
awkward questions.

"And what do you want me to do?" he asked cautiously.
Rash promises, he felt, could all too easily lead to a reversal
of their roles.

Miss Corsa was kind. "It's very simple," she reassured him.

The Sloan, like all self-sufficient worlds, was far more pre-
occupied with its own concerns than with those of alien
territories. As a matter of politeness, as a matter of relief
from temporary tedium, it might summon a passing interest
in outside affairs such as Presidential elections and space
probes. But at the moment, with drama rampant in every

109

corridor, it had no time for sabotage and murder in places so distant as New Jersey and Maryland.

As Miss Corsa elaborated her proposal, it was borne in on Thatcher that while he had been frittering his time away on the travails of Chicken Tonight, preparations for the Trinkam Anniversary Celebration were nearing climax. The solicitation phase was over. Munificent contributions had flowed in from people as far apart—in every sense of the word—as the bank tellers on the first floor and the directors in their tower suite. The final sum was so staggering that gift selection posed unprecedented problems. Gone were thoughts of luggage, gold watches or portable bars. Indeed, at first there had seemed to be only one solution—gutting Charlie's office completely, then transforming it into a bower of roses.

Cooler heads prevailed. The Committee had formed a subcommittee, on which every power bloc in the bank had tried for a seat. Miss Corsa's simple narrative of the complexities that ensued irresistibly reminded Thatcher of the Vietnam peace talks. The delegates finally chosen were, to a man, battle-hardened office politicians.

"And who," asked Thatcher, "is representing the Trust Department?"

"Mr. Gabler is acting for the senior trust officers. And Mr. Nicolls for the junior trust officers."

There was clearly no need to worry about a department that could collar two such coveted seats.

"And I suppose there's been trouble about coming to a decision?" Thatcher pursued, wondering where he came in.

Indeed there had. The negotiators had avoided taking hard positions. Instead, they had adopted a "here's a top-of-the head suggestion, see what you think of it" posture during open meetings, while caucusing savagely in the smoke-filled employees' cafeteria. Special interests had emerged. The lower ranks were all in favor of an object they had located at Hammacher Schlemmer which would enable Charlie to take a sauna bath, acquire a sun tan and do isometric exercises while enjoying a professional massage. In short, he could occupy all his office hours without having to fall back on the tasks for which he was paid. This choice seemed inspired by a burning desire to keep Mr. Trinkam in good condition for as long as possible.

The front office, with the conservatism that had wafted

its members to their current eminence, was opting for a Persian rug of incomparable silken splendor. Everett Gabler had warned against the introduction of Oriental opulence: there was already too much of the sheik in Charles F. Trinkam. His animadversions had been a tactical error; they almost succeeded in swinging the secretaries over to the pro-rug faction.

The junior trust officers wanted to enrich Charlie's life with a miniature Henry Moore sculpture—overlooking the fact that he had been having a roaring good time for years without benefit of aesthetics. The Investment Division had alienated everybody by shameless self-touting; they wanted to give Trinkam a baby portfolio of selected stocks. Other elements favored an astrakhan coat from London, a directoire desk allegedly used by Napoleon, and a set of Renaissance banking texts from the Palazzo Medici.

Not for the first time, Thatcher marveled at the riotous imaginations concealed beneath the Sloan's staid exterior.

"And do you foresee any resolution of this conflict, Miss Corsa?"

Miss Corsa told him that the time for electioneering was over. The subcommittee must come to a decision that very day. It was, therefore, planned that their final session should take place in Mr. Trinkam's office where they could view with their own eyes its deficiencies and its amenability to improvement. Mr. Thatcher's role was to lure Mr. Trinkam out of his den and keep him occupied for at least two hours. Did he think he could do that?

"I could call Mr. Trinkam now," Miss Corsa murmured helpfully.

Thatcher was fully alive to the benefits of a plan that insulated him so completely from the final convulsions of the subcommittee.

"Do so," he directed. "And after an hour or so you might send Mr. Bowman in."

Miss Corsa departed to alert all outposts. Her activities shortly produced Charlie Trinkam, insouciant as ever.

"Well, John, so the fuzz let you go?" he greeted his superior. "Don't you rank as a suspect?"

"As a matter of fact, they let us all go. They didn't have enough to hold anyone. That's the trouble, too many suspects. But I find it hard to believe that they're seriously concerned with Tom and me."

"Robichaux!" Charlie brayed. "One look at his record and they'll cross him off the list."

Thatcher raised his eyebrows.

"Anybody with his marital problems who settles for the divorce court hasn't got the stuff for a good murder."

For years Charlie had been predicting that Tom Robichaux would finally marry someone who would dig in her heels and resist termination.

"No." Thatcher shook his head. "Tom has got some secret selectivity principle of his own. It's like calling to like."

"That sounds," said Charlie comfortably perching on a corner of the desk, "like a couple of dinosaurs baying at each other. But about this murder. The papers didn't have much in the way of facts. Said it all happened at some sort of hunt club. What were you doing there?"

"Oh, they use it as a country club. But the setting was a godsend for the murderer." Thatcher explained about the horse show and the consequent disruptions. "The place was unbelievable pandemonium. Inside, the normal dining and dancing. Outside, horses and grooms and trucks. And both coming together in the parking lot where the murder took place. As a result, the police haven't been able to make any headway tracing movements in the lot and on the grounds— and I don't think they will. For instance, Sweeney could have been hanging around for the better part of the day, and everybody would have assumed he had something to do with the horse show."

Charlie swung a gleaming shoe in small arcs. "Well, a couple of motives leap to the eye. I suppose that's what the police are concentrating on. First and foremost, there's Frank Hedstrom. Sweeney was strangled, wasn't he? Say Hedstrom sees him and recognizes the man who's ruined his business. He goes into a blind rage and throttles him on the spot."

"Even the police rejected that theory. Sweeney wasn't strangled with bare hands. First he was struck over the back of the head, then he was strangled with Mrs. Hedstrom's scarf."

"All right," said Charlie with unimpaired gusto. "Hedstrom's afraid that office living has made him soft. So he rewrites the scenario. First he picks up a rock and cracks Sweeney over the head. Then the scarf!"

Thatcher looked up alertly at the reference to soft office living. Had Charlie heard rumors of the sauna-cum-masseur? "No," he said regretfully, "it's not that easy. Sweeney was bludgeoned with some kind of sandbag. Probably a sock filled with sand. And Mrs. Hedstrom's scarf was brought by someone from the Hedstrom house. All of which suggests premeditation."

Charlie tut-tutted. "That's a nice bunch of playmates you had down there," he said disapprovingly.

"Efficient, anyway," Thatcher grunted. "It was a bloodless murder. Anybody could have done it, then walked back onto the dance floor without a sign."

"Like those typewriter ribbons you're supposed to be able to change in white gloves," Charlie mused. "That seems to dispose of the maddened-rush theory. I never liked it, anyway. For one thing, it didn't explain what Sweeney was doing down there."

"That's the point which Hedstrom and Young seized on. If you assume that Sweeney was killed by the man who employed him to poison that truckload of chicken Mexicali, then his presence follows naturally enough. Either he came down to see his employer or he came down to tell all to Hedstrom. In either case, the employer killed him to seal his mouth." Thatcher paused before adding, "And that, unfortunately, leaves the field wide open."

Charlie had an objection. "You mean Hedstrom too?"

"At least provisionally. Though nobody has come up with a reasonable theory as to why he should poison his own product."

"Whereas everybody can think of a reason for this Ted Young. The number-two man trying to discredit the number-one man."

"There's more against Young than just that." Briefly Thatcher recapitulated the police disclosures of the Young-Sweeney encounter in Trenton. "So they have strong grounds for believing that Young would have recognized Sweeney if he had seen him. And I have grounds for believing that he did." Thatcher repeated the conversation on the terrace between Iris and Ted. "At the time, his wife thought he was lying about seeing someone in the parking lot. She thought he was trying to distract her. I did, too, for what that's worth. I only overheard a fragment of their talk. But now . . ."

Charlie whistled soundlessly. "Yes. If he hired Sweeney and then suddenly saw him at the club, apparently waiting for Hedstrom, Young really would have stiffened. That would explain a lot."

"It explains something else that has been bothering me. If Young was behind the sabotage, there's no mystery about how Sweeney's employer found out about Sweeney's existence." Thatcher used a finger for punctuation. "Young already knew about him."

"You mean it was no accident that Sweeney was perfect for the job—a drifter with no family who'd just been fired. Someone who'd have no objection to skipping town for a couple of months."

"Exactly. You know yourself how hard it would be to pluck just the right man from the roster of a company that you didn't know anything about."

Charlie was politely incredulous. "Oh, come on, John," he said. "Fifty dollars to a girl in the personnel office? It's done all the time."

Thatcher agreed up to a point.

"Yes, it's done all the time by, say, companies who are looking for technicians with rare skills. But then there's no troublesome aftermath. But if you're planning a wholesale poisoning, you can't rely on the girl's keeping quiet. Not to mention the fact you have to find the girl first and that too leaves a trail."

Charlie had a sudden thought. "Good God, there haven't been any sudden accidents to people in the Personnel Department of Chicken Tonight, have there?" he asked, horrified.

"The police thought of that one." Thatcher smiled grimly. "Hedstrom tells me they've put the personnel people through a fine sieve. Everybody is alive and accounted for. And the police are convinced that no girl was asked to run through the files and produce somebody with Sweeney's peculiar qualifications."

"You're right, then. That points the finger at Young."

Discontentedly, Thatcher thrust his feet into a low desk

drawer and tilted his chair back. He looked out the window a moment before summarizing.

"Not very conclusively. Not in the light of everybody else's behavior. But, regardless of whether Young really was up to anything, I'd be prepared to wager good money that his wife thinks he was. It wasn't until police suspicion veered toward him that Mrs. Young became hysterical and started to lash out at Hedstrom. She was in perfect control until then."

Charles laughed shortly. "That was some party. First a murder. Then a police investigation. And finally a raving hysteric."

"Not so hysterical if her outburst was planned to shift suspicion away from her husband," Thatcher said dryly.

"Was there any suggestion that the murderer had to be a man? Was it physically impossible for a woman?"

"With Clyde Sweeney unconscious? I imagine a ten-year-old child would have been strong enough. But it doesn't seem like a woman's murder, does it?"

"Wonderful what they can do when they set their minds to it," Charlie said with the cheerfulness of the lifelong bachelor. "And it would explain the scarf."

"Yes, as far as the scarf goes, premeditation applies only to the men. Either of the women could have brought it accidentally."

"Then, for my money, Mrs. Young is still on the list. And not so far down, either."

"Oh, they're all still on the list. It's not just confined to the Youngs and the Hedstroms, either. Morgan Ogilvie and Pelham Browne could both do a lot of explaining. Ogilvie's insistence on this merger verges on the pathological. He's trying to ram it down Hedstrom's throat."

"Now, John, you're prejudiced. Admittedly, the idea to have this conference down on the Chesapeake didn't turn out well, but that doesn't affect the business decision."

"Quite apart from the murder, it's incredible," Thatcher insisted quietly. "I would give a great deal to know how much Ogilvie has riding on the merger, how much he expects to make from it. You know, Pelham Browne is a director of Southeastern Insurance. I got the impression that he was taken aback at Ogilvie's activities. He certainly did his best to disassociate himself from them. First he was reluctant to join us, then he disappeared. Of course, if he hired Sweeney to sabotage the merger and then arranged to meet him at the club, he had every reason for acting the way he did."

Charlie grinned. "From what you say, human instinct would explain the desire not to join your party. But look here, the papers said this house of Hedstrom's was new, that the Hedstroms had never been there before. So how come an appointment with Sweeney down there? Did they themselves know they'd be there?"

"Yes. One of the features of this house was that they'd been planning—all four of them—to open it this weekend for over a month. And they've never deviated from that plan. The men, incidentally, haven't been there before, except for one trip to buy the land over a year ago. It might make sense to meet Sweeney someplace where they wouldn't be recognized. Certainly Maryland would be better for a meeting than New York or Trenton."

Thatcher was still speculating on this point when Walter Bowman came breezing in. The bulky chief of research directed a number of alarming grimaces across the desk which Thatcher took to mean that Miss Corsa's plot was unfolding. Charlie Trinkam looked concerned.

"Anything wrong, Walter?" he asked.

"No, no," Bowman hastily denied. "Except that trying to stay on top of Chicken Tonight is taking years off my life."

"How's the stock doing?"

"It's sort of seesawing. Opened up, went down, now it's climbing again. The market can't make up its mind." Bowman adopted a leisurely, diffuse manner indicating he was prepared to spin this out indefinitely.

Obedient to his cue, Thatcher said, "What can't they make up their mind about, Walter?"

"How this murder is going to affect consumer response to Chicken Tonight. If everybody thinks that Hedstrom strangled Sweeney on sight, then they may decide that here's a company that really stands behind its product. On the other hand, if they figure that Young was causing the shenanigans to lever Hedstrom out, then they're not going to want to buy chicken from a company that spreads poison every time it has a little front-office rivalry.

Charlie Trinkam recognized derangement when he heard it. "Now, Walter, baby," he began warily.

"The sooner this murder is cleared up, the better," Thatcher declared stoutly. "I know Wall Street is always at least three removes from reality. But it seems to be receding further and further."

"Of course," said Bowman, settling down for an analysis of the finer details of his argument, "this just applies to Chicken Tonight's normal residential sales."

"What other kind did you have in mind?" Thatcher was not sure that he was prepared to countenance outright idiocy on the part of his research chief merely to keep Trinkam from his office.

"College sales." Bowman's reply came like a pistol shot. "Home deliveries at Chicken Tonight are still fifty percent down, but dormitory deliveries are back to eighty-five percent of normal."

Charlie had the solution. "The kids don't scare easy."

"Don't you believe it! I say there's something else." Bowman was mysterious.

"Oh?" Thatcher was curious.

"The kids found out about sniffing glue, didn't they? They're the ones who found out about taking a trip on LSD. Well, then," Bowman said darkly, "there may be more to these zinc salts than meets the eye."

Inevitably Charlie was attracted by this speculation. "It may be simpler than that," he observed. "After all, if you spend your time smoking pot and downing amphetamine pills, you probably don't notice a little thing like zinc poisoning. Hedstrom's probably selling to every acidhead in town."

"If there are enough of them," said Walter Bowman, staunchly pious, "we may save our twelve million yet."

Thatcher had listened to this exchange absently. His thoughts were still with his earlier statement.

"Clearing up this murder and the Sweeney mess, Walter, would enable Chicken Tonight to appeal to a larger clientele."

Charlie Trinkam had heard that tone before. He leaned forward. "Just remember one thing, John. This bozo has already killed once to keep his identity hidden. He may not be through with Chicken Tonight."

CHAPTER 16

SQUEEZE THE LEMON

BACK IN New Jersey, Captain Johnson of the State Police was still concerned with the damage which had already been done to Chicken Tonight. The news of Clyde Sweeney's murder and urgent requests for cooperation from the Maryland police did not cause him to renew his efforts along these lines. They had never flagged. He had been quietly working, extending the inquiry to include Sweeney's bowling team and bookie, his fellow truck drivers and roomers. At the same time, earlier witnesses had been reinterrogated.

Mrs. Menotti, as the most likely source of hard information, got special treatment. Captain Johnson was inclined to view the landlady as a mass of sludge which might, with luck, contain a nugget of gold. He acted accordingly. The men he sent to interview her were so many strainers. Each time she was put through a finer mesh.

It was not until the day after Sweeney's murder that this delicate dredging operation, to a limited extent, paid off.

"The old lady finally came up with something," Sergeant Bousquet announced.

Johnson sat up. "Something about the actual doping of the Mexicali?" he asked hopefully.

It was already established that Clyde Sweeney had used Mrs. Menotti's cellar one day. There, undoubtedly, he had opened his pilfered boxes, introduced the zinc salts and resealed the cartons. Captain Johnson was convinced that their best hope of progress lay in further information about those moments. The packets of zinc salts had probably come from Sweeney's employer. They might yield a clue to his identity. They might even carry fingerprints.

Bousquet shook his head. "No, not about that. You know how it goes. Mrs. Menotti knew damn well that stuff in her basement was stolen. She thought Sweeney wanted a safe place to store it. She figured he was paying her five or ten bucks to turn a blind eye, and that's exactly what she did. Her story is that she was out of the house while he was using the cellar and, when she came back, the cellar had been cleaned up. She's got no idea what he did there or what happened to any trash, like empty packets. The hell of it is, it's probably just like she says."

Johnson sank back. "Then what did you get out of her?" he growled.

"I was taking her through that phone call again, the one Sweeney got to meet someone who paid him a thousand dollars."

"The guy in an orange-and-brown sport shirt and tan slacks," murmured Johnson, who knew the description by heart. "If she's been sitting on the fact that he also mentioned that he was six feet one and a quarter, weighed two hundred and seven pounds, had red hair, green eyes and a wart on his nose, I'm going to go out there and have a little talk with Mrs. Menotti."

"It's not anything like that good," Bousquet said sadly. He was tired of Mrs. Menotti. "But she did manage to remember that Sweeney repeated the place of the meeting. The lobby of the Hotel Granada, over in Bellsboro."

Johnson was skeptical. "And she's just happened to remember now?"

"Well, she says she would have forgotten all about it. The Granada didn't mean anything to her. But her nephew got a job in the kitchen there this weekend, and that brought the whole thing back."

Both men silently pondered this explanation. This, they finally agreed, was the way that the memory of a Mrs. Menotti worked.

"It's nice to know," Johnson summarized. "But if the guy was a stranger around here, it's not going to do us much good until we've got him in the lineup."

Bousquet sighed and rose to his feet. "And that's not going to happen until somebody finds out where Sweeney beat it to when he blew out of Willoughby."

The New York City police were doing just that.

From the point of view of the authorities, a dead Clyde Sweeney had some advantages over a live Clyde Sweeney. Backtracking over the last few days of his life was easier than searching for a fugitive.

"Surprising how much difference that haircut made, isn't it?" commented an officer in the precinct house.

Clyde Sweeney had not attempted much in the way of disguise. He had taken his long dark hair and his sideburns to a barber and they had been ruthlessly shorn to a minimal crew cut. The results were out of proportion to the effort. The shape of Sweeney's skull seemed different. The forehead had been heightened and the jaws broadened. His ears stuck out at a noticeable angle.

The mortuary photographer in Maryland had worked hard to produce a publishable picture, emphasizing these changes and glossing over the effects of strangulation. The picture had appeared in the morning papers. The first fruits had been a visit from a barber on West Forty-second Street and a telephone call from a hotel manager around the corner.

"Martino's identification was positive," the officer continued. "Says he's not likely to forget that haircut in a hurry. But the important thing is that he remembers the date."

"And it fits in," the detective across the desk said. He was brooding over a list of dates with scribbled notes. "That morning the story about the poisoning hit the papers. They didn't know it was deliberate poisoning. They didn't even know it was Chicken Tonight then."

"But they knew it was chicken. Seventy-six people in the hospital after eating chicken, that was the story. And they made a big splash with it, warning everybody about the symptoms and telling them to get pumped out. It's easy enough to see what happened. Sweeney knew he'd put something into that mix, but he thought it just had nuisance value. Then he wakes up, sees the headlines, and knows he's in big trouble. He realizes there isn't going to be any problem fingering him. So he gets off his ass and hightails it to a barber."

"And then?"

But the officer had come to the end of his reconstruction. "Maybe they can tell you that at the hotel. You'd better get on down there, Dougherty."

The West End Arms was not as magnificent as its name. This came as no surprise to Dougherty, who had visited it professionally before. It was one of the innumerable small, shabby hotels clustered around Times Square. Here, on the night of his departure from Willoughby, Clyde Sweeney had registered under the name Curt Slattery.

"Sure, I remember him. I signed him in," said the manager, a small, moist man called Sert. "He was just like all the rest. Got his bags upstairs and then went out to have himself a time." He leered hopefully across the counter. "Didn't get back till three or four in the morning."

Dougherty remained expressionless. "And the next day?"

"Same thing. Slept late, sat around, then went out for the night." Sert paused dramatically. "Next day, he started to act different. Had his hair cut, stopped going out at night, hung around the bar and grill next door."

"And didn't you make anything out of that?" Dougherty asked.

"Jesus Christ! It happens all the time!" Sert was indignant. "You know how it is. They come to the big city with a roll. They give themselves a big time until the roll starts to run out. Then it's all different. They're up early. They buy themselves a paper first thing to read the help wanted. They get their meals on the cheap, they spin out their beers in the bar. Then they leave."

Sert rattled off glibly a routine he had seen a hundred times.

To Dougherty's final question he also had a pat reply. "No, that picture they ran last week didn't mean a thing to me. I didn't see much of him those first two days. Afterwards, he was around all the time. I get my beer next door, too. That's the way I remembered him, with the crew cut."

Sert's analysis of Sweeney's behavior was rejected, however, by the newsie in the lobby.

"Nope," he said unshakably, "he wasn't after the help wanteds. I can spot them a mile away. You can tell a lot by the way a guy opens his paper. This one, he was the kind who takes a look at the headlines, then folds to the sports page."

The denizens of Riley's Bar and Grill were even more helpful. They had seen a lot of Curt Slattery and, for once, were not averse to talking. It was, Dougherty knew, the thrill of being associated with a sensation. These men spent their lives on the periphery of experience. They were not going to waste the chance of being, for once, at the center of things.

If Dougherty had seen the bar and grill down the street from Mrs. Menotti's in Willoughby, New Jersey, he would have recognized that he was now in its spiritual twin. In his hour of need, Clyde Sweeney had returned to the surroundings which spelled security. Here he could forget anxiety, talking about the Celtics, discussing the events of the day, drinking beer, eating corned beef and cabbage.

"He was in here most of the day," the bartender told him. "Sat around with the others. Didn't seem to have anything else to do. Quiet, worried sort."

"Curt was okay," protested a regular. "Didn't make any trouble. We used to have our openers together."

"What did he talk about?" Dougherty asked.

"The usual stuff. He'd read his paper then. He got all shook up about that chicken poisoning. Don't seem possible he was the one who did it." For a moment the regular was awed by the duplicity of human nature. "Then he kept up with the sports page. Liked to read Red Smith. That's how we pass the time of day."

Dougherty knew all about those endless talks. He shifted his bulk restlessly and ordered another round.

"I suppose," he said resignedly, "Sweeney never said anything about his plans."

"Didn't seem to have any." There was surprise that anybody should. "At least, not until that last morning."

Dougherty came to attention. "What happened then? You were with him?"

"Sure. It was like I was telling you. We were having a quick one. He was going over all the stuff about that Chicken Tonight mess. I was reading about the Green Bay Packers myself. Sounded as if they were going to have their work cut out for them on Sunday. Let's see, that must have been Thursday. So I ask Curt if he wants to put money on the game. He didn't seem to hear what I was talking about. I had to ask him twice. Then he started to fold up his paper and said he wasn't going to be around on Sunday. In fact, he had to leave town right away. Next thing I knew, he was walking out." The regular shrugged. "That was the last I saw of him."

Dougherty was thoughtful. He already knew that Clyde Sweeney had gone straight back to the West End Arms and packed his bags. Then he checked out and late that Thursday morning disappeared into the blue.

But not for long. While many people have dropped totally from sight in this vast continent, successful vanishing acts are usually open-ended. One moment, a housewife is in her kitchen in Lexington, Massachusetts, or a counterfeiter is in his basement in Milwaukee, Wisconsin—then, nothing!

But Clyde Sweeney had been in New York on Thursday morning. On Saturday night his body was on the Eastern Shore of Maryland. While no policeman thinks that a straight line is the shortest distance between two points, criminologically speaking, the area between New York and Maryland does not constitute the blue, either.

"'Course, with planes, he could have been anywhere," somebody observed to Captain Stotz over a ream of reports from hotels, motels, boardinghouses, railroad stations, bus stops and similar facilities in four states. "No reason he had to hang around here."

"It's possible," Stotz conceded. He was as amiable to his subordinates on the Maryland State Police as he was to witnesses—and a good deal more forthcoming. "But I don't think so, Will. Planes—I don't figure they're Sweeney's style."

Will was a good deal younger than Captain Stotz. "These days planes are everybody's style, Captain. And Sweeney sounds just like the kind of guy who'd want to fly to Las Vegas first chance he got." He brandished a teletype from New Jersey and recited, "Plays the ponies . . . always in to the bookies . . . likes cheap night spots. I'll bet . . ."

But police work, like gambling, is a matter of probabilities. Captain Stotz was proved right before Will really got going on how Clyde Sweeney could have been in Las Vegas, Lake Tahoe or Reno en route to the Calvert Hunt Club.

First, the owner of the Chesapeake Bay Motel recognized a circular thrust at him by a weary detective. Second, Ed Twombley, of Paton, Maryland, reported a car abandoned in a lane on his farm.

"And two and two make four," Stotz observed. Clyde

Sweeney had rented a car in New York, driven south to Maryland, and registered on the Eastern Shore on Thursday night as Curt Slattery. Then—sometime—he had driven fourteen miles to Paton, left his car in a dirt track, and walked a half mile to the Calvert Hunt Club.

High-speed machinery and routine leg work pieced that much together from a registration number and an identification. Captain Stotz hoped that Mr. Larue Voorhis, of the Chesapeake Bay Motel, could flesh out the picture.

At first glance, this did not seem likely.

Mr. Voorhis, like Will, was younger than Stotz. But he had already matured a commercial philosophy. His forty-eight units (plus coffee shop) were not a business; they were a credo.

". . . the human touch," he said earnestly. "We try to give everybody that little special touch, Captain—like coffee *and doughnuts* free in their rooms for breakfast. The ice is free, of course. But we provide soda water too! You take your big impersonal chain of motels . . ."

Stotz did not have time to, so he led Voorhis to more germane matters by flourishing photographs.

"Absolutely," Voorhis said, eyes glistening with Rotarian zeal. "I'm sure they're the same man. And I'll be glad to view the remains."

That, Stotz replied absently, was not necessary. Police officers in Unit Twenty had already found Clyde Sweeney's union card and a driver's license—the latter crudely but efficiently altered. Voorhis assumed an expression of solemnity and said that he wanted only to do his duty. If more citizens cooperated with the police, why . . .

"Sure," said Captain Stotz. He had been a policeman for many years. He had a fairly good notion of what Mr. Voorhis would now be saying if Clyde Sweeney's body had come to light at the Chesapeake Bay Motel. "Now, what can you tell me about Sweeney?"

Voorhis ushered Stotz and Will into a small office leading from the reception counter and switchboard.

"I jotted down some notes," he reported proudly. "Once Detective O'Brien told me . . . wanted to get myself organized . . . Let's see. Oh, here it is, Slattery—that is, Sweeney—registered here Thursday evening. New York plates three-four—oh, you've got that? Yes, said he wasn't sure how long he'd need to be here. I put him down as a salesman of some sort. You know, dealing with the public as I do—"

Stotz was not interested in character analyses, particularly when they were inaccurate.

"Did you see him after that?" he interrupted to ask.

Mr. Voorhis was reproachful at this cavalier treatment of a citizen's attempt to cooperate with the police.

"Don't you want to know about the telephone calls?" he asked smartly.

Stotz glanced at Will with long-suffering and allowed as how, yes, he did want to know about any phone calls.

"Sweeney made two telephone calls Thursday night," said Mr. Voorhis in thrilling accents.

"Where to?" Will asked patiently.

That, Voorhis replied, he could not say. He had logged two calls from Unit Twenty on Thursday night, but he did not record the numbers.

Stotz sighed. "Tell me, Mr. Voorhis, how do you handle long-distance calls?"

"That's right! I got the charges on long-distance calls," Voorhis shouted triumphantly. "That means they were local calls! I knew they were important!"

"OK," said Stotz. "Then what?"

Then, unfortunately, there was little more that the voluble Mr. Voorhis could recall. Sweeney-Slattery had stopped by the office Friday morning to say he would be winding up his business on Saturday night. He would check out early Sunday morning. And that was all that Mr. Voorhis knew, for a fact. When the cleaning woman found Sweeney's possessions still in Unit Twenty after checkout time on Sunday, when Mr. Voorhis saw that the car was gone, when Detective O'Brien showed him the circular, why, Mr. Voorhis got thinking . . .

Stotz left Mr. Voorhis still talking and proceeded to Unit Twenty, where three policemen were methodically searching. In the spotless Danish impersonality that would always defeat Mr. Voorhis' best efforts, Clyde Sweeney's possessions were pitiful and few: a pair of cheap suitcases, with clothes jammed carelessly into them. A jacket, flung across a chair. A grimy hairbrush and, in the bathroom, bottles of hair conditioner and cologne. A few meretricious objects, and the full pathos of Clyde Sweeney's dreams stood out vividly.

"But he could have done better," commented one policeman, straightening from the suitcase lid he was examining. "He had a roll." Carefully, holding it by the corners, he handed Stotz an opened registered envelope.

The late Clyde Sweeney had left turtleneck sweaters, an imitation alligator wallet, some gaudy shirts behind him. He had also left three thousand dollars in fifty-dollar bills, and one thousand dollars in hundreds.

"Four thousand dollars," muttered Captain Stotz disgustedly. "A poisoner's pay."

CHAPTER 17

THICKEN THE DRIPPINGS

WHILE AUTHORITIES in New York, New Jersey and Maryland were painstakingly re-creating the immediate past, another branch of government was probing the future.

"It's a shame that Sweeney is dead," said Dr. Mosby. "Have they found out who did it?" He asked the question without much interest.

"They're keeping us informed," said Mr. Denton in equally desultory tones. "Seems they've tracked him from New York to Maryland. Who knows what it all means?"

The Public Health was not interested in the murder of Clyde Sweeney, per se; far less, in attempts to apprehend his murderer. Clyde Sweeney, to them, had been a grave health menace, like infectious hepatitis. Until the investigation unearthed medically useful facts, it would receive only tepid attention from the Public Health. And as yet, Sweeney's movements had shed no hard light on the introduction of zinc salts to chicken Mexicali.

So it was only right and proper that the Public Health should be planning a more relevant investigation. And, as Dr. Mosby put it, Sweeney alive would have been a good deal more useful than the entire police forces of New Jersey, New York and Maryland combined were proving.

"Until now," said Denton. "They may still come up with something."

"They may," Mosby replied militantly. "But we would be remiss in our responsibilities if we did not take steps."

In short, the Public Health was forging ahead with plans to subject the Chicken Tonight episode to searching scrutiny. The scope of the forthcoming hearing was very broad. In fact, a captious critic might have claimed it exceeded the powers of the Public Health. For there was no real question about the actual source of the threat to public safety: for a price, Clyde Sweeney had introduced an alien substance into a commercial food product.

"Although there seems to be some question about whether he knew how dangerous it was," Mosby began.

Denton waved this aside. "Let Hedstrom—or the police—worry about that. No, our interest is . . ."

Dr. Mosby listened, although he already knew that the Public Health grew fanatical over the possibility of food sabotage. Clyde Sweeney's success had opened a terrible vista. After all, one Cuban hijacks a plane to Havana and soon whole air fleets are detouring past Miami. How easy was it for madmen or criminals to poison American food?

The Public Health was going to find out.

"Now," said Denton, warming to his subject, "we've got a list of the people we'll want to summon to the hearing. Do you want to look it over?"

Dr. Mosby did look it over, mentally coming to a conclusion that John Putnam Thatcher had reached before him. Mr. Denton was an enthusiast.

Enthusiasts sometimes go too far.

"Why on earth the sixth and seventh grades from the Englewood School?" he inquired humbly. "Don't think I'm criticizing, Denton. But what can forty-two schoolchildren—"

Denton waxed eloquent. Those forty-two schoolchildren had taken the guided tour through Chicken Tonight's test kitchens. Could they have dropped bubble gum into a gleaming cauldron? Mrs. Collins, the dietician, said no. But could they be sure? And, indeed, what made people think that the mask of danger could not be worn by a pre-adolescent? Had Mosby read . . . ?

If Denton had his way, Chicken Tonight was in for the investigation of all time. Already, teams of Public Health authorities (with aides co-opted from the Department of Agriculture) were readying questions for every single firm who sold supplies to Chicken Tonight, which included broiler producers like Pelham Browne, and the Morton Salt Company.

Furthermore, analysts from many agencies were peering into Chicken Tonight's business activities. Did the Sloan Guaranty Trust, one of Hedstrom's creditors, harbor an unscrupulous desire to use that power unworthily? What had Southeastern Insurance discovered when it was studying merger proposals? Could any Chicken Tonight stockholder slip past security . . . ?

("You know, Denton, you may be overdoing.")

Then, what about outsiders? The schoolchildren? The garden club from Leonia, New York? What precautions did Chicken Tonight erect against owners, employees, creditors, debtors, visitors?

Or their relatives?

The Public Health's press-relations officer was a man who knew how to transform molten lava into pure lead:

> . . . announced today an impartial study of standards obtaining in major U.S. food processors. Among the firms cooperating in this venture is Chicken Tonight . . .

Chicken Feed, house organ of the Chicken Tonight organization, was not due for three weeks. This was just as well. These were hard times for the relentlessly cheery. Moreover, Chicken Tonight's franchisees were not, on the whole, particularly happy to be part of the great Chicken Tonight family.

Unfortunately, their common plight was generating news items in other places. There was still much time for reading in most Chicken Tonight franchise kitchens. On most tables in such kitchens were newspapers and magazines that held a dreadful fascination. (Mr. Chet Brewster, would-be doyen of the area's franchisees, took one look at *Time* magazine and thought of libel actions.)

In Willoughby, Dodie Akers was reading aloud.

"'. . . no reason for suspicion, said Mr. Larue Voorhis, owner-manager of the Chesapeake Bay Motel. Late police releases confirm earlier reports of money found in Sweeney's possession. According to informed sources, in addition to undisclosed amounts in Sweeney's wallet, four thousand dollars cash was found hidden in a suitcase. Police now theorize that Sweeney was paid one thousand dollars as down payment and received three thousand dollars through the mail on the morning of the crime . . .'"

"Four thousand dollars!" said Vern Akers bitterly, interrupting Dodie's reading. "That's what Clyde took to put us out of business."

Customers were returning slowly to most Chicken Tonights—except those unlucky enough to have been in the news. Unfortunately for the Akerses, Clyde Sweeney had earned his four thousand dollars in their back yard.

Dodie put down the paper with a sigh. "I'll never understand it. Not if I live to be a million years old."

Vern looked at her with concern. It was not like Dodie to sound so defeated; for more than twenty years, she had been the one who kept him looking on the brighter side of things. It shook him to see her shoulders sag.

"I don't understand it, either," he said gruffly.

She smiled gratefully at him, and Vern put a huge paw over her hand.

They sat in the Chicken Tonight kitchen, alone and in silence. But even silence has its own emotional color, and this was the silence of despair, not anticipation. Tonight would see no noisy jangle of telephones, no rushing of delivery boys in and out, no alarm bells sounding on ovens, no prosperous bedlam. Tonight there would be perhaps six calls for a delivery of Chicken Tonight—perhaps seven.

Last night there had been four calls.

Vern Akers, Dodie and Sue, together with Sue's boy friend, were determinedly cheerful about the business outlook during the long hours when Chicken Tonight should have been humming.

"You see? I told you people are getting over it!"

"Sure it's going to take time. But we'll be back on schedule in a week."

"It won't be long before we have to get Neil and Peter back on the trucks."

It was exhausting enough to display this optimism through the long evenings, to reveal nothing but confidence when only two small orders had arrived by eight-thirty. The Akerses all did it.

But by day, when Sue was safely off at school, Vern and Dodie Akers were too drained to face events with anything but complete honesty.

"I never liked Clyde," said Dodie, resolutely picking up the paper again and letting her eye fall on the thick headlines. "But I honestly would never have believed he could do a terrible thing like this."

Vern stared hard at his own reflection in a gleaming oven door. Chicken Tonight was, in many ways, like the Army, he thought. Whenever there was a lull, the troops cleaned the gear. But cleaning up, brushing, polishing and shining did not keep a man from thinking, in Chicken Tonight or the Army. Vern Akers, who was not an introspective man, had had too much time to think recently.

"You know, Dodie," he said slowly, "I've been thinking . . ."

She put down the paper and waited for him to continue. Vern had never been one to talk your ear off; Dodie was still interested in what he had to say.

"I've been thinking about Clyde," he said, unconsciously tightening a pump handle. "You know, what happened to Clyde is kind of like what's happening to me."

Dodie was a kind and tolerant woman. But she knew her own worth and, more important, she knew her husband's worth.

"You and Clyde? Vern Akers, have you gone crazy? I never heard anything—"

Still groping, Vern barely heard her. "What I mean," he said with furrowed brows, "is that we both got mixed up in this big business. And it's beginning to look like maybe it was too much for us."

Dodie was still a ruffled mother hen, ready to counter any threat to her brood. "Humph!" she said, crossing plump arms pugnaciously.

Vern took this as skepticism. He persisted.

"Dodie, from what the papers say, somebody offered Clyde a chance at an easy four thousand bucks. If it had been a question of lifting a couple of cases of beer from the PX or of kiting a check—well, that wouldn't surprise you at all. Clyde cut corners all his life. But Clyde was a lightweight. This whole thing was too big for him."

He paused to see if he had made himself clear.

"And what does that have to do with the Akerses?" Dodie challenged, tacitly conceding his point.

Vern rubbed his chin thoughtfully. "Somebody slipped Clyde dough to put zinc in the Mexicali mix. Why? Big business, that's why! Somebody was out to get Chicken Tonight. Not you and me, or any of the rest of the guys, but all of Chicken Tonight."

"You mean Mr. Hedstrom?" Dodie asked, interested despite herself.

"That's right," her husband said. "Now, Dodie, that's big business. I don't know who did it, or why, but it wasn't for nickels and dimes. It was just Clyde's tough luck that his easy money came from someone who has so much riding that a murder or two don't make much difference to him."

Dodie weighed this. "All right," she said. "But where do you fit in?"

Vern approached a conclusion. "I've been thinking," he said again, leaning persuasively forward. "I guess I made a mistake. Dodie, when I was mustered out, I could have got a good steady job—"

"Night watchman," she said with scorn. "Salesman! Vern, after twenty years in the Army, we wanted to be our own bosses. To have our own business."

"Sure we did," he said, slipping back into an argument they both knew by heart. "But instead we got into big business. Oh, we run this Chicken Tonight—but, Dodie, we're a little cog in a big machine. God, look at the franchise committee I'm stuck with. That's a lot of people like you and me, but you add them up and you're talking about millions of dollars. And I'm supposed to go up to Mr. Hedstrom and bargain with him. Dodie, Mr. Hedstrom is big business. It's like . . ." he searched for an illustration. "It's like I should go in and bargain with General Westmoreland!"

He sat back, looking both troubled and determined.

She nodded at him. "I see what you mean."

Together they sat in silence until Dodie said finally, "But, Vern, you know what the difference is?"

He waited.

"We *are* big business," said Dodie Akers seriously. "I'm not saying it's turned out the way we expected. I guess we thought we'd have our own little place and do our own work. But you know what *Chicken Feed* says. We're all partners. Sure, Mr. Hedstrom and the company, they're big business, and they sell on Wall Street and all that. But where would they be without us, Vern? You're not one of their employees. You're one of their partners. So you *are* big business. And when you go in to talk to Mr. Hedstrom—well, it's not Sergeant Akers, it's Mr. Akers, with a couple of million dollars behind him!"

He widened his eyes at her, blinking at a new view of himself.

She gave a sudden warm laugh.

"What?"

Dodie gestured around the gleaming empty Chicken Tonight, and in the gesture encompassed the ruined business, the damage done by Clyde Sweeney, even the murder of that insignificant little man. For a moment, Vern sat stolidly; then his heavy features creased into a grin as he too saw the absurdity.

"There's always that job as custodian up at the junior college," he said. "If I have to leave big business, that is."

He was giving her a huge, reassuring hug when the tinkle of the shop door caused them to stand apart and look at each other with surprise.

"A walk-in," said Dodie, round-eyed. "Well, maybe things are looking up!"

Even in its palmy days, most of Chicken Tonight's customers used the telephone to summon the gold-and-orange truck for their chicken Mandarin. Still, each day from three to five o'clock a small band of walk-in customers stopped by on the way from work: blue-overalled men with empty lunchboxes, harried working mothers racing from four-thirty office closings to five-thirty dinners for hungry husbands and sons. Occasionally there was an agitated young wife, desperate over the collapse of some grandiose culinary project.

With a welcoming smile, Dodie hurried forward, leaving

Vern ready to press the buttons that would produce chicken Milanese, chicken Paprika or chicken Jamaican, then tidily box it in an orange-and-gold container to be carried out. He looked around with a surge of irrepressible hope. Vern Akers loved the whole panoply of equipment. And with Dodie beside him—well, maybe they could ride it out. Maybe his talk with Hedstrom would help.

In the tiny shop, Dodie was gaping at the newcomer.

The walk-in was a beautiful raven-haired woman with green eyes. Her clothes were not part of Willoughby, New Jersey, let alone Willoughby's Chicken Tonight. Dodie wished that Sue were here to see her.

"Mrs. Akers?" the woman asked with a flashing smile. "I wonder if your husband is available. I'd like to talk to both of you, about some business matters. My name is Mrs. Young. I hope you'll call me Iris."

CHAPTER 18

SEASON WITH CARE

"VERN!" DODIE yodeled. She was irritated to hear herself sound flustered. Mrs. Young, at any rate, bestowed on her a reassuring smile, then gazed about politely.

"Vern!" Dodie repeated, going to the door. "Somebody here to see you!"

Now she sounded like an Okie, she scolded herself. With an effort, she steadied her voice. "Vern, there's a Mrs. Young . . ."

He was wiping his hands on a towel when he came through the doorway. Except for a fractional rise of his graying eyebrows, he was unmoved by their visitor, Dodie was pleased to see.

"Vern," she said calmly, "Mrs. Young here wants to talk to us about business."

"We're not buying anything," he said without hesitation.

Was there a flicker of anger across that lovely face? Perhaps not, but Dodie was cheered by her husband. And she let Mrs. Young do her own explaining.

"No, I'm not selling anything," Iris said. "I want to talk to you about Chicken Tonight."

Vern looked at her quizzically. Then, after a glance at Dodie, he replied, "You'd better come in and sit down. Want a cup of coffee?"

In a way, Iris Young was incongruous in the large Chicken Tonight kitchen, but to Dodie her crisp self-possession and her polished appearance mirrored the glittering efficiency of the machinery.

Mrs. Young settled at the table, pulled out a pack of cigarettes and waited impatiently. Opposite her, Vern assumed the look of wary blankness that had seen him through twenty successful years in the service. Clearly, Dodie was the only one present afflicted by absurd fancifulness.

"I understand that you represent the organized franchisees of Chicken Tonight," Iris Young began. "So I decided that we should talk—"

Vern raised a big hand and, without hostility or heat, said, "Just a minute! First you'd better tell me what your interest in Chicken Tonight is. And tell me exactly why we should talk."

Iris Young bent her attention on stubbing out a half-smoked cigarette. Her downcast eyes belied a voice that was creamily confident. "I represent a group of minority stockholders of Chicken Tonight. Actually, it's more than that. My husband was one of the founders of Chicken Tonight, and he is probably the most important executive in the company."

Akers was disingenuous. "I don't remember any Youngs, lady. And I've been dealing with the company for over two years now."

How flat and unforthcoming Vern could sound. More as a note of hospitality than anything else, Dodie softened the blunt edges of his remark. "I think I remember a Mr. Young, Vern. They wrote him up in *Chicken Feed*. Ted Young, wasn't it?"

Her good intentions did not succeed. Certainly Mrs. Young showed no gratitude. There was slightly heightened color in her face when she replied, "Yes, it is Ted Young. And my husband has done most of the work inside the organization. For years, he's handled all the financial details of the company, including the real-estate developments. And he's in charge of the selling campaigns. Most of the advertising ideas are cleared through him. He doesn't deal directly with the individual kitchens, but he's really been in charge—behind the scenes. That's been very important, even if it doesn't get all the publicity!"

She paused, expecting some sort of response from Vern. Well, Dodie thought, she doesn't know Vern. He sat, stolid and waiting.

A shade more rapidly, Iris Young went on. "As I said, we ourselves own a considerable block of Chicken Tonight stock. And with the cooperation of some others—including the owners of the franchises . . ."

Again she did not want to spell out her message. Again, the pause failed to elicit help. Finally, with a minute shrug, she said baldly, "What we have in mind is a change of management."

"You mean, get rid of Mr. Hedstrom?" Dodie asked forthrightly. She had decided that the elegant Mrs. Young was not the general's lady. Far from it. And, like her husband, she liked to get things clear in her own mind without a wrapping of verbiage.

"Mr. Hedstrom!" said Iris Young venemously. "That's exactly what I mean. Until we get rid of Frank Hedstrom, we're all going to be in danger of losing everything we own, everything we've worked so hard for. What has Frank Hedstrom done for Chicken Tonight! I'll tell you—almost nothing. He's been sitting back, taking the credit, but it isn't Frank Hedstrom who's done the work. No, he's just been taking the money that other people—like you and the other franchisees, like my husband—make for him. And what's he doing to Chicken Tonight now? He's ruining it. And he's going to ruin us too. All he cares about is saving his own skin. He can't afford to worry about anything else. How can we hope to rebuild Chicken Tonight, under a man who's up to his neck in murder! You've read the papers, haven't you? Well, everybody else has, too. Our only hope is to get rid of Frank Hedstrom!"

The passionate words rang oddly in the functional kitchen. Helplessly, Dodie stared at Iris Young. But Vern Akers might have been listening to a sermon, for all the response he showed.

"If we get rid of Frank Hedstrom," Iris went on, "we may be able to save ourselves. But Ted and I don't have enough leverage through the stockholders, because Hedstrom saw to that. But you franchisees—you can push through a change. You've got him where you want him. What's Frank Hedstrom done for you? He's taken your money. He's destroyed your business. What you should do is insist that he resign!"

"And put your husband in his place?" Vern made Dodie jump by asking.

Iris Young bit her lip at his tone. "Ted is the backbone of Chicken Tonight. He's done all the work. He's your only hope. You stick with Frank Hedstrom, and you're going to be out on your ear."

"Just asking," said Vern mildly. Dodie wondered if he too registered the coarsening of Mrs. Young as she was caught up by her own words. If Vern did not, Mrs. Young herself did. Drawing a deep breath, she again produced that flashing smile and slowed her pace.

"Look, Mr. Akers—do you mind if I call you Vern? Vern, let's start from the beginning. You can't deny Chicken Tonight is in terrible trouble. Just how much business have you been doing? I don't have to guess—I know. Not much. And why? Because of Frank Hedstrom, that's why. And Frank Hedstrom isn't going to get out of trouble soon, believe me. For all we know, the worst is yet to come. What does that mean for you and me? It means we've got to save our own necks."

Vern listened carefully as she continued. He entered no objections and offered no criticism. So she thought she was convincing him, Dodie realized. Iris Young was confident that her fluency was sweeping Vern and Dodie along with her.

How could she know better?

". . . so you organized franchisees should demand a change in management. I *know* Ted thinks Chicken Tonight should be worrying more about the individual operations. He always has. You don't know him yet, Vern, but Ted has always been the best friend you franchisees have at Chicken Tonight . . ."

"I see," said Vern.

How could this beautiful creature know that Vern was analyzing what she said, following, not quickly but surely, each argument? Dodie knew the Mrs. Youngs of the world put a lot of stock in cries of comprehension, in nods, even in contradiction.

Wooden immobility was beyond them.

How long she would have pleaded her case, and how much more she would have said about Hedstrom, they were never to learn. With a flurry, Sue Akers burst through the back door, pink-cheeked from a nippy wind.

"Hi, everybody— Oh, I'm sorry!"

In the midst of introductions, Iris Young was quick to sense that her moment was gone. With fluid grace she rose.

"I'm so glad to have caught you, Vern and Dodie. I hope you'll give a lot of thought to what we've been talking about. It's really important, to all of us. And I hope you'll talk to the others as well. I'll be in touch with you in a few days. . . ."

She was gone in a moment. The impression lingered on.

"What did Her Royal Highness want?" Sue asked with the cruelty of youth.

"I'm not quite sure," Dodie retorted.

They both looked at Vern.

"Something's wrong," he said slowly. "On top of everything else, this woman trying to put the skids under Mr. Hedstrom. All that garbage about how her husband really runs Chicken Tonight. You know, this is beginning to have a real funny smell."

While he spoke, Dodie and Sue were beginning to make preparations, bravely, for the evening rush that would not come.

Vern brought a hand down on the table. "You know, I'm beginning to be glad that I'll be talking to Mr. Hedstrom himself."

"You are?" his wife asked sincerely. If there was one thing that Vern did not like, it was the kind of confrontation he faced with Hedstrom.

"You're damned right I am," he said robustly. "No, I'm not crazy about haggling over money! Or even griping about who's to blame. Hell, we're all in this together—no matter what Gatto says! But you know, I want to get the measure of Hedstrom himself. Because, sure as hell, there's something about him that's causing a lot of people a lot of trouble."

His womenfolk exchanged meaningful looks. This, those looks said, sounds more like Vern.

As she swung her convertible back to the city, Iris Young was reviewing the past hour. Her talk with Vern Akers had not gone exactly as planned.

"Fool!" That's what Vern Akers was—a fool. Too much of a fool to see she was offering him the only chance he had.

"What's the matter with him? Is he blind?" This time she actually spoke aloud. She knew how much money the franchisees were losing; Ted's desk was piled high with pleas and threats, with letters and reports about defaulted loans, plummeting sales and back pay. And every publicity blast was hurting, not helping. Clyde Sweeney's corpse, practically lying at Frank Hedstrom's feet, wasn't going to help Chicken Tonight—not by any stretch of the imagination. Iris knew this; Vern Akers knew it; the world knew it.

He should have jumped at any opportunity to bail himself out. But when Iris Young offered him one, what did that fool Akers do? He sat there, gaping. And his little wife.

"You mean Mr. Hedstrom?"

Iris could hear that flat, unfriendly voice. Her lip curled. Sure she meant Mr. Hedstrom. She still did.

She pressed down on the accelerator and passed a truck. Now what?

She reviewed the possibilities. Clearly, she had to make another approach to the franchisees. But somehow, after the Akerses, she really didn't want to venture into another Chicken Tonight to try to talk sense to a harried man and his depressing wife. She had Ted's list of the important local franchisees in her purse at the moment—but she'd go to them later. Every damned one, if she had to. But later.

There must be something more immediate she could do.

Iris' life and temperament had not left her so honest with herself as Dodie Akers was. As she sped back to New York it never occurred to her that she was driving erratically and dangerously.

Nor did it occur to her that she was playing a dangerous game in other ways.

On the contrary, everything was clear, crystal clear, in Iris' mind. Frank Hedstrom had to go. It was now or never —and if she had anything to do with it, it was going to be now.

Vexed, she groped for a cigarette.

Approaching the franchisees had seemed like a brilliant idea. Now she saw that it would be like trying to herd sheep.

Suddenly Iris Young knew what she should have done, and what she was going to do. To hell with sheep! She'd take care of them in the future. She was going where the power was—the power that could be exercised with a snap of the fingers.

Iris was so pleased with her insight that she even hummed a sprightly tune.

She was on her way to see Tom Robichaux.

No one had ever accused Tom Robichaux of keeping his troubles to himself. Before Iris Young was out of the office, he was reaching for the phone.

"You won't believe it," he confided. "Spent the damnedest half hour I've ever had."

Thatcher reviewed some of Robichaux's half hours and waited hopefully. But Robichaux knew a good story when he had one by the tail. John was not going to get a blast of indignation. He was going to get a dramatic reading.

"Guess who just breezed in here?" Robichaux began theatrically, the ace all too obviously up his sleeve.

"General de Gaulle?" Thatcher suggested, throwing the timing off.

"General— Oh, come on, John! Would I be bothering you with some politician? No, you'll never guess. Mrs. Young. You remember, Ted Young's wife."

Thatcher remembered all too well, in view of his most recent exposure to Ted Young's wife.

"That must have been fun for you," he observed with malice.

Robichaux made a noise Thatcher took to be protest.

"No, I'm absolutely sincere about that, Tom. I was privileged to watch the lady having a tearing bout of hysterics— and I deeply regretted your absence."

"Cold water," said Robichaux, a man who knew. "The only good thing for hysterics."

"Unfortunately," Thatcher reminded him, "the only water readily available was the Chesapeake Bay."

"John!" said Robichaux sternly, calling him to order.

Thatcher grinned to himself and prepared to listen. He was, after all, going to have an opportunity to hear this notable womanizer on the subject of Iris Young. Better late than never.

Surprisingly enough, Robichaux was terse.

"She's crazy," he said authoritatively.

Thatcher's ears pricked up. By rights, Robichaux should have been expansive.

"I take it you mean that Mrs. Young didn't drop by to see you because of your fatal charm," Thatcher said.

"She dropped by," Robichaux rejoined grimly, "to talk business with me."

"Oh ho!" said Thatcher, interested. "The plot is thickening. What business does Mrs. Young have, Tom?"

Robichaux was blunt. "The woman's a damned fool. Sat there fluttering her eyelashes at me, talking the silliest damned nonsense I ever heard. I could hardly get rid of her . . ."

"Ye-es?" said Thatcher invitingly.

"She's hatched this lunatic scheme," Robichaux explained. "Seems to think I can fire Hedstrom—"

Thatcher could follow the line of reasoning easily. "And have Ted Young move in as president of Chicken Tonight. Right? You don't really surprise me. She was approaching that position when last I saw her. I confess I took it to be an excess of feminine sensibility—but perhaps I was wrong."

"Woman's crazy," Robichaux rumbled.

"I wonder," said Thatcher thoughtfully.

"What do you mean?" Robichaux exploded. "Hedstrom is Chicken Tonight's only chance. This woman doesn't understand which way is up."

"No, Tom. I grant you Mrs. Young has a brutally simple way of looking at business. But forget about her—as a woman and a personality."

"I'd be glad to," Robichaux said.

"Look at it this way. Here's an attempt to change Chicken Tonight's management by getting rid of Frank Hedstrom.

In view of what's been happening, I'd like to know just how serious this attempt is."

Light dawned and Robichaux gasped. "You mean . . . ?"

"Yes, I do," said Thatcher firmly. "And I'd be even more interested to know just how far . . . er, anybody . . . would go to get rid of Frank Hedstrom."

CHAPTER 19

KNEAD THE DOUGH

NOT EVERYONE might like it, but Frank Hedstrom was still very much the man in charge at the headquarters of Chicken Tonight.

Arriving at his office shortly after noon on Monday, he nevertheless put in more than a full working day before leaving for home, undeterred by police interruptions, the clamor of the press, and even his wife's fears that the children might have heard about Clyde Sweeney's murder.

Tuesday morning he scheduled more marathon activity. But his plans were altered by telephone calls that he received and telephone calls he made.

One of them produced John Thatcher.

"They should be here in ten minutes," Hedstrom explained as he gestured Thatcher to a chair.

"You said over the phone that they were representatives of your franchise operators," said Thatcher, disposing of his topcoat and briefcase. "I don't understand what the sudden rush is about."

"Neither do I. They were due here for a meeting next Friday. Then they called up first thing this morning and insisted on coming up right away." Hedstrom shrugged a silent comment on the inexplicability of human nature. "By the way, it's Mr. and Mrs. Akers. You remember, the couple we met in Willoughby, New Jersey."

Thatcher nodded slowly. "Yes, I remember. They knew Clyde Sweeney. Does this have something to do with his murder?"

"They didn't say. But the murder was in the papers Sunday. And yesterday too, for that matter. I don't think they would have waited so long to call. This is probably something else."

"And you thought I would be interested?"

A sudden grin lit Hedstrom's face. "Well, after all," he said apologetically, "it is your twelve million dollars."

And with that remark, everything became clear to Thatcher. Ever since entering the suite, he had been bothered by the atmosphere. There was no frenzied hysteria, no sense of impending doom. The secretaries and administrative assistants were, if anything, calmer than in the salad days of Chicken Tonight. As for the president himself, Frank Hedstrom sat behind his desk with the confident authority of a poker player holding a royal flush. All of which would have puzzled the spectator who knew only that the chief officers of this company had barely emerged from a mass poisoning in time to become embroiled in a murder.

But it was not puzzling to a man of Thatcher's experience. He knew that they had passed a traditional watershed. When trouble befalls a debtor, there is a period when he covers up, when he minimizes his predicament, when he responds to pressure. When, in short, he is the one who does the worrying. But let things go really sour and positions get reversed. The creditor does the worrying, and the debtor holds the whip hand. Frank Hedstrom's attitude told Thatcher as clearly as words that this was now the case. If Chicken Tonight were auctioned off on the spot, there wouldn't be twelve million dollars' worth of assets. The only way the Sloan would ever see its money again was by helping Hedstrom back to solvency.

Which made Thatcher very grateful that Frank Hedstrom had enough acumen to recognize this. The Sloan Guaranty Trust had a big interest in Frank Hedstrom's acumen right now.

The buzzer interrupted these speculations. Vern and Dodie

Akers entered the room, acknowledged greetings, and then sat, looking rather lost.

"I understand you've been elected to represent the franchise operators, Mr. Akers," Hedstrom prompted when silence threatened to descend.

"Yes, that's right. That's why we set up that meeting for Friday." Vern Akers paused.

"But you decided not to wait that long. Was it because of the story about Sweeney's murder?" Frank Hedstrom spoke slowly and calmly. He reminded Thatcher of a naturalist stalking a wild animal.

"Not exactly." Akers took a deep breath. "Look, Mr. Hedstrom, you may think it's none of our business how you run your office here. And maybe it's out of line for us to barge in, but we've got a lot riding on Chicken Tonight."

Dodie Akers decided to take a hand. "Now, Vern, you know we decided that Mr. Hedstrom would want to know."

Thatcher had to give Hedstrom full marks for the way he reacted. He had obviously decided that Vern Akers was the one who needed reassurance. Hedstrom swiveled around for a direct view.

"Of course it's your business. Look, I know how close to the bone a lot of you are operating. Our credit arrangements weren't designed to handle a real disaster like this. And while I don't know what Mrs. Akers is talking about yet—" he turned to smile at Dodie—"I want to know every single thing of interest to Chicken Tonight. Now more than ever."

"There!" Dodie was triumphant. "What did I tell you? Now go ahead and tell the man, Vern."

Thus encouraged, Vern Akers plowed ahead. "It's like this, Mr. Hedstrom. I had it all set to come up and see you on Friday. We were sitting around, hashing things over, when suddenly there's a ring at the door and in walks this Mrs. Young." He looked up, half hoping that further explanation would be unnecessary.

Hedstrom had been playing with a ruler on his desk. Now his hands froze, the knuckles whitening as his grip tightened.

"Iris," he breathed softly.

"Yes, that was her name." Dodie's snort was eloquent. "She asked us to call her Iris."

Hedstrom ignored the interjection. "And what did Iris want?" he demanded harshly.

"That woman must be nuts," Akers burst out. Thatcher noted with appreciation that his original embarrassment was dissipated, thanks to Hedstrom's skillful handling. "She gave us a lot of crap about how you're just a figurehead, that the really important man up here is her husband. Except when it comes to troubles. Those are all your fault. So then, after she'd softened us up with that routine, she got down to brass tacks. Said if all the franchise people got together and cooperated with the stockholders, we could bounce you in favor of her husband."

"And then?"

"And then everything would come up roses," Vern Akers said with fierce sarcasm. "All our problems would make themselves into a little ball and just roll away. It's like I said, she's crazy."

"No, she's not crazy, she's just a troublemaker." Hedstrom was very sober. "Iris always has been. I hate to think what Mrs. Sussenberger would say to this."

"Mrs. Sussenberger?" Thatcher was perplexed. "Who is Mrs. Sussenberger?"

"Iris' mother. A real sweetheart. I've always liked her, but she never realized what she hatched out."

It was rare in Thatcher's circle to hear business maneuvers condemned on grounds of maternal disapproval. But, he realized as he remembered the Hedstroms and the Youngs, he was dealing with something closer to a tribal clan than a corporate hierarchy. Still, was this the time for old-fashioned kitchens, floury hands rolling out pastry, and cooky jars filled for the neighborhood children?

"She's dead, I suppose," Thatcher murmured.

"Dead?" It was Frank Hedstrom's turn to be puzzled. "Hell, no! She's just divorced her second husband. And high time, too!"

So much for floury hands. Once again Thatcher had forgotten how incredibly young all these people were. He did some fast calculating. My God! Mrs. Sussenberger, sweetheart or not, could be a very youthful—and active—fifty.

He had been distracted from the active middle-aged woman in their midst.

"We didn't like it," said Dodie Akers, flushed by recollection of Iris Young. "We could see what she was up to, trying to take advantage of what Clyde did. But it wasn't just that. When we sat down to think about it, that's when we really got upset. Because . . ."

Now it was Vern who came to the rescue when his wife faltered. "Because we think the front office should be concentrating on us, the franchise operators. We're going to go under if we don't get help now. And I don't mean in a month or two." He was looking Hedstrom straight in the eye. "We don't want this Mrs. Young acting as some kind of red herring, getting all the attention we should be getting. Nobody has to tell us that Chicken Tonight is in trouble. It's not going to help if headquarters is all knotted up with some power play. That's why we came right up."

Frank Hedstrom nodded and was silent. Very few men on Wall Street would have been capable of as much, Thatcher realized. They would never understand the world of Vern Akers. But then, Hedstrom came from the same world. Some of his high-school classmates had probably gone into the service as a career. In fifteen years they, like Akers, would be ready to take on a franchise. If Hedstrom kept up with Mrs. Sussenberger, he might well keep up with them. He knew by instinct what response they valued—a studied answer after a long pause for review and thought.

"I'm glad you did," he said slowly. "I didn't know what Iris Young was up to, but you're right. Whatever it is, we don't have time for it. You can forget about it. I'll take care of her. But you said you had problems and needed help. The best thing I can do is get started on that. Suppose you tell me your ideas."

In unison, the Akerses let out sighs of relief. Vern drew out an envelope from his inner jacket pocket, produced a sheaf of rumpled notes and, rather unexpectedly, donned a pair of stylish eyeglasses.

"This is a list we got together on. But before I read it to you, there's one thing I'd better explain," he began scrupulously. "Not all the operators agree with it. A couple of them are big enough so they're not as worried as the rest of us. People like Chet Brewster have been in business long enough so they've got cash reserves. They figure they can ride this one out. And then, of course, we've got some guys who are real complainers. They've got a list of gripes a mile long.

This is a sort of . . ." He looked into recent political history and produced the *mot juste*. "This is a consensus."

Everybody nodded.

"I guess you could say Dodie and me are about the average. And this is where we stand. . . ."

The facts were simple enough. The Akerses' original investment had gone into building alterations and delivery trucks. Their obligations to Chicken Tonight included a lease for their equipment and a credit line for supplies. In addition, they had to meet the rent, the payroll and utility bills.

"I know," Hedstrom said. He then proceeded to outline his proposal. As he systematically moved from one point to the next, Thatcher realized that each one of them had been carefully prepared in advance. Hedstrom, for one, was taking the problem of his franchisees seriously.

In essence, Chicken Tonight was offering its operators a moratorium on their lease payments, an increase in their credit lines, a massive promotion campaign and, under special circumstances, loans for payments to outsiders.

"Not many loans like that," he warned. "They'd just help out individual franchisees. It wouldn't be fair. Publicity is more important. That'll help all of you."

"I suppose you're right," Vern conceded, inspecting the advertising figure unenthusiastically. "Somehow it doesn't seem right to spend that much money on anything that isn't hard."

Dodie did not agree. "You've got to remember that Clyde's murder is going to keep things stirred up. We need advertising, Vern. People won't just forget. It's not like that cranberry sauce we read about when we were in Germany."

"Don't be too sure," Hedstrom commented. "It all depends. Maybe people will decide that Sweeney's murder winds up the whole thing. If they do, they'll forget about the poisoning faster than you think, Mrs. Akers. Either way, advertising should help a lot."

Hedstrom did not have to describe the other possibility, at least not to John Thatcher. If people decided that Sweeney's murder was just the beginning, then not even the Sloan could float Chicken Tonight.

"There's one other thing," Vern Akers said, crossing off as he went. "The breather on our lease payments and a bigger credit line will help tide us over. If everything works out, that's fine. But still, it's costing us money every day we stay open." He squared his jaw. "If Chicken Tonight is going to fold, the sooner we know about it, the better. We don't want to be conned into piling up our debts, if the end is already in sight. We realize you're an important man with a lot of other interests, Mr. Hedstrom. You may decide it's not worth fighting for. The papers say you were down in Maryland about buying some kind of insurance company. Well, then—"

"Get that out of your head," Hedstrom ordered brusquely. "I'm fighting with everything I've got, just the way you are. If Chicken Tonight goes down, I'm going down with it!"

"But what about the insurance company?" Akers persisted.

"That merger is dead as a doornail. Southeastern wouldn't touch it, and neither would I. I don't have time for anything but keeping Chicken Tonight alive. And, by God, I'm going to do it! You're going to get your money, and you're going to stay open. Iris Young is going to get kicked in the pants —she's had it coming for a long time. Don't worry, the minute you leave, the first thing I'm going to do is order enough broilers to keep Chicken Tonight hopping for the next six months. Chicken Tonight isn't going under, and no-one's edging Frank Hedstrom out, either! You come back in five years and this office will be right here, with me in it!"

Vern Akers was unabashed. "Well, it's nice to get things out in the open," he said peaceably. Clearly he was pleased by this declaration of intent.

Hedstrom's tension dropped a notch. "Besides," he said almost lightly, "you don't seem to realize that I'm the middle of a sandwich. Mr. Thatcher here represents the bank that's financing me. You're not the only ones who want to keep me on the straight and narrow. He feels exactly the same."

Thatcher recognized a cue. He assured the Akerses that the Sloan did not intend to see its twelve million dollars frittered away on nonessentials. Whether he was unusually convincing or whether the Akerses were heartened to learn that Big Brother was watching the front office, Vern and Dodie departed looking ten years younger than on entry.

When they left, Frank Hedstrom seemed abstracted. After remarking casually that Vern Akers had his head screwed on the right way, he lapsed into silence.

"I should listen more to Joanie. She knows Iris like a book," he finally muttered to himself.

Thatcher remembered Joan Hedstrom's lack of surprise at Iris' hysterical attack on Hedstrom.

"You mean that Mrs. Young hates you?" he asked, half suspiciously. Could these people be so blind that they did not see the obvious? This was no time to accuse anyone of hating Frank Hedstrom. Not when someone who hated him might have poisoned over a hundred people and strangled Clyde Sweeney. Or were they more subtle than they seemed?

"No, no. That's not what I'm talking about," Frank Hedstrom sat up straighter. "Iris is just a born troublemaker. I suppose if she didn't have her claws into me, she'd have them into somebody else. But Joanie has another idea about Iris I should have listened to. That, even if Iris is crazy about Ted, she doesn't understand him at all." Hedstrom paused to examine this statement and added, "Even I'll give her that much. I don't think she's looked at another man since she was sixteen."

Thatcher was taken aback. He had come for a business conference. At Hedstrom's first word he had braced himself for a discussion, however veiled, of murder and murder suspects. Now he was being propelled into marital analysis.

"Oh, yes?" he said neutrally.

"I don't know if she understands him," Hedstrom continued, missing his guest's wariness. "But I'd say Iris isn't very good for Ted. You see, Ted's not the easygoing kind. He can't help letting things get to him. And Iris is even worse. Whenever he's wound up, she winds him up tighter. So before you know it, the two of them can take any molehill and turn it into a mountain. And Joanie says they both probably enjoy it!"

Thatcher could have sworn that the last sentence was genuinely indignant.

"Some couples do like to live on their nerves. They have an appetite for crises," he offered, amused despite himself.

Hedstrom flicked a hand as if he were brushing away a fly. "Maybe you're right. Maybe Ted does enjoy being all the way up or all the way down. As far as that goes, Iris should know. It's nobody's business if they like to . . . like to . . ."

"To live the rich emotional life?" suggested Thatcher, feeling his years.

Hedstrom was grateful. "That's it. But Iris doesn't have a clue about the *things* he wants. Hell! I understand him better than she does that way. All this running down to the Akerses to start some kind of revolution! Her big dump-Frank scheme! That isn't what Ted wants. Look, the last thing Chicken Tonight needs right now is someone rocking the boat. Ted knows that. He's sweating his guts out in the opposite direction. We've both got better things to do, but I'll have to tell him about this—and he'll have to choke Iris off. Ted can handle her, when he wants to. And he'll be able to get a list of the people she contacted. I don't suppose she stopped with the Akerses."

"I don't suppose so," said Thatcher, reminded of Iris' descent on Robichaux.

"Then," Hedstrom continued blandly, "Ted should be able to stop this thing before it gets off the ground."

"And that's what he'll want to do?" Thatcher asked curiously.

Frank Hedstrom's blue eyes widened. Momentarily, he looked very much like his wife.

"Well, naturally!" he said.

CHAPTER 20

ROAST THE NUTS

FRANK HEDSTROM might not notice every complexity in his personal relationships. There was, however, nothing dormant about his commercial instincts. Within five minutes Thatcher was learning that more was expected of him than witnessing the session with the Akerses.

"I know it may not fit in with your schedule," Hedstrom said with the barest sketch of apology, "but, if you can manage the time, I'd like you to come down to Pelham Browne's place in Maryland with me."

"You mean now?" Not unnaturally, Thatcher was reluctant to return to a locale which spelled police detention and domestic discomfort.

Hedstrom organized himself for a selling job.

"That's right," he said. "The weekday schedule isn't bad. We can be back in time for dinner."

Thatcher did not need extrasensory perception to see how useful his presence might be. "What time is Browne expecting you?" he asked.

"He isn't," Hedstrom replied forthrightly. "I want to take him by surprise. I don't know if you've seen enough of him to get an impression of what he's like . . ." His voice trailed off suggestively.

Unbidden, Thatcher's mind conjured up the vision of Pelham Browne acting out the territorial imperative in the Calvert Hunt Club men's room.

"I may not have seen him at his best," he equivocated.

"Browne doesn't have a best," Hedstrom retorted. "But right now he's suspicious of me. God knows why! I suppose he's afraid he isn't going to get his money. At the same time, he's lazy. If I call him for an appointment about a new broiler contract, he'll want to squirm out of it. He'll start hunting other markets for his birds, he'll talk to people, he'll have time to think of objections. But if I go down with a contract in hand, with you beside me as proof of payment— well, he'll be so glad not to do any work, he'll sign on the spot."

Thatcher was beginning to appreciate why Frank Hedstrom had shot to the top in the business world. Understanding money is a rare talent. Understanding people is even rarer. Understanding both is damn near nonexistent.

"I'd better call my office and let them know where I'll be," he capitulated.

Hedstrom's motives were clear enough. Nothing is more useful during commercial bargaining than a Wall Street banker, on tap as it were, to guarantee good faith, cold cash —or both.

Not much later, they were on a Baltimore-bound plane.

As he ate plastic food off a plastic tray, Thatcher admitted that his own conduct did not bear close examination. The Sloan's twelve million, of course, explained this trip adequately for the rest of the world. Thatcher knew better. The alacrity with which he had accepted these arrangements argued a less reputable motive than concern for the well-being of the Sloan. Thatcher was normally able to defend its interests without resorting to commando raids.

He glanced at his companion. Hedstrom, in the window seat, was working his way through lunch in silence. He might be analyzing his interview with the Akerses, particularly with reference to Iris Young. Or again, he might be planning his strategy with Pelham Browne.

The plane began to circle. Thatcher rejected a pseudo pastry and told himself that Frank Hedstrom might well be pondering the subject of precooked food. Surely the expert in him must be roused by what Eastern Airlines had the effrontery to offer its passengers.

Reminding himself that he really should sample Chicken Tonight's menu one of these days, Thatcher appraised Hedstrom. What kind of man was he? Robichaux's answer, he recalled, was simple: a money-maker.

Thatcher leaned back, closing his eyes against a demented smile from the stewardess. What did this morning add to Robichaux's summation? Hedstrom was straightforward—and devious. Witness his handling of the Akerses, and his tactics with Pelham Browne. That guileless look of youth was deceiving—no doubt about that. At the moment, for instance, Thatcher would not willingly go bail for what Hedstrom was thinking as he gazed down at the dense cloud cover.

And that, Thatcher reflected, was one reason to let himself get lassoed into bizarre expeditions.

"Are we bearding Browne at the poultry plant?" he inquired as they were taxiing into the landing area.

Hedstrom was assembling his belongings. "I don't think so," he said. "Browne's got an efficient manager running the show. He doesn't spend much time on it himself."

One question answered, Thatcher told himself. Pelham Browne had not struck him as a man who kept his nose to the grindstone. And Frank Hedstrom knew it, and knew about that efficient manager as well.

If nothing else, Frank Hedstrom was a man who valued efficiency. This trip proved it. Hedstrom's office could deal with jump starts, to judge from the smoothness with which transport had been arranged at two airports. Within a commendably short time after touchdown, Thatcher and Hedstrom were heading back to the Eastern Shore in a chauffeur-driven limousine.

Hedstrom decided he had been incomplete. "Browne handles the over-all business," he said to Thatcher. "His manager supervises the actual poultry production. So Browne does most of his work out of his own house. I think that's probably the best place to catch him."

"I see," said Thatcher. And in a very short time he did. Journey's end, Pelham Browne's home, was nothing like Hedstrom's sprawling new country place, some thirty miles farther south. Nor did it suggest work, in the strict sense of the word.

The chauffeur swung off the highway to a dirt road, then onto grounds protected by cross-barred white fencing. Respectfully the car crept up a tree-lined alley to a Southern Georgian mansion, complete with antebellum columns. The circular lawn before the house was manicured within an inch of its life, but, beyond the driveway, field grass stretched down to the bay.

Stepping out of the car, Thatcher took a closer look at Pelham Browne's working quarters. There were hitching posts in the driveway, careful rattan chairs on the veranda, and two well-placed magnolia trees at the cutoff to the stables. There was a Land Rover pulled alongside the house.

There was also a trimly uniformed maid at the door. Before she could announce them, Browne himself came hurrying down the stairs. He did not seem ruffled by their presence.

"Come on in!" he shouted athletically as he swung himself around the newel post, every inch the gentleman farmer. His bulky frame had been crammed into trim jodhpurs; his weatherbeaten face emerged from a bright-red turtleneck. In his hand he carried a riding crop and a green tweed jacket.

"Glad you dropped by," he said vaguely. "But you're too late, you know."

Hedstrom showed no emotion as they were ushered

toward the rear of the house. "I'm sorry about that," he said easily, "but it never hurts to talk things over."

Had some competitor nipped in and secured the future output of Browne's poultry operation? If so, it was quick work. Thatcher reminded himself to have a talk with the Sloan's recruitment officer. Why, he would ask, are all the bright young men going into chicken franchises while we get left with the dummies?

He had drawn the wrong conclusion. He discovered his mistake when a figure rose from a chair on the sun porch. It was Morgan Ogilvie.

"Morgan and I just got back," Browne explained during the handshaking. "He's waiting for Margo to be through in the stables. But it's all over. The board voted against you."

"The board?" When Frank Hedstrom wrote off a project, he did so completely. "Oh! Southeastern!"

Browne was indignant. "Well, what did you think I was talking about? The vote was nine to one, if you want to know. Morgan stayed with you right to the bitter end."

"That's nice." Hedstrom was clearly marking time; he had been thrown off balance by the unexpected reminder of the merger. Now he tried to look appreciative. "You did more than I had any reason to expect, Ogilvie. Your board must have been pretty leery of me already. Sweeney's murder must have been the finishing touch."

"You can say that again!" Pelham Browne was relieved by Hedstrom's attitude. "Most of our directors thought the vote was just a formality. Even Morgan couldn't find a word to say in favor of the merger. As for me," he took a deep breath and looked his guest in the eye, "I say, business is business! You may as well know that I told them that I wasn't too happy at being tied up with Chicken Tonight already. That I've got too much riding on you as it is."

Morgan Ogilvie stirred unhappily. He was not used to these artless disclosures about board discussions. "Pel is leaning over backward to give you a picture of his position. Actually he did not speak up until after the vote had been taken. And I think that's all that would really interest you about our meeting. In fact, it did turn into a mere formality. I'm sincerely sorry about this, Hedstrom. I think we might have worked well together."

Thatcher was amused to see that, for one brief moment, Hedstrom's composure threatened to crack. Buying out Southeastern Insurance had never, in the planning of Frank Hedstrom and Ted Young, entailed working with Morgan Ogilvie. Thatcher had already heard Young's views on the subject of the archaic management which had made Southeastern ripe for the plucking. A modest pension and a dignified early retirement would have been more like it. Frank Hedstrom escaped the need to frame a diplomatic reply.

"I would have said it before the vote, if I'd had to," Browne said stubbornly.

"I don't blame you." Hedstrom was eager to develop the theme. "This is no time for a merger. But I hope I can make you feel better about your contract with Chicken Tonight. Really, that's what I wanted to talk to you about."

Browne was openly alarmed.

"The contract? Look, you've got almost four weeks left to go. At a rate of thirty thousand birds. It's all cut and dried."

"Not that contract."

"Then *what* contract?"

Morgan Ogilvie cleared his throat loudly. He seemed relieved at the change of subject. Attempts to save Browne from the results of his own rough-edged candor had been made and had failed. Now Ogilvie could leave the field with honor.

"You won't need me for this," he said rising, "and I'm anxious to get home. So, if you don't mind, Pel, I'll go down to the stables and see what's keeping Margo."

Pelham Browne's slightly protuberant eyes rolled in entreaty, but Ogilvie was adamant. Pausing only for brisk farewells, he departed.

"I've got to hand it to Ogilvie," Browne began rapidly, all innocent admiration, "the way he voted today. Of course, it didn't do any good. Nothing could. But everyone noticed. Hell, his uncle told him he was crazy to be so loyal to you. Said that in business, when someone's in a mess, the healthy thing is to put distance between you and him. That's old Buell Ogilvie, his uncle," Browne concluded in a doomed attempt to spark genealogical interest.

"I came to ask you about a six-month contract," Hedstrom announced remorselessly.

Browne shied. "Oh, now, I don't know about that."

"That would be six months starting from the termination date of the contract we've got now," Hedstrom continued without pause. "It would mean a guaranteed market for your total output."

"I thought you were supposed to be in trouble," Browne said sullenly. "And here you are, offering better terms than anyone else in the business. It sounds fishy to me. What protection have I got?"

"That's why I asked Thatcher to come with me. I thought you'd like to know that the Sloan is financing me." A half-smile twisted Hedstrom's lips. "That means that the money is there."

Pelham Browne regarded Thatcher doubtfully. Again Thatcher took up his cue. He recited the terms of the Sloan's loan agreement, adding that Hedstrom had already signed an amendment restricting Chicken Tonight to the franchise business. Its outlays were limited to those necessary for normal operations. Surely Mr. Browne must see that poultry purchases would rank high on the list of such outlays.

"It sounds all right." Presumably Browne was in a quandary. The only visible sign was a look of sadness.

Frank Hedstrom started to play his fish.

"Of course," he said slowly, "I know that there are other things you can do. You don't have to stay tied up with Chicken Tonight. You'll want to think about this from your point of view. Maybe you'd like to try working with some other franchise outfit. Naturally, this isn't a very good time to approach them. With chicken sales off, they're taking a beating on the suppliers they've already got. So maybe that isn't a very good idea. Then there are the city markets. You've got a big layout here. You might have to hustle a bit. But I know you wouldn't mind that. Even if you couldn't unload entirely in one place, you've got an ideal location. By pressing a little, you could cover New York, Philadelphia, Baltimore and Washington. Hell, you might even be able to take in Boston. On the other hand, you might not like the idea of heading into November without a sure customer."

If Pelham Browne had been sad at the beginning of this cunning speech, he was looking downright suicidal by its end. For a man averse to "hustling a bit," the program Hedstrom unfolded was anathema. Even more important, Browne liked to know where his income was coming from. Wildly, he bleated about other possibilities.

Nothing loath, Hedstrom launched into a systematic review of the disadvantages attaching to a Browne alliance with any big canner or freezer. By the time he finished (with pressed-chicken-breast rolls), Browne had been bludgeoned into regarding Chicken Tonight as his one salvation.

"But look here, this six-months business. I don't go for that!" Peevishly he swished his crop against a boot.

The gesture gave Thatcher a clue to at least one of Browne's dilemmas. Pelham Browne thought he was dealing with a man on the way out, a man struggling for survival. Under the circumstances, any business done should be a benefit conferred by Browne. He wanted to crack the whip, but he had hoped for at least some cooperation from his victim. He wasn't getting it.

"What don't you like about six months, Mr. Browne?" Thatcher asked kindly.

"Anything can happen to the market. Poultry prices might shoot up."

"Naturally, we've included a sliding scale," Hedstrom said briskly. "It's tied to market prices on the East Coast. That way, you're protected against any rises. And, let me say it for you, we're protected against drops."

"Hell, prices can't go lower. They've got no place to go to. Do you know," Browne said hotly, turning to Thatcher, "that even before this whole poisoning mess started, you could buy a beautiful bird, over three pounds, for under a dollar in any supermarket? When steak's selling for around a dollar-fifty a pound?"

Browne leaned back, defying Thatcher to cope with the shock of this revelation. Since broilers could be sold cheaply only because of giant producers like Browne—and, conversely, giants could sell their huge output only at low prices —Thatcher was shocked all right, if not the way Browne intended. Did this highly educated simpleton understand the amount of breeding effort behind today's hybrid broiler? Did he know it constituted a major technical breakthrough? Did he realize that his day-old chicks arrived complete with metabolism designed to work overtime for fifty-six days, from the first peck through the shell to the last beautiful moment?

Or, more probably, was this Abercrombie-Fitch rustic merely trying to allay suspicion?

If so, Thatcher wanted to know what that suspicion was. He glanced over to see if Hedstrom shared his reaction. But the younger man was about to land his catch.

Hedstrom had produced two copies of a contract. He was directing Browne's fretful attention to several clauses. Patiently, question after question was answered. Then, setting a good example, Hedstrom produced a pen from his breast pocket almost casually.

Mesmerized, Browne followed suit. His pen was actually hovering over the signature line when he looked up.

"And after the six months? What happens then?" he asked.

Hedstrom was thrown off stride. His energies were directed toward staying alive for six months. He had not really looked beyond.

"What do you mean?" He stared at Browne. "More contracts and more chickens, I suppose. You mean, now you want a longer contract?"

"No." Browne paused to summon resolution. "I heard you were planning to go into broiler production yourself," he blurted. "So, what if everything pans out? What if you live down this Sweeney mess? Do I get the boot then?"

Once the problem became apparent, Hedstrom addressed himself to it wholeheartedly. He did not make the error of looking at pen or contract. He did not rush into improbable denials.

"Sure, I've been thinking about it," he admitted seriously. "I was meaning to talk to you, if we got the idea off the planning board. But there wasn't any sense talking when the roof fell in on me. I won't be doing anything like that for a year at least now."

"And then the boot?" Browne pressed.

Hedstrom's air of confusion was, in Thatcher's opinion, a work of art.

"The boot?" Comprehension was allowed to dawn. "For God's sake! What do you think I plan to do? Buy a hundred thousand day-old chicks and try to hand-raise them? Ask Joanie to get out the medicine dropper? I was thinking of amalgamating with you! Then, if it worked out, we could think about taking over broiler outfits in other sections of the country. We'd be integrated right down the line!"

"Why the hell didn't you tell me this before?" Browne demanded, his ready color rising.

"It doesn't seem like a very good time to talk to you about mergers with Chicken Tonight." Hedstrom was neatly sarcastic. "You told us yourself today how you feel about that. Would you have raised the subject in my place?"

He'll have Browne apologizing before he's done, Thatcher thought to himself.

And that was exactly what Frank Hedstrom did. Having thrown Pelham Browne into confusion, he adopted the air of a man resentful at having honest intentions misinterpreted. He demanded to know how long Browne had distrusted him. How long had suspicion been tainting their relations?

"So that was why you were avoiding me at the club!" he exclaimed.

He informed Browne that a little openness on Browne's part would have cleared up this misunderstanding at inception. Then he softened. He generously conceded that Browne had some cause for concern. Particularly if he could trust his sources of information. Hedstrom even admitted that if he had been in Browne's shoes, then maybe . . .

Frank Hedstrom got more than Browne's apology. By the time he left, he also had a contract duly signed "Pelham Caldwell Browne."

"But there's one thing I didn't get," Hedstrom observed as they were flying back to New York. "I didn't get the name of his source."

"Does that worry you?" Thatcher asked.

"It sure does! The whole idea of Chicken Tonight going into broiler production was under wraps. Nobody outside our head office should have known about it."

Thatcher reminded him that Wall Street made a living out of picking up these snippets of news. Tom Robichaux might well know of Hedstrom's plans. Even Walter Bowman might have heard something.

"I doubt it. Your people pick up things when a move is made, not before. This was still in the casual conversation stage. And I don't have anybody in my office who's making a sideline of peddling information." Hedstrom was very positive. Then he relaxed enough to add, "I'm not big enough yet. Give me another two or three years, and I will have someone."

Thatcher encouraged this realism. "Then I don't think you have very far to look for a source, do you? Ogilvie and Browne seem to live in each other's pocket. And Ogilvie has just subjected your company to a very close scrutiny. He probably found out about your plans. After all, Southeastern had a vital interest in your future activities because of the merger."

"I suppose you're right," said Hedstrom discontentedly. "But I'm not sure. Either Ogilvie was picking up more information about Chicken Tonight than I ever thought or Browne has got better contacts than you'd expect."

Now was Thatcher's moment.

"Tell me, has Browne always played this game of being a rough diamond who's not up to subtlety? I found all that innocence about the retail price of broilers a little excessive."

"The price of chicken is a specific fact," Hedstrom said simply. "Browne doesn't know many."

Thatcher was unconvinced. "And he hasn't deduced that his way of life on the Eastern Shore is dependent on that fact?"

"I doubt it. Of course, he plays other games too. All that business with his clothes, for instance."

"You mean red turtlenecks?" Thatcher's previous view of Pelham Browne had been at the Calvert Hunt Club, where he had been rumpled but formally attired.

"You haven't seen the half of it," Hedstrom replied. "He comes up to conferences in New York in work shoes and tweeds. Hell, once he was wearing a cap." A reminiscent chuckle was forced from Hedstrom. "Ted went wild about that cap, for some reason. And Ogilvie tells me he turns up at the clubhouse at the Garden State Race Track in plaids that have to be seen to be believed. But, like you said, it's a game. It's a funny way to show that he went to Princeton, but that's the way he does it."

"That's one method of flaunting social invulnerability," Thatcher commented. "They dress like race-track touts to prove they're part of the elite."

"I guess so." Hedstrom sounded detached. "It was a real eye-opener to me. We don't see much of that sort of thing in Oak Park."

Hedstrom was tolerant, and Thatcher honored him for it. Nevertheless he was inclined to believe that there might be more to Pelham Browne than what met the eye so strikingly.

CHAPTER 21

SKIM THE FAT

MISS CORSA greeted Thatcher's second return from Maryland with reserve. But when he arrived at his office the following morning without displaying any inclination for further travel, she thawed perceptibly. A second day of commendable attention to desk work, and Miss Corsa unbent enough to cater to weakness.

"I thought you might be interested," she reported, handing him a newspaper with the relevant item carefully outlined in red.

"Thank you," he replied docilely, glancing at the headline: "PUBLIC HEALTH PROBE OF CHICKEN TONIGHT."

"Humph," said Thatcher, tossing the paper aside without reading on.

Miss Corsa was gratified enough to become reckless.

"Mr. Bowman is just finishing a study of how this hearing will affect Chicken Tonight sales," she reported. "I'll bring you a copy as soon as it's typed."

"Fine," said Thatcher. "I'll look forward to it."

For, perversely, Thatcher's rehabilitation in Miss Corsa's esteem had been accompanied by mounting discontent on his part.

And even Bowman's forecast that a public which could take poison in stride was not going to boggle at a Public Health hearing did very little to cheer him.

The trouble went deeper. Thatcher lacked Tom Robichaux's capacity to harrumph his way through life's vexations. Nor did he resemble his eminent subordinate Everett Gabler, the personification of virtue confronting decay and degeneration. On the contrary, Thatcher was a man to take things as they came. He rarely wasted time or energy on what might have been.

This, he had long since concluded, was not more than efficient, and efficiency went far toward explaining his success on Wall Street. Certainly two other characteristics were no help at all. Thatcher had what he liked to think was a speculative turn of mind (Miss Corsa, he knew, had another name for it). He wanted to know the whys and wherefores of his own back yard. There was, for instance, a small firm in South Dakota, headed by an Armenian-American, staffed by Swedish-Americans, that was currently producing miniature cameras more cheaply than its Japanese competition. Everybody else on Wall Street was happy with Atamian Instruments' growth and dividends. Not Thatcher. Sooner or later he would find out why this unlikely meld could do what the rest of the Western world found impossible.

Only because his curiosity so often paid off did Wall Street and Miss Corsa tolerate it.

Wall Street and Miss Corsa were divided on Thatcher's other idiosyncrasy. He was, essentially, a man who liked to complete his packages before they were tied up and put away. Miss Corsa too opposed loose strings, but since she regarded an orderly desk as the outward manifestation of an orderly mind, Thatcher did not earn many credits from her along these lines. With his professional colleagues, the gulf was more profound. Wall Street is, *par excellence,* the home of fad, passion and craze. Last year's favorites are not only dropped, they are cut dead. Even Gabler, a walking compendium of little-known facts, immersed himself in what was happening now. The bowling-equipment producers, who had commanded his horrified attention ten years ago, were now only history to him. Although, if prompted, he could still dredge up the bare bones. Robichaux, who had spent countless hours touting bowling leagues and automatic pin setters, would probably deny that such a game had ever existed.

Thatcher not only recalled the bowling mania, he occasionally thought about it. Were fevered hordes still lining up

for an alley? What had happened to those ambitious over-
seas plans to introduce bowling to Manchester, Blackpool
and Glasgow? Would he ever know?

So, in the days that followed, Thatcher fell prey to a
rare mood of Robichauvian dissatisfaction. Things came to
a head with a call from Hedstrom.

". . . finally turning a corner," he announced. "We're getting our first comprehensive reports from New England.
Sales are finally beginning to move. In Boston alone . . ."

Thatcher did not repeat Charlie Trinkam's hypothesis about
college youth and zinc salts. Hedstrom continued, ". . . . almost up to seventy percent of normal. That's way beyond
our most optimistic estimates. Our marketing people . . ."

Hedstrom's marketing people said much what Walter
Bowman said.

"The hearing?" Hedstrom asked. "No, we don't expect it
to have much of an impact."

Thatcher heard him out, offered congratulations, and hung
up. He sat for a moment, glowering at a report Trinkam had
forwarded on the eccentricities of Texas utility regulation.
Then, as an afterthought, he stabbed the buzzer.

"Maitland," he ordered Miss Corsa. He was tempted to
thank her for tearing herself away from the Trinkam Anniversary Committee long enough to devote token attention to
his needs.

Instead, he relayed Hedstrom's good news to Maitland as
unencouragingly as possible. Temperately he agreed that
Chicken Tonight might be getting out of the woods and that
the Sloan's twelve million dollars looked like a better bet.
But, on the subject of the absolution of Maitland and Commercial Credit, he was unforthcoming.

No sooner was this over than he fell back into a steady
simmer. The basic trouble was that everything had come to
a halt. Three separate police forces were still documenting
Clyde Sweeney's life, career and death. Judging from the
story's steady recession from page one to page twenty-seven
in all newspapers, landladies, rented cars, fifty-dollar bills
and beery conversations about horses were adding up to
very little.

And the forthcoming Public Health hearing was unlikely
to explode any bombshells.

In fact, Thatcher thought, Miss Corsa was right: his various forays to warehouses in New Jersey and hunt clubs in Maryland were so much wasted time. There seemed to be a fighting chance that Frank Hedstrom would salvage Chicken Tonight—and the Sloan's twelve million. Unless, of course, the Public Health people had something sensational up their sleeve. But twelve million dollars alone could not justify Thatcher's recent activities. Not if they left unanswered the questions plaguing him.

Who had killed Clyde Sweeney? And why?

Thatcher was reflective when Miss Corsa did what no one else in the Trust Division dared. She demanded his attention.

"Yes?" he inquired.

Miss Corsa recognized that this was to be a contest of wills.

"Mr. Thatcher," she declared. "The Committee would like you to accompany them to the Parke-Bernet Galleries. The selection for Mr. Trinkam has narrowed down . . ."

"I would be delighted," replied Thatcher, who knew that there are times when only the big lie is enough. "Unfortunately, I have a luncheon appointment. And several afternoon engagements. Important engagements. And I don't know when I'll be in tomorrow morning, either."

While the guardian of his appointment book prepared to remonstrate, Thatcher rose, snatched up hat, topcoat and umbrella, and fled.

He had just challenged fate.

Fate retaliated with a chance luncheon encounter at Eberlin's.

". . . tried to be reasonable with her," Robichaux said, salting his steak with gusto. "But I can't sit still for this. Not after that damned hairdresser. I ask you, John! A Polish prince!"

He paused, hoping for comment.

"Aren't Polish princes rather old-fashioned?" Thatcher inquired. But Robichaux swept into a complex discourse centering on the needs, desires and activities which were shortly going to divorce Loël from Robichaux himself, if not from a healthy portion of his income.

Had he been feeling more charitable, Thatcher would

have spared a thought for Francis Devane, Robichaux's partner and a prominent Quaker. Devane always suffered during these misadventures. Instead, Thatcher recalled his own discomforts and cut into some ribald speculations about European royalty.

"You know I went down to talk to Browne? I saw Ogilvie too," he said.

"Ogilvie?" said Robichaux blankly. "Oh, Ogilvie. What did you want to do that for?"

"I did not want to do it," Thatcher growled. "It was a matter of Chicken Tonight—as usual."

Loël could be expected to monopolize Robichaux for several months henceforth. But he was not as yet fully immersed. To Thatcher's surprise, he still retained some grasp of the Chicken Tonight situation.

"Why is Ogilvie still hanging around?" he asked. "Everybody knew the merger was off the minute that poisoning broke."

"Everybody but Ogilvie," Thatcher remarked.

Possibly because of the Polish prince, Robichaux was taking a large-minded view of all things American. "You know," he said, "I'm really sorry that merger didn't come off . . . What's that, John? No! I am not talking about Robichaux and Devane's commission. I'm looking at the big picture."

Thatcher indicated interest in the big picture as Robichaux saw it.

"Well," Tom ruminated, "you know how some mergers are. But this one would have made everybody happy. Southeastern's stockholders were going to make money. Hedstrom would have gotten a foot in the financial world, so he wouldn't have all his eggs in one basket." He stopped with a vagrant puzzled look. "Now, why does that sound so strange?"

Thatcher ignored this. "Tell me, Tom. During the preliminary negotiations was everybody enthusiastic?"

"Everybody," said Robichaux firmly, by inclination a sundial who recorded only cloudless hours.

This brought out the worst in Thatcher. "Oh, come on, Tom. You're not claiming that Ted Young was a booster."

Robichaux darkened. "Young," he exclaimed. "A man who can't control his own wife—"

"Or won't," Thatcher interjected, struck by an idea.

Robichaux, possibly reflecting that his current situation left his views on marriage suspect, continued, "Everybody else was for it. And why not? It was a sweet deal. Good God, John, you should see the reports. Hedstrom hired Goodoe and Wiley to give Southeastern the once-over, and what did they find? A conservative outfit. Maybe not making as much as it should, but beautifully situated. It was a perfect setup for Hedstrom. Gave him a good chance to diversify, at a really good price. And Southeastern got Bly Associates to be sure that Chicken Tonight wasn't some fly-by-night operation. What did they find? Southeastern could become part of a first-rate organization. It was a perfect marriage—"

"Until the poisoning," said Thatcher, registering the influence of preoccupation on metaphor. "So everybody, except Ted Young, saw all this, and cheered wildly?"

Robichaux shrugged philosophically. "That's the way it goes. You have to take things as they come. Give a little, take a little . . ."

Rightly assuming that these thoughts derived from Loël rather than Chicken Tonight, Thatcher let the subject drop. But after Tom had bustled off to alert his lawyers, Thatcher was still thinking about Chicken Tonight.

"Hmm," he said finally.

Outside Eberlin's, he hesitated for a moment, assailed by impulse. He reminded himself that returning to the Sloan and Miss Corsa would constitute defeat. That was to be avoided at all costs. He turned his steps elsewhere.

"Mr. Hedstrom isn't in this afternoon," said the receptionist at Chicken Tonight before Thatcher spoke. "He's out touring the franchises. I can get in touch with him in Willoughby—"

"No, no," said Thatcher, docketing the fact that Hedstrom was spreading the good news where it was most useful. "Is Mr. Young in?"

Ted Young, scanning page after typewritten page, was possibly surprised at this unheralded descent, but he was courteous. Abandoning his studies, he welcomed Thatcher, and waited.

"What I'd like to know," Thatcher began, "will probably

seem remote to the situation at hand. But I would like to learn something about your investigation of Southeastern Insurance when you were first considering the merger."

Young's response, he would have sworn, was discreet amusement.

"We got a report as thick as the phone book," Young said. After shouting a request to his secretary, he continued. "We knew everything about them but the color of their eyes. Sales, the staff, their salaries—the works. Goodoe and Wiley are about the best industrial investigators in the business and they didn't leave out anything. Here it is." He indicated Thatcher, and the secretary handed over the thick paperbound volume.

Thatcher dutifully flicked pages, noting the endless lists of data. This, however, was not what he had come for. Facts do not determine policy, and it was on policy that Frank Hedstrom and Ted Young differed.

"Why did you dislike the merger?" he asked.

Young's lips tightened. But twelve million dollars protected Thatcher from the reply he deserved: None of your business. Young chose his words.

"Nothing against Southeastern," he said. "Somebody could take it over, shake it up and really get it moving. But I felt that until we consolidate our own situation . . ."

It was a careful argument, carefully marshaled. No doubt with Hedstrom, Young had been more emphatic. But Thatcher would be willing to guess that he had been logical then too.

Young was warming to his theme. "I said we weren't really set up with Chicken Tonight. God, we are—we were— opening so many franchises that we couldn't really keep tabs on them. Didn't have enough inspectors to check around. And that's important in this business, Mr. Thatcher. You've got to be sure everybody's doing things right, so you build the Chicken Tonight name. That's what I kept telling Frank—when we still had a lot of work to do in our own shop, that was no time to branch out. Oh, sure, once we got in shape here—"

Thatcher watched the younger man halt suddenly.

"Hell," said Ted Young, almost stricken, "I keep forgetting."

Thatcher sympathized. "Say what you will, you have your chance to . . . er, consolidate now."

Young sat absolutely still for a second. Then, straightening his shoulders, he said, "We will, Mr. Thatcher. Did Frank tell you about our New England sales? I think we're over the worst. By the end of the year . . ."

Thatcher left Chicken Tonight after a brisk sales talk. He left also with a new impression of Ted Young; whatever his wife's feelings about the role, Young gloried in his position at Chicken Tonight. A less intense man might be concealing resentment, envy, hate. But Young was transparent.

Thatcher was in the lobby when he heard himself hailed.

"I beg your pardon," he said, finding Joan Hedstrom before him.

"You were thinking hard," she said in forgiveness.

Thatcher regarded Frank Hedstrom's wife with approval. Here was a wealthy, uncomplicated woman. No Polish princes here—if several packages from F.A.O. Schwarz meant anything. And, in the midst of a prolonged business crisis, here was a woman who retained serene confidence in her husband and life.

". . . that terrible weekend," Mrs. Hedstrom was saying. "You know, I'm not sure that we're ever going to feel comfortable in that house. Somehow it's been spoiled."

Was this Mrs. Hedstrom's way of preparing to lose the Maryland house, and a good many other things? Aloud, Thatcher said, "I recall that it was your first stay down there. I can sympathize with your feelings."

She sighed. "It really was an awful disappointment. We'd worked so hard planning it, Iris and I. And it was going to be the perfect weekend—you know. Then, first, there was all the trouble—"

She never got nearer than that to the poisoning of chicken Mexicali, Thatcher realized.

"—and then, well, we thought the boys needed a rest even more. But everything went wrong. First Mr. Ogilvie insisted on talking business. Oh, I know business is important, Mr. Thatcher. But you have to get away from it once in a while."

Thatcher agreed and she shook her head at him, smiling. "Men! You're all the same. Still, it really was a silly time to talk business. And getting dragged off to hunt clubs—good heavens, Frank and I aren't the hunt-club type!"

"Who is?" Thatcher asked.

"Unless," she said with a twinkle, "I meet a really good dancer, of course. Then it's different."

A nice woman, Thatcher thought. For her sake, he hoped that Frank Hedstrom came through his difficulties unscathed.

"Mrs. Hedstrom," he said. "It occurs to me that you're just the person I'd like a few words with. Won't you come and have a drink with me?"

A small, worried frown appeared, but Joan Hedstrom replied promptly, "Of course, but let's go upstairs instead. We keep a tiny apartment here, because Frank can't always get home."

"Well, Mr. Thatcher?" she asked when they were settled in the small living room.

"I've just been talking to Ted Young," he began.

Her expression lightened. Admirably, she did not inquire about the subject of that talk.

"Oh, yes?"

"He's a very capable man," said Thatcher.

"I know that Frank would be lost without him," she replied.

Thatcher doubted this, but he realized that Joan Hedstrom would always say the correct thing.

"I got the impression that he's happy in his work," he said.

She was briefly puzzled. Then, with real merriment: "Happy in his— Oh, my goodness! You're still worrying about what Iris said about second fiddle, aren't you?"

"Not exactly," said Thatcher evasively. No use airing phantom thoughts roused by Robichaux's remarks.

". . . loves his job," she was saying. "Why, Ted lives for Chicken Tonight. That's the trouble, don't you see? Ted gets all tensed up about his work—that's what upsets Iris. Mr. Thatcher, Iris doesn't really mean half what she says. I know. She's just—she just can't keep calm about things."

"I recall," said Thatcher dryly. Was this reading of Iris Young accurate? He had not known in Maryland, and he did not know here. For that matter, did Mrs. Hedstrom know what her good friend had been up to since?

"But Ted?" Joan Hedstrom went on, gaining confidence. "Why, Ted *does* live for Chicken Tonight. Honestly!"

"More than your husband does," said Thatcher unguardedly.

Startled, she looked at him inquiringly. "Well, in a way, yes," she replied. "Frank is a different type altogether. He's always got so many different irons in the fire that he's . . . he's . . ."

Once again she did not want to put thoughts into words. Out of deference to her loyalties, Thatcher did not do it for her this time.

"I mustn't keep you," he said, rising. "And I should be going myself. I had almost forgotten that I have another appointment this afternoon."

Deference to Mrs. Hedstrom's feelings also kept him from specifying where he was going.

"Where did you want to go?" Miss Corsa's voice was frigid. It had, unfortunately, been necessary to revert to her sooner than Thatcher felt desirable.

"To Willoughby, New Jersey. Have them send the limousine to the Hotel Montrose as quickly as possible," he said. "I'm in a hurry."

"Certainly, Mr. Thatcher," said Miss Corsa.

The limousine arrived within ten minutes. Miss Corsa did not stoop to pettiness. She would make Mr. Thatcher pay in other ways.

The devil with it, Thatcher thought as he settled back for the interminable drive to New Jersey. A costly gift would only make things worse. And, of course, it was impermissible to dream of informing Miss Corsa that he was beginning to piece together some strange fragments . . . casual comments about marriage . . . how men feel about their work . . . loyalty and independence . . .

It was a long drive, even at speeds well over the posted limits. At its end, however, Thatcher's mounting impatience received a setback. He had not fully assimilated what increasing sales meant to Chicken Tonight.

"Two chicken Mandalays and a side order of Apple Rummy," Dodie Akers was saying happily into the receiver. "Yes, we'll get them on the six o'clock truck, Mrs. Hunniker.

Now, that's three-six-one Mulberry Lane . . . right here in Willoughby. Fine. . . ."

Vern Akers was at the gleaming bank of knobs, yanking levers and simultaneously answering the warning bell that signaled the emergence of completely cooked, assembled and bagged orders.

"Four more ready, Gil," he said as a gangling youth in orange-and-gold coveralls swung a wire carrier through the serving window. Sue Akers loaded it and the boy pivoted to the truck behind him to begin tucking packages into the heating unit.

Thatcher had not bargained for a conversation punctuated by chicken-to-go orders.

"Oh, no," said Akers, without stopping his swift movements. "No, we're still below normal business. But . . ."

At the small table by the telephone, Dodie looked up from the order forms she was filling out. "Oh, Vern!" she said joyfully. "You're the limit! You really are! It's just wonderful, Mr. Thatcher. One minute we were dead. Then, all of a sudden, the phones began to ring—" She broke off to laugh as the phone did ring. "Chicken Tonight! . . . Yes, that's six Bavarians. What about a side order of cranberry wriggle? . . . Fine. . . . Buns? Good. What was the name? . . . "

For a variety of reasons, Thatcher was sincerely happy at the improvement now unfolding before him, and said so. He added that he did not want to interrupt. But happiness after sorrow is an expansive emotion. Even someone as chary with words as Vern Akers was moved to speech.

"No . . . no trouble. If you don't mind that I keep going. Sue, check if the truck will be ready to go after this order, huh? Too bad, Mr. Thatcher. You just missed Mr. Hedstrom. Thanks, Sue. He must have been here, talking with us, oh, at least an hour. Here you go, Sue. All done."

Thatcher, feeling rather out of things, took the sheaf of orders that Dodie brandished as she returned to the phone. He handed it to Akers.

"Thanks."

Orders started moving down the line again.

"Yeah, Mr. Hedstrom sounded real good," said Akers, watching an instrument panel with an array of lights and meters. "I guess you've heard about what's happening up in New England?"

"Yes, indeed," said Thatcher, watching an almost human steel claw press tops on cardboard cups.

"Looks like it's just reaching us," Akers said in a burst. "Boy, if only this upswing isn't a flash in the pan!"

"Vern!"

"Dad!"

The Akers ladies, Thatcher could see, were fighters.

"That's what Mr. Hedstrom says," Akers replied with a chuckle. "He says that this Public Health thing is going to help us, not hurt us. It'll show how carefully everything is handled."

"I'm sure it will," said Thatcher. Since the phone rang at that moment, and a warning bell sounded, it was unlikely that Akers would detect anything but courtesy in this sentiment.

". . . and a big publicity campaign, he says. Television! And maybe sponsor a football game or two. Boy, would that be something! That'd be worth a couple of hundred orders every Sunday, at least. And Mr. Hedstrom says they're going to beef up their inspecting systems so guys like Gatto don't keep giving us a black eye. You know that guy buys his onions on the sly? Me, I told Mr. Hedstrom we got enough people checking on us. What the company's got to do is to crack down on these guys who don't cooperate. But Mr. Hedstrom says no, he's going to really go all out—"

"You see, Mr. Thatcher," said Dodie, flushed and bright-eyed. "All of a sudden, Vern Akers is giving Mr. Hedstrom advice on how to run the business!"

"Dodie! There are just some things they don't see up there. What, Sue? . . . Oh, tell him to turn up at six. We're gonna need two trucks out tomorrow night. I'm sure of that!"

He had arrived at Chicken Tonight, Thatcher saw, at a moment to be remembered. Here was authentic happiness, pervasive as the exotic aromas filling the kitchen.

". . . introducing *two* new flavors next month and giving us a volume discount," Akers said. "Hey! I'll bet Chicken Tonight would be a big success down where you work."

He looked at Thatcher. So did Dodie and Sue. Hungrily.

Thatcher himself was taken with the number of Chicken Tonight orders lunchtime Wall Street could generate.

"Of course, the big trick is a low rental. I expect you know all about that."

If he didn't escape soon, Thatcher was in some danger of becoming silent partner in the Akers take-over of lower Manhattan.

"How is your organization of franchisees doing?" he inquired hastily.

"Yes . . . four-three-two Morton Avenue," said Dodie into the phone.

"The organization? Oh, we're having a lot of meetings— Hey, Dodie, does this say Tropicali or Tripoli? Sorry, Mr. Thatcher. Well, we're still meeting. As a matter of fact, we're supposed to meet tomorrow, but, like I told Mr. Hedstrom, I don't know if I've got time."

Thatcher retreated. The Akerses were not particularly curious as to why he had come in the first place. They were filled with the wonder of it all, and assumed that the whole world would want to be witness.

For that matter, Thatcher was pleased he had come.

And, more important, he had learned what he wanted to know. Without asking.

Thatcher went home with the deep sense of satisfaction that comes to a man who has solved an abstruse mathematical problem. Nor did he have any difficulty falling asleep. All that he needed now was confirmation.

He knew where to find it.

"Good morning, Mr. Thatcher."

"Good morning, Miss Corsa." Thatcher's buoyancy was proof against the prevailing chill. "Miss Corsa, I have a few things that I want done immediately. . . ."

Almost immediately they were done.

In very short order, Thatcher was reading down a list of the stockholders of Southeastern Insurance and Chicken Tonight.

These held no real surprise for him.

Frank Hedstrom and Joan Hedstrom, jointly, were Chicken Tonight's largest stockholders. Farther down the roster, after several institutional investors, came the names of Ted and

Iris Young. And, just as Thatcher had expected, at the very end of the list, still accounting for a large holding in her own right, was Iris S. Young.

"Tom Robichaux," said Thatcher to himself, "would never believe it."

Stockholders of Southeastern Insurance included fewer Wall Street institutions and more of the Philadelphia Social Register, with the Ogilvie family represented by Buell Ogilvie, that mainstay of the U. S. Lawn Tennis Association for the last fifty years. Apart from him, Thatcher found no one else of interest.

He was still reading when Miss Corsa rang through with another item he had requested: a name Robichaux had mentioned yesterday.

"Thank you, Miss Corsa."

"You're welcome, Mr. Thatcher," she replied punctiliously.

"Oh, just a minute, Miss Corsa. I want you to make another call."

The intercom was elaborately patient while John Putnam Thatcher did a little fast thinking. He had the quarry. But before he could call out the hounds, he needed an accomplice. He reviewed the people he had met and would meet again. Then, in a determined voice, he said, "Miss Corsa, I want you to put me through to a Mr. Denton who is associated with the U. S. Public Health."

That, he knew, would be enough for Miss Corsa.

And what he had, he was equally sure, would be enough for Mr. Denton.

CHAPTER 22

STIR THE BATTER

PYROTECHNICS ARE not a standard weapon in the armory of the United States Public Health. Great conflicts over great issues occupy arenas from the U.S. Supreme Court to the Bureau of Standards. Even traffic courts in Georgia get their share of homely drama. Public Health hearings, however, rarely rise above chagrin. A contest, after all, needs adversaries. And no one is seriously opposed to public health on principle. Partisans of the spread of disease and contamination can be numbered on the fingers of one hand.

Even when vigilance unmasks a miscreant, does the villain fight like a trapped rat? Does right vanquish wrong? Does society exact its price for sin?

"Fat chance," as Mr. Denton once put it in a low moment.

The Public Health isolates the guilty party, and the guilty party, nine times out of ten, is more horrified than anybody else. Fish filleters in Gloucester, frozen turkey purveyors in Pennsylvania, even bakers selling custard pies in July, react the same way—with stunned disbelief, with horror at what they have unknowingly done, and with touching gratitude to the Public Health for bringing them to their senses.

The Public Health, in short, does all the work and gets very little of the fun. Unless, of course, you count grave editorial commendation from *The New York Times* or approbation from Consumers' Union as fun. And who does?

It is, therefore, doubly admirable that the U. S. Public Health is as dedicated and indefatigable as the FBI.

Naturally, at the barest suspicion of genuine malice aforethought, the Public Health turns giddy. The Chicken Tonight case had held out the intoxicating prospect of a criminal for the Public Health to smite. But Clyde Sweeney's emergence—and, even more, his departure—had put those enticing aspects of the case into the hands of the police. Hopes blasted, the Public Health was again falling back on "a hearing to ascertain whether vendors of precooked chicken products maintain adequate standards . . ."

But the meek are blessed. A day before the Public Health hearings were scheduled to open in the Federal Building in Trenton, Mr. Denton was summoned from a conference.

"Yes," he told the phone. "Oh, Mr. Thatcher. . . . Yes indeed, I remember. . . . What? Ye-es? . . Ye-es?"

Rapt, Mr Denton listened for twenty-five minutes without once interrupting. When Thatcher asked his final question, Mr. Denton's answer held the reverence of a knightly pledge to the Holy Grail.

"You can rely on us. Absolutely! I assure you—we can and will do it!"

Mr. Denton looked straight into the Promised Land. Then, recovering, he added, "Now, if you'll excuse me, Mr. Thatcher. There's a good deal that I'm going to have to do."

"Why are there so many people here?" asked Ted Young, looking around the hearing room, which was filled to capacity.

Young and Hedstrom studied the chamber. They did not like what they saw.

"My God," Young continued. "What kind of hearing is this going to be?"

Hedstrom did not bother with reassurance. "I don't know," he said in an odd tone of voice. "Ted, something must be up. They've got everybody here."

He was very nearly right. Across the aisle from the Hedstroms and the Youngs sat Vern Akers. Beside him was Dodie, her hair for once brushed into place. Farther along sat other Chicken Tonight franchisees: the Horvaths, Mr. and Mrs. Gatto, the Zabriskies from Buffalo. Mr. and Mrs. Chester Brewster, she in a mink stole, sat four rows ahead. They were not franchisees, they were prominent business people.

Mrs. Collins, from the test kitchens, wearing a dashing mauve satin hat, headed a delegation of her staff. Perhaps because of coaching by the Legal Department of Chicken Tonight, the test-kitchen personnel strongly suggested an underdog football team prepared for, but not resigned to, the drubbing in store.

Among those present was John Putnam Thatcher. Like Frank Hedstrom, he was registering the unusual crowd in the room. As he watched, Pelham Browne strode down the aisle.

"What was that, Tom?"

Robichaux repeated his question with some heat.

"When the Sloan has to testify before the Public Health," Thatcher said, "I like to follow what's going on."

Robichaux inspected him. "I don't believe you," he said bluntly. "Normally you would have sent Maitland. For that matter, I would have . . ."

It was easy to underestimate Robichaux's common sense, Thatcher reminded himself. Aloud, he said that the Sloan was reserving Maitland for lost causes.

"Stands to reason," Robichaux agreed after thinking it over. "Pretty wet fish, I've always said."

Thatcher was momentarily diverted from other thoughts. It had not escaped his notice that when Robichaux wanted to hook the Sloan he made a beeline for Maitland.

"I believe, Tom," he retorted rather grimly, "that Maitland will be putting in for early retirement."

Since this meant retirement early enough to be sensational, Robichaux looked around the room with elaborate innocence.

"Lots of people, aren't there? Good God, they've dug up Ogilvie. And that's his Uncle Buell with him. What on earth does the Public Health want with them?"

He got his answer from a Mr. Levin, a tall and professorial man. After brief consultation with colleagues, Mr. Levin cleared his throat into the microphone. The ensuing detonation silenced the hum of conversation and brought the meeting to order.

"Good morning— What? . . . Oh, yes. Can you hear me in the back of the room? How's that? Fine. Er, good morning. We are going to open this hearing of the Public Health inquiry into the food industry, with special emphasis upon those who vend precooked meals and deliver them . . ."

"Marvelous how those fellows learn all that by heart," murmured Robichaux, much impressed.

". . . complete inquiry into Chicken Tonight from a rather broad point of view. Before we commence our formal hearings, on behalf of the Public Health I want to thank Chicken Tonight for their frankness in cooperating with our many questions . . ."

From where he sat, Thatcher could see Hedstrom, rigidly still. Ted Young was rubbing a hand against the back of his neck.

". . . all other parties," Mr. Levin continued, consulting a note, to Robichaux's disappointment. "Our interest, of course, has been sparked by recent tragic developments revealing that unauthorized personnel could introduce contaminants into Chicken Tonight products . . ."

"Why doesn't that fellow speak up?" a cranky elderly voice demanded. Uncle Buell, Thatcher inferred. Mr. Levin pursed his lips, then said, "And our first witness, Mrs. Vera Collins."

Bosom uplifted, Mrs. Collins rose and accepted Mr. Levin's invitation to sit beside him. Whether she made herself comfortable, as he also suggested, was anybody's guess.

Mrs. Collins had herself well in hand. If anything, she was tediously forthcoming. With Robichaux growing restive, Thatcher, like everyone else, heard an exhaustive rehearsal of every single process employed by Chicken Tonight, from test kitchen to orange-and-gold delivery truck. Unfortunately, she set the tone for succeeding witnesses.

The cigarette break came none too soon.

"Let me tell you, John," said Robichaux, getting to his feet. "If things go on this way, we're all going to be asleep."

Thatcher was thinking ahead. "I'm sure," he said vaguely, "I'm sure things will become more entertaining."

Again Robichaux projected suspicion, but before he could voice it they were surrounded by spectators, witnesses and officials.

"You too, Robichaux?" asked a voice from behind them. "And Mr. Thatcher? I don't know if you gentlemen have met my uncle."

Buell Ogilvie exercised the prerogative of extreme age and took charge of the conversation. "First time I ever heard of bankers getting dragged in by the Public Health," he said with relish. He was blocking the path of everybody behind him with splendid indifference.

Inevitably, Morgan Ogilvie was diminished by the presence of his relative. "As I've already explained, Uncle Buell, we're simply here because we made inquiries about Chicken Tonight—"

"About the merger! I know that!" Uncle Buell snapped while Ogilvie looked deprecatory. "But that's ancient history, even if you can't get it out of your head, Morgan!"

"Well, that's one of the good things about getting older," Robichaux confided after Uncle Buell had been led away. "You start outliving some of them— Oh, hello there, Hedstrom. Mrs. Hedstrom—"

To Thatcher's genuine admiration, Tom Robichaux's *savoir-faire* did not falter when the crowd parted to let Ted and Iris Young join them. "Ah, yes," he said meaninglessly. "Well, it all seems to be cut and dried, doesn't it?"

"Let's hope so," Young remarked dully. "I don't see what good they hope to accomplish. No, we are not giving interviews!"

This last was addressed to a reporter thrusting himself forward.

"Hold it," said Frank Hedstrom. "Sure, we'll give you a statement. You can say we're following the hearings with interest. And, of course, Chicken Tonight not only has nothing to hide . . ."

"Come on, Tom," said Thatcher, suddenly oppressed.

Robichaux showed no inclination to linger in the vicinity of Iris Young. He followed Thatcher back into the hearing room. Mrs. Hedstrom and Mrs. Young, Thatcher noted during his hasty farewells, both wore the fixed painful smiles of political wives.

"And now," said Mr. Levin, frowning at latecomers, "we'll proceed to Mr. Frank Hedstrom."

There was an expectant hush.

"Mr. Hedstrom?" Levin raised his voice and there was an answering hum throughout the room.

"Frank Hedstrom!" called a second man loudly.

Heads at the front table were raised from folders and charts. For the first time, Thatcher located Mr. Denton, eyes bright and watchful as a squirrel's.

And that large man in the corner, watching with sleepy interest? Johnson? Jackson? A policeman, whatever his name.

He was not the only policeman present.

"Frank Heds—"

"Here!"

The youthful voice from the back of the room cut confidently through the mounting tension. "Sorry to be late. I got caught . . ."

He hurried down the aisle to the front of the room while his wife and the Youngs hovered uncertainly in the doorway until people started making room for them in the last row of seats.

Thatcher was leaning forward. The proceedings he had come to see were beginning.

"Mr. Hedstrom," Levin began, "you are the president and chief stockholder of Chicken Tonight?"

"I am," said Hedstrom. But Thatcher gave him full marks for a sensitive ear. He had flicked a look toward Young at Levin's unusual identification.

Mr. Levin consulted a note. "I wonder, Mr. Hedstrom, if you would tell us something about your background."

"My background?" Hedstrom repeated blankly. His lawyers, in the front row, stirred.

"Your business background, of course," Mr. Levin said encouragingly.

After hesitating, Hedstrom complied with a brief outline of his career, from the first take-out restaurant in Oak Park, Illinois, to the expansion that had culminated in a nationwide chain. His voice remained steady.

"That's word for word from his publicity releases," Robichaux said.

"I know," said Thatcher absently.

"Fine, fine," said Mr. Levin, not sounding as if it were fine at all. "Now just a few additional points, Mr. Hedstrom . . ."

He then put Hedstrom through a series of questions about the organizational structure of Chicken Tonight, its financial situation and current prospects, that would not have disgraced a Wall Street banker.

Thatcher wondered how many spectators could sense Mr. Levin's basic unfamiliarity with the terms he was using so fluently. Not many, he thought, glancing around. It was the human confrontation that captured attention.

Frank Hedstrom passed rapidly from wariness to hostility.

"I don't think that's a question I should be asked," he protested to a query about personal finances.

"Of course," Mr. Levin soothed, "if you do not wish to cooperate—"

"Dammit, I am cooperating!" Hedstrom exploded.

Abruptly, proceedings were interrupted by a conference at the front of the room between Hedstrom and his lawyers.

"At least things are livening up," Robichaux observed. "Still, those are strange questions. For the Public Health, that is."

He was going to hear stranger questions.

The exchange between Levin and Hedstrom resumed, with Hedstrom barely able to control his temper.

"No," he finally snarled. "Chicken Tonight was not in financial difficulties! It has never been in financial difficulties! It is not now in financial difficulties!"

"There's an optimist for you," commented Robichaux.

"Thank you, Mr. Hedstrom. Next, Mr. Theodore Young, please."

Young walked up the aisle, paused for a whispered word that drew a grin from Hedstrom, then composedly proceeded. He was confident, Thatcher thought, because he had all the details at his fingertips.

The question, when it came, was not what he had expected. "Mr. Young, what is your precise official title at Chicken Tonight?"

"Senior vice-president," said Young, wondering what was coming.

"And would you please describe to us your exact duties?" Mr. Levin sounded disingenuous.

He continued to be patient as Ted Young, frowning, described an array of duties far too extensive for any single man or job. Then Levin paraphrased. "I see. In reality, you are Mr. Hedstrom's assistant, aren't you?"

Thatcher was happy not to be sitting next to Iris Young.

"That's one way to put it," said Young, reddening slightly. Then, glancing to the back of the room, he added, "In a way, almost everybody at Chicken Tonight is an assistant—to Mr. Hedstrom."

"Yes indeed," said Mr. Levin, dismissing the comment. "Now, in connection with your responsibilities in personnel training, I understand that you frequently give courses to introduce new methods when, for example, new cost-cutting techniques are begun?"

"I do," said Young, through stiff lips. He was not the only one in the room recalling that training course in Trenton with Clyde Sweeney.

For another ten minutes, Levin conducted Young through the labyrinth of Chicken Tonight. Whether by accident or by design, one unmistakable theme emerged: there was nothing at Chicken Tonight, from poultry purchases to truck deliveries, in which Young did not take a hand.

And, somehow, Mr. Levin managed to make that sound very incriminating.

Young was floundering when Levin indicated that he was satisfied. Mr. Levin himself was showing signs of fatigue. First he sipped a glass of water. Then he coughed unconvincingly once or twice. Finally he bent down for a whispered colloquy with his colleagues. As a result, two things happened simultaneously: the Public Health sent in Mr. Denton as pinch hitter and the clerk called the next witness:

"Mr. Thomas Robichaux."

Once his initial gobbling was over, Robichaux proved a seasoned and responsive witness. Due, Thatcher had no doubt, to the body of experience accumulated in one divorce court or another. He admitted that he was a partner of Robichaux & Devane, investment bankers. He further admitted that Robichaux & Devane had been party to negotiations aimed at promoting a merger between his client, Southeastern Insurance, and Chicken Tonight.

In fact, Robichaux had barely hit his stride, and was leaning back comfortably waiting for more, when Mr. Denton said quietly, "Thank you very much. Next. Mr. Morgan Ogilvie."

Ogilvie was looking harassed. Small wonder, Thatcher reflected. The combination of Uncle Buell, on the one hand, and the random-shot pattern of the Public Health, on the other, was enough to perplex less conventional men.

Pelham Browne, he saw from the corner of his eye, was goggling.

Ogilvie identified himself as executive vice-president of Southeastern Insurance Company, of Philadelphia, and agreed that the firm had once contemplated merging with Chicken Tonight.

"Unfortunately," Ogilvie offered, unsolicited, "the merger came to nothing. Due, let me hasten to add, to purely . . . er . . . technical financial considerations. We still regard Chicken Tonight as an outstanding firm, one which has conducted its business with uniquely high standards . . ."

A snort from the front row spoiled his effect.

"Yes indeed," said Mr. Denton, consulting notes more attentively than Mr. Levin had done. "Now, perhaps we could go back, Mr. Ogilvie, to your investigations of Chicken Tonight during the proposed merger. Could you tell us . . . ?"

Like Frank Hedstrom, and Ted Young before him, Morgan Ogilvie was not completely happy with the line of questioning.

"Tell you? Well, let me see . . . I'm not sure . . . When Robichaux and Devane broached the possibility of the Chicken Tonight merger, we felt we had to undertake a thorough investigation—as we knew very little about the firm."

"What did that investigation reveal?" Mr. Denton had pounced, sounding rather like Uncle Buell.

Ogilvie was firm. "We assured ourselves that Chicken Tonight was an opportunity not to be missed. A first-rate organization. Not only was it an excellent financial prospect, it was an exceptionally up-to-date business operation."

He sounded stubborn, and Robichaux leaned over. "Sticks to his guns," he whispered. "You have to hand it to him."

Mr. Denton too seemed impressed by Ogilvie's fervor in the cause of Chicken Tonight.

"And no one was more surprised than you, then, when Chicken Tonight fell victim to the terrible events about which I need not remind you?"

"I was very surprised indeed," said Morgan Ogilvie.

"And nothing uncovered by your investigation hinted at laxity or negligence?"

Mr. Denton might have thought that Morgan Ogilvie was, for some reason, protesting too much.

"On the contrary." Ogilvie's voice rang with sincerity. "I was very much impressed by their exceptionally rigorous security methods."

"Oh, you were?" said Mr. Denton. "Well, thank you, Mr. Ogilvie."

With the air of a man satisfied by his own performance, Ogilvie rejoined Uncle Buell, who had, Thatcher saw over intervening heads, quite a lot to say.

By now, the Public Health had baffled everybody present. There must be a pattern to these hit-or-miss questions, but it was a pattern that was eluding almost everyone. As a result, there was a good deal of informal talk, curious in most areas, anxious in some. Mr. Denton smiled benevolently at the assembly and, in a voice pregnant with significance, said, "Next we will be calling Mr. Giles Bly!"

"And who the hell is Giles Bly?" Robichaux demanded indignantly.

Thatcher was genuinely curious. "You mean you don't remember him?"

"Why should I?"

"Listen!"

"Mr. Bly, you are the senior partner of Bly Associates, are you not?"

"I am," said Mr. Bly with pride. He went on to describe Bly Associates as a firm of industrial consultants. This, Thatcher knew, was euphemism with a vengeance. Bly Associates was a firm of industrial detectives. Their customers wanted information; they provided it.

". . . an analysis of Chicken Tonight, for purposes of determining whether a merger was in the best interest," Mr. Bly read.

Mr. Denton was also consulting documentation.

"Fine," he said. "Now, Mr. Bly, we would like to hear about the areas of Chicken Tonight to which you paid particular attention."

Mr. Bly shot a cuff and delivered a speech about thoroughgoing study of the whole panorama. Bly Associates were well known—

"Yes, yes," said Mr. Denton hastily. "But surely you addressed more than usual attention to certain areas, in view of the special needs of your client."

Mr. Bly looked wise. When it came to mergers, he confided, the financial structure came first. "We want to be absolutely sure that financial resources exist."

"And?" Mr. Denton prodded.

"And," said Mr. Bly, "operating procedures. We ascertain if, for example, Chicken Tonight is a stable business with a real future." He beamed at the thought. "That's one thing we're very very careful about."

Mr. Denton was nodding frenetically. "I see," he said, taking a turn around the table.

"And, Mr. Bly, what did you determine about Chicken Tonight?"

Mr. Bly might have been reporting to a client. "Our survey revealed that Chicken Tonight is a well-managed, stable firm. It has excellent internal controls, a more than adequate research and development program, and exceptionally promising growth potential. After long consideration, Bly Associates judged it to be an excellent partner in any proposed merger."

The Chicken Tonight franchisees buzzed happily. Not so Mr. Denton. He rocked back on his heels and contemplated Mr. Bly.

"That's very interesting, Mr. Bly. But perhaps you can explain the grounds for your conclusion in everyday language. Those of us who aren't as expert as you find it astonishing that this paragon of a company should have become involved in poisoning and a financial crisis that destroyed all hopes of merger—so soon after your thorough investigation."

Professional pride struggled with discretion in Bly's breast. Then, as Thatcher had hoped, he bit.

"We had plenty of grounds for our conclusions," he retorted hotly. "We gave Chicken Tonight the full treatment."

Mr. Denton was outdoing himself. "Er, what exactly is the full treatment, in layman's terms?"

Mr. Bly was unconscious of his audience. The audience, however, hung on every word.

"I had men at their franchises," he rapped out. "I had men in the warehouses. I knew every machine they bought. They didn't hire anybody or fire anybody that I didn't know all about. Listen, there are guys at Chicken Tonight who haven't told their wives they're going to quit—and I can give you their name, rank and serial number."

Mr. Denton was purring now. "Very impressive," he said. "You must have compiled volumes of data."

"You're damned right I did!" Bly replied. "When I tell a client something, I back it up with cold, hard facts. If I say a cost-cutting program works—I can show him the personnel files on the guys who got bounced, and just how much salary is being saved. I can—"

Mr. Denton's voice had changed. "You studied cost-cutting in Trenton, didn't you? You got data on discharged truck drivers, didn't you? You found out about Clyde Sweeney, didn't you?"

If Mr. Denton had seen the Promised Land, Mr. Bly had seen something else. "But—" he began a protest, then broke off. Helplessly he searched for one face in the audience.

Mr. Denton was remorseless.

"Do you want to tell us to whom you passed this information, Mr. Bly? Who learned about Clyde Sweeney—from you?"

His answer came in an unexpected form. Suddenly there was a confused scuffle in one corner of the room. On all sides, people rose, craning to see. They were too late. The side door slammed behind a frantic, hurrying figure.

Once again an elderly voice took charge.

"Always knew he was a damned fool," said Buell Ogilvie bitterly.

Thatcher was inclined to agree.

CHAPTER 23

TAKE A DISJOINTED TAIL

"MORGAN OGILVIE, eh?" Tom Robichaux growled indignantly. "So he's the one responsible for all this!" He examined his surroundings with burning reproach.

Thatcher's reply was diplomacy itself. "Yes, it was Ogilvie who first hired Clyde Sweeney to poison chicken Mexicali and then murdered him."

This was not what was exercising Tom, as Thatcher knew all too well. It was a bare two hours since Morgan Ogilvie's dramatic exodus from the Public Health hearing. But in that brief period his earlier crimes had been eclipsed, at least in Robichaux's opinion, by subsequent atrocities.

Ogilvie's flight had left the hearing in pandemonium. Mr. Samuel B. Levin had pounded his gavel, the press had streaked for telephones, bailiffs had arrived from nowhere to bar the doors. Women had screamed. The turmoil had continued unabated until word filtered back that Morgan Ogilvie had been arrested in the parking lot. Thereupon Mr. Levin wisely adjourned the hearing for a week. Thatcher and Frank Hedstrom paused only long enough to thank the elated Mr. Denton. Then the whole party had strolled out in high spirits.

The festive mood had dissipated rapidly when they learned the consequences of Morgan Ogilvie's abortive escape. He had seized Frank Hedstrom's car and sped into the arms of the waiting police. More precisely, he had crashed into the Sloan's limousine.

"I can have them both ready to roll by seven-thirty or eight," the garage man had said uncompromisingly. "Not a minute sooner."

Everybody had huddled deeper into his collar. An icy rain was falling, driven by winds of gale force. The two courses open to them were unappealing. They could commandeer transport from the Chicken Tonight warehouse in Trenton and go home. But that would leave four cars out of place. Alternatively, they could endure several dreary hours and retrieve their cars.

Two factors influenced the final decision. Vern and Dodie Akers, hearing of the predicament, offered hospitality in Willoughby's own Chicken Tonight.

And John Thatcher remembered that seven-thirty would hear the opening guns of the Trinkam Anniversary Celebration. In the chair would be George C. Lancer, chairman of the board; in the wings would be personnel from the Parke-Bernet Galleries standing guard over the Table on Which

Washington Had Drafted His Farewell Address; and in the offing would be speeches, sentiment and, inevitably, hurt feelings. At first the resentments would be institutional. The Accounting Department would feel slighted. It always did and, for that matter, it always was. The Investment Division would know that it had been shouldered aside by the Trust Division. But, as time and liquor flowed on, the personal element would intrude. Someone would imply that a file clerk was no better than she should be. The girl would threaten to resign. Someone else would suggest that a stenographer was still a virgin. *She* would threaten to burn the whole bank down. Several junior trust officers would act in a manner unworthy of their high calling—God willing, with secretaries other than their own.

"I vote for Willoughby," Thatcher had said unhesitatingly.

The Akerses had made it clear their hospitality was informal. They were now all crowded into the back room. The ladies had been provided with chairs. The men were perched on counters while Vern and Dodie bustled to and from the kitchen. There was no question of entertaining guests there. The kitchen hummed with activity; oven doors were slamming, phones were jangling and the whole effort was being directed by Sue Akers and her invaluable Bob.

"Our orders are just coming out," Dodie declared from the doorway. "Sue had to squeeze them in."

As she hurried back to the kitchen, Frank Hedstrom capitalized on the lull before the storm.

"But why did Ogilvie want to ruin Chicken Tonight?" he asked.

"Oh, he didn't care about ruining Chicken Tonight. He was simply determined to stop the merger," Thatcher said.

Ted Young was shocked. "And for that he poisoned over a hundred people and killed a man?"

"He killed two men. You're forgetting that poor old guy in Elmira," corrected Hedstrom, who had a soft spot for patrons of Chicken Tonight.

"I always said Ogilvie was crazy." Tom Robichaux wagged his head sadly. So this was what clients of Robichaux & Devane were coming to.

"I doubt if he intended to kill anybody," said Thatcher before Robichaux could get them all pounding after some false hare. "He probably made a mistake in dosage on the Elmira box. And I'm certain he didn't expect to kill Sweeney. He was convinced he would never have to see Sweeney again."

"Hey!" Vern Akers protested, arriving with the food. "I want to hear about Clyde. Don't explain yet."

Obediently Thatcher waited, surprised to find how hungry he was. He eyed Dodie's tray with interest when she rejoined them. It held onion rings, french-fried potatoes, cole slaw, rolls and relishes. Tantalizing smells eddied around the table. Thatcher's salivary glands answered the call of duty. Meanwhile Vern was isolating subgroups.

"Chicken Mandarin for the Youngs," he murmured, "chicken Creole for the Akerses, chicken Tarragon for everybody else."

Dodie started to serve out heaping plates. Thatcher had wondered at first how the Akerses would react to their reunion with Iris Young. But the problem had never materialized. The smartly styled Iris who had tried to spearhead a dump-Frank movement was not in evidence tonight. This was largely thanks to the weather and the style of transport acquired by Hedstrom.

The party had split up in Trenton. Robichaux and Thatcher had driven to Willoughby with the Akerses while the others waited for a vehicle from the warehouse. In the interim the women, mindful of cold ears and wet hair, acquired wool caps. They had already been wearing fashionably high boots. The long stocking caps, red for Iris and blue for Joan, made them look ready for an ice-skating party. On top of that, the Trenton warehouse had come through with the familiar orange-and-gold-striped truck. It was this vehicle which had pulled up in the Akerses' back yard, horn tooting loudly. Ted Young had been at the wheel; the other three were sitting in the rear, feet propped on a crate of beer acquired, and opened, en route. They were all singing with tuneless gusto:

> *Give a cheer! Give a cheer!*
> *For the boys who drink the beer,*
> *In the cellars of old Oak Park High!*

As a quartet, they seemed a good deal younger than Sue Akers and Bob, more like the tag end of a high-school cheering section than anything else. And Dodie treated them accordingly.

"All right, Mr. Thatcher," said Vern Akers at last. "Now tell us about Clyde. I didn't follow what that man said about Bly Associates. I thought he was just talking about some merger."

"That's how it started. Morgan Ogilvie hired Bly Associates in good faith to investigate Chicken Tonight. He asked for a very thorough study."

"I knew he was doing it," Hedstrom said quietly. "And I circulated the word to cooperate. I never realized how far he'd go."

"Of course not. Because when the reports started coming in, Ogilvie realized that the merger offer was too good for him to stop by ordinary means. He decided to stop it by starting a poisoning scare and causing the stock of Chicken Tonight to nose-dive. That may sound easy, but it meant he had to find a very special kind of man at Chicken Tonight, a man like Clyde Sweency. And that isn't easy to do, not without leaving a trail. It bothered me, and I know it bothered the police. That's why they found it difficult to believe an outsider had been behind the scheme. What we didn't realize was that Morgan Ogilvie very cleverly used Bly Associates as camouflage. He demanded the names of personnel who had left the company or were thinking of leaving. Then he wanted lists of employees terminated because of cost-cutting programs, supposedly to judge if the programs were efficient. So you see it's not surprising that no one remembered furnishing him with particulars about Clyde Sweeney. The girls in the personnel office, acting under instructions, pulled literally hundreds of records for Bly Associates, as part of a routine business transaction."

"The smart bastard," said Ted Young, almost admiringly. "He didn't try to wipe out his tracks. He just buried them under a snowdrift."

"Exactly. It seems to have been a natural instinct with him, as you'll see," Thatcher promised.

Vern brought them back to essentials. "All right. But what about Clyde?"

"You already know how he was hired. It was exactly as Captain Johnson postulated. Ogilvie telephoned and arranged one meeting. Naturally he didn't give his real name. That was supposed to be his only personal contact with Sweeney. Then it didn't make any difference to him whether Sweeney was arrested or not."

"But they must have met down in Maryland," Iris Young objected. "What happened? Did something go wrong?"

"A great deal went wrong, from Ogilvie's point of view." Thatcher smiled at the Youngs and the Hedstroms. Ted Young, he noticed, was getting through a remarkable amount of beer. "And he immediately involved you in his troubles. Try to think back to the Thursday before the murder. Sweeney was in hiding at a hotel in New York. He was frightened, he had no plans and he had no one to turn to. Then he opens his morning paper, checks the progress of the police search for him, turns to the sports page and what does he see?"

Thatcher's attempt at drama was promptly torpedoed. Tom Robichaux had not been listening to a word.

"This isn't so bad," he said into the silence, having cautiously essayed his chicken Tarragon. Surprise yielded to judicious savoring. In spite of themselves, the Akerses, the Hedstroms and the Youngs were professionally riveted, until finally the gourmet said, "Not bad at all!"

Vern Akers was the first to recover. "What did Clyde see on the sports page?" he almost howled.

"He saw a picture of the horse which had won the Garden State Futurity. Next to the horse was the owner, described as 'Morgan Ogilvie, owner of the Ogilvie Stable in Paton, Maryland.'"

"Good heavens!" exclaimed Joan Hedstrom. "That was the horse Mrs. Browne kept talking about."

Thatcher refreshed himself from his can of beer and continued explaining to the Akerses. "You see, against all odds, a horse owned by Morgan Ogilvie had won a race that week. The picture was picked up by a good many papers and carried on the one page Sweeney never missed. As soon as Clyde Sweeney saw that picture, he packed his bags and started south. By Thursday evening he had checked into his motel and was calling Ogilvie to announce his arrival."

"The phone never stopped ringing all day," Iris Young suddenly echoed in genteel tones. She blinked when everyone stared at her. "I'm sorry. I was remembering what Mrs. Ogilvie said."

"It must have been a real boot in the belly for Ogilvie," said Frank Hedstrom with every sign of approval.

"I'm sure it was. And I'm sure at first he panicked, agreed to everything that Sweeney demanded and arranged to meet him at the parking lot of the Calvert Hunt Club on Saturday night. He may have been instinctively stalling for time. But you have to admit that he recovered magnificently."

Dodie Akers was indignant. "You mean murdering poor Clyde!"

"Certainly not!" Thatcher was outraged himself. "I mean that, having made up his mind to kill Sweeney, he decided to flood the Calvert Hunt Club with murder suspects! His old snowdrift principle, you see."

The trouble with Tom Robichaux was that his deafness was highly selective. Now he rounded on Thatcher in righteous wrath.

"Do you mean to tell me that he got us down there to—?" He became speechless at the enormity of the suggestion.

Thatcher smiled beatifically at his old friend. "That's right, Tom. We were gulled from the start. Morgan Ogilvie had been behaving fairly reasonably about the merger until that Friday, if you remember."

Hedstrom remembered, if Robichaux did not. "That's right. He said he was sorry about our troubles and hoped things would work out. But that was all politeness. He was preparing to cut the rope."

"Then suddenly we had to rush down and save the merger," Ted Young contributed briefly. He did not have much attention to waste on speech. He was emerging as one of those small, spare men who eat like horses. He was surrounded by debris. On one side there was a plate with the carcasses of several chickens, on the other a neat pyramid of empty beer cans. "I said it was crazy."

"I said the same thing myself," Robichaux began expansively.

"We all said it." Thatcher was dampening. "Instead, we should have wondered why he suddenly cast himself in the role of lunatic. The reason was plain enough. He wanted as many people connected with Chicken Tonight as possible on the scene of his murder. That is also why he insisted we dance. He knew that with an uneven number of men and women, there would always be some men wandering about without an alibi."

"I did wonder about that. But then," said Hedstrom simply, "I thought maybe that was how they did things at these hunt clubs."

"Not with that ill-assorted a party. And when Ogilvie had us all where he wanted us, he went out to the parking lot, met Sweeney, mugged him and strangled him."

Hedstrom's voice grated. "With Joanie's scarf."

"He must have taken it when he came over to pick you up for your business conference," Joan said calmly. "There were all those open suitcases in the hall."

"Yes. I'm afraid he believed in improving on the occasion," Thatcher answered. "He was desperately anxious to tie the murder in with your house. Because he was enormously vulnerable if the police ever started to look at him. In fact, from what Mr. Denton tells me, his machinations didn't succeed very well. Captain Stotz started narrowing down to Morgan Ogilvie almost immediately."

"You're joking!" Frank Hedstrom was incredulous. "What about the grilling they gave us?"

"That was at the beginning, before they located the motel owner. Stotz is not a man who can't see the forest for the trees. He is not afraid to ignore the trees. As soon as he knew that Sweeney had been making local calls in Maryland on Thursday night, apparently arranging appointments for Saturday night, he became very suspicious of Ogilvie's invitations —on Friday. Then, he appreciated that Ogilvie, in addition to stage-managing that weekend, was the one with local knowledge. You didn't even know where the hunt club was. And it was extremely unlikely that any of you knew there would be a horse show to add to the confusion."

Iris' eyes darkened dangerously. "Do you mean that Frank and Ted have been in the clear for days and nobody has had the decency to tell us?"

"You'll have to ask the police about that. But I do know that Stotz had very few doubts. Not since he learned that Ogilvie knew Sweeney's bribe was four thousand dollars long before he should have."

"Ogilvie did say something about that," Hedstrom murmured. "But for the life of me, I can't remember when."

Thatcher was relieved to see that Hedstrom was not the perfect machine. "Apparently Ogilvie was incautious enough to repeat that remark to Stotz. They had just searched Sweeney's room, and at that time only the police should have known the total amount."

"It sounds pretty watertight. But about that local knowledge. I know it may sound nuts"—Hedstrom grinned apologetically—"but did anybody ever consider Pelham Browne? After all, he had local knowledge, too. He'd know about the horse show and that sort of thing."

"Browne certainly acted oddly enough, but Stotz refuses to believe in miraculously good luck. Assume Browne set up an appointment with Sweeney on Thursday night, long before Ogilvie broached weekend plans to anybody. He would have to be the luckiest murderer in the world to have a crowd of suspects descend on the scene at the critical moment without any contrivance on his part."

Hedstrom continued to argue thoughtfully. "But he could have heard that we were planning to open the house. We'd ordered the utilities turned on, and that sort of thing gets around."

"No." Thatcher shook his head. "What good would it do him to have the four of you playing bridge, under the eye of a maid, twenty miles from the scene of the murder? And you could easily have been doing that. Besides, there were other points against Browne as a candidate. He had no access to the scarf. He had no access to Sweeney. And, finally, his motive doesn't hold water. That is where I feel you and I fell down. We should have been able to distinguish the motive."

Before Hedstrom could speak, Vern Akers leaped at the chance for enlightenment. "Yes, what was so special about this Ogilvie's motive? You said he wanted to stop the merger with his insurance company. Why didn't he just say no?"

"Oh, Vern! You know it's going to turn out to be the kind of thing they do in big business." Dodie didn't believe rational explanations applied.

"Not often, Mrs. Akers," Thatcher replied gravely. "You see, it wasn't Ogilvie's insurance company. He just worked for it. But it had once been a family company. I am afraid Morgan Ogilvie came to look on Southeastern Insurance as a cow designed for milking by the Ogilvie family. His uncle and he both drew handsome salaries. His nephew was an executive in the company. And—"

Robichaux interrupted. "He said his son was going into it, too. Makes your blood run cold, doesn't it?"

"There you are," said Thatcher. "Everything in that family was planned around the company. But if the company was merged, those plans would all come to nothing. There wouldn't be any more handsome incomes. And there certainly wouldn't be the civic position that Ogilvie held in Philadelphia as a leading businessman. To add insult to injury, Morgan Ogilvie no longer held any substantial amount of stock. So he wouldn't reap any of the profit coming to the stockholders."

"Jesus!" Hedstrom exclaimed. "Do you think he had the gall to sell out and invest in a stock that paid better?"

"I wouldn't put it past him. But to return to Mr. Akers' question. Morgan Ogilvie couldn't say no. He didn't have the power to. All he could do was object as long as possible, and then give in gracefully when the other directors made up their minds. But he was determined to stop the take-over just the same. His difficulty was that the directors thought the offer too good to turn down. He decided to do something that would make the offer much less attractive."

Vern nodded. "Now I understand."

Dodie looked skeptical, but Thatcher plowed on.

"When I said Ogilvie's motive was distinguishable, I meant it had a time dimension. We all know that a merger offer is never valid for long. Conditions change too rapidly. Either the offer is taken at flood tide or it disappears. That's why Ogilvie arranged the poisoning in the manner he did. He wanted one short, very sharp blow. He wanted a public scandal and a fall in the value of Chicken Tonight. If he had wanted a different effect, he could have instructed Sweeney to distribute his poison, or even a noxious taste additive, in the boxes in the warehouse. That way he would have achieved a much less intensive but more protracted result. Now, if Pelham Browne had a motive, it was to distract you from going into the broiler business. He would have wanted to tie you up with problems. He wouldn't have wanted to destroy his customer."

Hedstrom had caught the hint of reserve in Thatcher's voice. He was half smiling as he challenged, "And?"

Thatcher met the challenge. "And if anyone inside the company had wanted to dispossess you—like Mr. or Mrs. Young—" Thatcher very carefully did not look at Iris, "then they would have even more reason to space out their program. The whole point of such an operation would have been to preserve the company while undermining you. There wouldn't be any point to killing the goose that lays the golden eggs."

Ted Young had long since leaned back against the wall and closed his eyes. Now he half opened them.

"The golden chicken," he chuckled sleepily.

Thatcher risked a glance at Iris. She was deep in thought, heedless of his accusations. If his ears did not deceive him, she was crooning over and over again, "Sam Levin . . . Sam Levin . . . Sam Levin . . ."

Hedstrom had risen to his feet and was giving a mighty stretch. "I guess that about ties it up. You're right, we got misled by the trees. Ever since we heard the description of the man who met Sweeney—you know, the sport shirt and slacks—I've been thinking about Browne. It's just the sort of outfit he'd wear to a downtown hotel."

Thatcher began to help him collect dirty plates. As he added Robichaux's to the pile, he noted that Tom had somehow equipped himself with a copy of the gold-and-orange menu. He was deep in conversation with Dodie Akers.

"I think we can take it that the sport shirt and slacks represented an attempt at disguise by Ogilvie. He was trying to look different than he usually did, so that he would be safe from casual recognition by Sweeney. From what you tell me of Browne's habits, he would have to go into charcoal gray to achieve the same effect."

Thatcher looked about the room uncertainly. At some point they would have to collect themselves for the trip into the Trenton garage. Ted Young, now sleeping heavily with his fair hair ruffled into cowlicks, would have to be roused. Tom Robichaux would have to be pried loose from his study of the culinary delights offered by Chicken Tonight. Joan Hedstorm would have to be detached from her beer, for which she was showing a surprising partiality. His thoughts were interrupted by a sudden call for help from the kitchen. Vern Akers cantered off, to return a moment later grinning from ear to ear.

"A full buffet order for Friday night," he announced happily. "A hundred people at the Elks. They've heard about the arrest, and they say they want to support local business."

Dodie broke off her conversation to smile at him. "There, Vern, what did I tell you? We're going to make it!"

Robichaux disliked being deserted. "But there isn't any chicken with orange sauce," he said plaintively. "I like duck with oranges. Why not chicken?"

"That's an idea," said Hedstrom, his business instincts coming to the fore.

"Oranges!" Iris Young turned a sybilline gaze on Thatcher. "There may be something there."

Thatcher would not commit himself. "Possibly," he admitted.

"And Sam Levin," she continued inexorably. "There are millions of them."

Millions of oranges or millions of Sam Levins? Did it make any difference? Thatcher was growing restless under that intense, unblinking stare.

"Certainly," he said, turning away.

Conversations were swirling about the room.

"Étienne uses thyme," Robichaux was saying with animation.

"It's a funny thing about thyme," Hedstrom replied, one scholar to another. "You don't think of it as strong, but a little goes a long way."

Iris had retreated further into preoccupation. "Jerusalem . . . Haifa . . . Negev . . . Jaffa . . . Gaza," she intoned.

Vern and Dodie were looking to the future.

"We may have to start thinking about that extra truck again."

"And uniforms," Dodie prompted. "Probably six uniforms."

Suddenly Iris' voice rang out like a clarion. "Frank! I've got it!" she cried. "We'll make it with Jaffa oranges."

Frank Hedstrom came to attention immediately. "Yes, Iris?" he said respectfully.

Iris' head was thrown back. "We'll call it . . ." she said softly, as one who sees truth plain, "we'll call it chicken Sinai!"

There was a reverent silence.

It was Robichaux who responded with ready gallantry. He raised his beer can to Iris in a toast.

"To chicken Sinai!" Admiration was succeeded by awe. "It will make a mint!"

Rachel Monette's husband has been murdered, and her child has been kidnapped. Now she has gone hunting from New England to Morocco, from Old Jerusalem to the French countryside.

A Nazi secret buried for forty years holds the answer. An answer that will serve her quest for vengeance. And vengeance only will slake…

THE FURY OF RACHEL MONETTE

by Peter Abrahams

**TO THE NAMES LUDLUM, LE CARRÉ AND FOLLETT ADD PETER ABRAHAMS—
"DRUM-TIGHT TENSION…A PERFECT READ."**
—John Barkham Reviews

"CHILLING, SATISFYING…INGENIOUS FROM FIRST PAGE TO LAST."
—Eric Van Lustbader, author of *The Ninja*

**FROM POCKET BOOKS
WHEREVER PAPERBACKS ARE SOLD**

260